SNOWFALL ON HAVEN POINT

Center Point
Large Print

Also by RaeAnne Thayne and available from Center Point Large Print:

Riverbend Road
Evergreen Springs
Redemption Bay
Christmas in Snowflake Canyon

**This Large Print Book carries the
Seal of Approval of N.A.V.H.**

SNOWFALL ON HAVEN POINT

RaeAnne Thayne

CENTER POINT LARGE PRINT
THORNDIKE, MAINE

The text of this Large Print edition is unabridged.
In other aspects, this book may vary
from the original edition.
Printed in the United States of America
on permanent paper.
Set in 16-point Times New Roman type.

ISBN: 978-1-68324-448-6

Library of Congress Cataloging-in-Publication Data

Names: Thayne, RaeAnne, author.
Title: Snowfall on Haven Point / RaeAnne Thayne.
Description: Center Point Large Print edition. | Thorndike, Maine :
Center Point Large Print, 2017.
Identifiers: LCCN 2017013873 | ISBN 9781683244486
   (hardcover : alk. paper)
Subjects: LCSH: Large type books. | Christmas stories.
Classification: LCC PS3570.H363 S664 2017 | DDC 813/.54—dc23
LC record available at https://lccn.loc.gov/2017013873

When I'm writing a book, I spend a great deal of time in solitude, listening to the imaginary characters in my head all day (and sometimes long into the night, unfortunately!). It would be a mistake, however, to believe I labored alone in bringing *Snowfall on Haven Point* to life. Though my name is the one on the cover, in reality, many people play a vital role in the process, from the first tiny seeds of an idea germinating in my imagination to the final creation.

As always, I am deeply grateful to every single person at Harlequin—from the amazing art department for their stunning cover designs to the tireless marketing team to the fabulous HQN editors (especially the incomparable Gail Chasan, who has been with me through more than fifty books now!). Thank you also to my agent, Karen Solem, for guiding me through all the nitty-gritty details; to Sarah Burningham and Katie Olsen of Little Bird Publicity and everyone at Writerspace for helping spread the word; my assistant, Judie Bouldry; Tennis Watkins, my wonderful son-in-law who updates my website; my friend Jill

Shalvis, who always has my back when I need plot help or just to talk; my dedicated review crew; and all the bloggers and booksellers who work so hard to help my books reach my wonderful readers.

I must also thank my husband and three children for their patience, tolerance and endless cheerleading. I love you dearly.

Chapter ONE

She really needed to learn how to say no once in a while.

Andrea Montgomery stood on the doorstep of the small, charming stone house just down the street from hers on Riverbend Road, her arms loaded with a tray of food that was cooling by the minute in the icy December wind blowing off the Hell's Fury River.

Her hands on the tray felt clammy and the flock of butterflies that seemed to have taken up permanent residence in her stomach jumped around maniacally. She didn't want to be here. Marshall Bailey, the man on the other side of that door, made her nervous under the best of circumstances.

This moment definitely did not fall into that category.

How could she turn down any request from Wynona Bailey, though? She owed Wynona whatever she wanted. The woman had taken a bullet for her, after all. If Wyn wanted her to march up and down the main drag in Haven Point wearing a tutu and combat boots, she would rush right out and try to find the perfect ensemble.

She would almost prefer that to Wyn's actual request, but her friend had sounded desperate when

7

she called earlier that day from Boise, where she was in graduate school to become a social worker.

"It's only for a week or so, until I can wrap things up here with my practicum and Mom and Uncle Mike make it back from their honeymoon," Wyn had said.

"It's not a problem at all," she had assured her. Apparently she was better at telling fibs than she thought because Wynona didn't even question her.

"Trust my brother to break his leg the one week that his mother and both of his sisters are completely unavailable to help him. I think he did it on purpose."

"Didn't you tell me he was struck by a hit-and-run driver?"

"Yes, but the timing couldn't be worse, with Katrina out of the country and Mom and Uncle Mike on their cruise until the end of the week. Marshall assures me he doesn't need help, but the man has a compound fracture, for crying out loud. He's not supposed to be weight-bearing at all. I would feel better the first few days he's home from the hospital if I knew that someone who lived close by could keep an eye on him."

Andie didn't want to be that someone. But how could she say no to Wynona?

It was a good thing her friend had been a police officer until recently. If Wynona had wanted a partner in crime, *Thelma & Louise* style, Andie wasn't sure she could have said no.

"Aren't you going to ring the doorbell, Mama?" Chloe asked, eyes apprehensive and her voice wavering a little. Her daughter was picking up her own nerves, Andie knew, with that weird radar kids had, but she had also become much more timid and anxious since the terrifying incident that summer when Wyn and Cade Emmett had rescued them all.

"I can do it," her four-year-old son, Will, offered. "My feet are *freezing* out here."

Her heart filled with love for both of her funny, sweet, wonderful children. Will was the spitting image of Jason, while Chloe had his mouth and his eyes.

This would be their third Christmas without him and she had to hope she could make it much better than the previous two.

She repositioned the tray and forced herself to focus on the matter at hand. "Sorry, I was thinking of something else."

She couldn't very well tell her children that she hadn't knocked yet because she was too busy thinking about how much she didn't want to be here.

"I told you that Sheriff Bailey has a broken leg and can't get around very well. He probably can't make it to the door easily and I don't want to make him get up. He should be expecting us. Wynona said she was calling him."

She transferred the tray to one arm just long

enough to knock a couple of times loudly and twist the doorknob, which gave way easily. The door was blessedly unlocked.

"Sheriff Bailey? Hello? It's Andrea Montgomery."

"And Will and Chloe Montgomery," her son called helpfully, and Andie had to smile, despite the nerves jangling through her.

An instant later, she heard a crash, a thud and a muffled groan.

"Sheriff Bailey?"

"Not really . . . a good time."

She couldn't miss the pain in the voice of Wynona's older brother. It made her realize how ridiculous she was being. The man had been through a terrible ordeal in the last twenty-four hours and all she could think about was how much he intimidated her.

Nice, Andie. Feeling small and ashamed, she set the tray down on the nearest flat service, a small table in the foyer still decorated in Wyn's quirky fun style even though her brother had been living in the home since late August.

"Kids, wait right here for a moment," she said.

Chloe immediately planted herself on the floor by the door, her features taking on the fearful look she had worn too frequently since Rob Warren burst back into their lives so violently. Will, on the other hand, looked bored already. How had her children's roles reversed so abruptly? Chloe used to be the brave one, charging enthusiastically past any challenge, while Will had been the more tentative child.

"Do you need help?" Chloe asked tentatively.

"No. Stay here. I'll be right back."

She was sure the sound had come from the room where Wyn had spent most of her time when she lived here, a space that served as den, family room and TV viewing room in one. Her gaze immediately went to Marshall Bailey, trying to heft himself back up to the sofa from the floor.

"Oh no!" she exclaimed. "What happened?"

"What do you think happened?" he growled. "You knocked on the door so I tried to get up to answer and the damn crutches slipped out from under me."

"I'm so sorry. I only knocked to give you a little warning before we barged in. I didn't mean for you to get up."

He glowered. "Then you shouldn't have come over and knocked on the door."

She hated any conversation that came across as a confrontation. They always made her want to hide away in her room like she was a teenager again in her grandfather's house. It was completely immature of her, she knew. Grown-ups couldn't always walk away.

"Wyn asked me to check on you. Didn't she tell you?"

"I haven't talked to her since yesterday. My

11

phone ran out of juice and I haven't had a chance to charge it."

By now, the county sheriff had pulled himself back onto the sofa and was trying to position pillows for his leg that sported a black orthopedic boot from his toes to just below his knee. His features contorted as he tried to reach the pillows, but he quickly smoothed them out again. The man was obviously in pain and doing his best to conceal it.

She couldn't leave him to suffer, no matter how nervous his gruff demeanor made her.

She hurried forward and pulled the second pillow into place. "Is that how you wanted it?" she asked.

"For now."

She had a sudden memory of seeing the sheriff the night Rob Warren had broken into her home, assaulted her, held her at gunpoint and ended up in a shoot-out with the Haven Point police chief, Cade Emmett. He had burst into her home after the situation had been largely defused, to find Cade on the ground trying to revive a bleeding Wynona.

The stark fear on Marshall's face had haunted her, knowing that she might have unwittingly contributed to him losing another sibling after he had already lost his father and a younger brother in the line of duty.

Now Marshall's features were a shade or two

12

paler and his eyes had the glassy, distant look of someone in a great deal of pain.

"How long have you been out of the hospital?"

He shrugged. "A couple hours. Give or take."

"And you're here by yourself?" she exclaimed. "I thought you were supposed to be home earlier this morning and someone was going to stay with you for the first few hours. Wynona told me that was the plan."

"One of my deputies drove me home from the hospital, but I told him Chief Emmett would probably keep an eye on me."

The police chief lived across the street from Andie and just down the street from Marshall, which boded well for crime prevention in the neighborhood. Having the sheriff *and* the police chief on the same street should be any sane burglar's worst nightmare—especially *this* particular sheriff and police chief.

"And has he been by?"

"Uh, no. I didn't ask him to." Marshall's eyes looked unnaturally blue in his pain-tight features. "Did my sister send you to babysit me?"

"Babysit, no. She only asked me to periodically check on you. I also brought dinner for the next few nights."

"Also unnecessary. If I get hungry, I'll call Serrano's for a pizza later."

She gave him a bland look. "Would a pizza

13

delivery driver know to come pick you up off the floor?"

"You didn't pick me up," he muttered. "You just moved a pillow around."

He must find this completely intolerable, being dependent on others for the smallest thing. In her limited experience, most men made difficult patients. Tough, take-charge guys like Marshall Bailey probably hated every minute of it.

Sympathy and compassion had begun to replace some of her nervousness. She would probably never truly like the man—he was so big, so masculine, a cop through and through—but she could certainly empathize with what he was going through. For now, he was a victim and she certainly knew what that felt like.

"I brought dinner, so you might as well eat it," she said. "You can order pizza tomorrow if you want. It's not much, just beef stew and homemade rolls, with caramel apple pie for dessert."

"Not much?" he said, eyebrow raised. A low rumble sounded in the room just then and it took her a moment to realize it was coming from his stomach.

"You don't have to eat it, but if you'd like some, I can bring it in here."

He opened his mouth, but before he could answer, she heard a voice from the doorway.

"What happened to you?" Will asked, gazing at

14

Marshall's assorted scrapes, bruises and bandages with wide-eyed fascination.

"Will, I thought I told you to wait for me by the door."

"I know, but you were taking *forever*." He walked into the room a little farther, not at all intimidated by the battered, dangerous-looking man it contained. "Hi. My name is Will. What's yours?"

The sheriff gazed at her son. If anything, his features became even more remote, but he might have simply been in pain.

"This is Sheriff Bailey," Andie said, when Marshall didn't answer for a beat too long. "He's Wynona's brother."

Will beamed at him as if Marshall was his new best friend. "Wynona is nice and she has a nice dog whose name is Young Pete. Only, Wynona said he's not young anymore."

"Yeah, I know Young Pete," Marshall said after another pause. "He's been in our family for a long time. He was our dad's dog first."

Andie gave him a careful look. From Wyn, she knew their father had been shot in the line of duty several years earlier and had suffered a severe brain injury that left him physically and cognitively impaired. John Bailey had died the previous winter from pneumonia, after spending his last years at a Shelter Springs care center.

15

Though she had never met the man, her heart ached to think of all the Baileys had suffered.

"Why is his name Young Pete?" Will asked. "I think that's silly. He should be just Pete."

"Couldn't agree more, but you'll have to take that up with my sister."

Will accepted that with equanimity. He took another step closer and scrutinized the sheriff. "How did you get so hurt? Were you in a fight with some bad guys? Did you shoot them? A bad guy came to our house once and Chief Emmett shot him."

Andie stepped in quickly. She was never sure how much Will understood about what happened that summer. "Will, I need your help fixing a tray with dinner for the sheriff."

"I want to hear about the bad guys, though."

"There were no bad guys. I was hit by a car," Marshall said abruptly.

"You're big! Don't you know you're supposed to look both ways and hold someone's hand?"

Marshall Bailey's expression barely twitched. "I guess nobody happened to be around at the time."

Torn between amusement and mortification, Andie grabbed her son's hand. "Come on, Will," she said, her tone insistent. "I need your help."

Her put-upon son sighed. "Okay."

He let her hold his hand as they went back to the entry, where Chloe still sat on the floor, watching the hallway with anxious eyes.

"I told Will not to go in when you told us to wait here, but he wouldn't listen to me," Chloe said fretfully.

"You should see the police guy," Will said with relish. "He has blood on him and everything."

Andie hadn't seen any blood, but maybe Will was more observant than she. Or maybe he had just become good at trying to get a rise out of his sister.

"Ew. Gross," Chloe exclaimed, looking at the doorway with an expression that contained equal parts revulsion and fascination.

"He is Wyn's brother and knows Young Pete, too," Will informed her.

Easily distracted, as most six-year-old girls could be, Chloe sighed. "I miss Young Pete. I wonder if he and Sadie will be friends?"

"Why wouldn't they be?" Will asked.

"Okay, kids, we can talk about Sadie and Young Pete another time. Right now, we need to get dinner for Wynona's brother."

"I need to use the bathroom," Will informed her. He had that urgent look he sometimes wore when he had pushed things past the limit.

"There's a bathroom just down the hall, second door down. See?"

"Okay."

He raced for it—she hoped in time.

"We'll be in the kitchen," she told him, then carried the food to the bright and spacious room with its stainless appliances and white cabinets.

"See if you can find a small plate for the pie while I dish up the stew," she instructed Chloe.

"Okay," her daughter said.

The nervous note in her voice broke Andie's heart, especially when she thought of the bold child who used to run out to confront the world.

"Do I have to carry it out there?" Chloe asked.

"Not if you don't want to, honey. You can wait right here in the kitchen or in the entryway, if you want."

While Chloe perched on one of the kitchen stools and watched, Andie prepared a tray for Marshall, trying to make it as tempting as possible. She had a feeling his appetite wouldn't be back to normal for a few days because of the pain and the aftereffects of anesthesia, but at least the fault wouldn't lie in her presentation.

It didn't take long, but it still gave her time to make note of the few changes in the kitchen. In the few months Wynona had been gone, Marshall Bailey had left his mark. The kitchen was clean but not sparkling, and where Wyn had kept a cheery bowl of fruit on the counter, a pair of handcuffs and a stack of mail cluttered the space. Young Pete's food and water bowls were presumably in Boise with Young Pete.

As she looked at the space on the floor where they usually rested, she suddenly remembered dogs weren't the only creatures who needed beverages.

"I forgot to fill Sheriff Bailey's water bottle," she said to Chloe. "Could you do that for me?"

Chloe hopped down from her stool and picked up the water bottle. With her bottom lip pressed firmly between her teeth, she filled the water bottle with ice and water from the refrigerator before screwing the lid back on and held it out for Andie.

"Thanks, honey. Oh, the tray's pretty full and I don't have a free hand. I guess I'll have to make another trip for it."

As she had hoped, Chloe glanced at the tray and then at the doorway with trepidation on her features that eventually shifted to resolve.

"I guess I can maybe carry it for you," she whispered.

Andie smiled and rubbed a hand over Chloe's hair, heart bursting with pride at this brave little girl. "Thank you, Chloe. You're always such a big help to me."

Chloe mustered a smile, though it didn't stick. "You'll be right there?"

"The whole time. Where do you suppose that brother of yours is?"

She suspected the answer, even before she and Chloe walked back to the den and she heard Will chattering.

"And I want a new Lego set and a sled and some real walkie-talkies like my friend Ty has. He has his own pony and I want one of those, too.

Only, my mama says I can't have one because we don't have a place for him to run. Ty lives on a ranch and we only have a little backyard and we don't have a barn or any hay for a pony to eat. That's what horses eat—did you know that?"

Rats. Had she actually been stupid enough to fall for that "I have to go to the bathroom" gag? She should have known better. Will probably raced right back in here the moment her back was turned.

"I did know that. And oats and barley, too," Sheriff Bailey said. His voice, several octaves below Will's, rippled down her spine. Did he sound annoyed? She couldn't tell. Mostly, his voice sounded remote.

"We have oatmeal at our house and my mom puts barley in soup sometimes, so why couldn't we have a pony?"

She should probably rescue the man. He just had one leg broken by a hit-and-run driver. He didn't need the other one talked off by an almost-five-year-old. She moved into the room just in time to catch the tail end of the discussion.

"A pony is a pretty big responsibility," Marshall said.

"So is a dog and a cat and we have one of each, a dog named Sadie and a cat named Mrs. Finnegan," Will pointed out.

"But a pony is a lot more work than a dog *or* a cat. Anyway, how would one fit on Santa's sleigh?"

Judging by his peal of laughter, Will apparently thought that was hilarious.

"He couldn't! You're silly."

She had to wonder if anyone had ever called the serious sheriff *silly* before. She winced and carried the tray inside the room, judging it was past time to step in.

"Here you go. Dinner. Again, don't get your hopes up. I'm an adequate cook, but that's about it."

She set the food down on the end table next to the sofa and found a folded wooden TV tray she didn't remember from her frequent visits to the house when Wynona lived here. She set up the TV tray and transferred the food to it, then gestured for Chloe to bring the water bottle. Her daughter hurried over without meeting his gaze, set the bottle on the tray, then rushed back to the safety of the kitchen as soon as she could.

Marshall looked at the tray, then at her, leaving her feeling as if *she* were the silly one.

"Thanks. It looks good. I appreciate your kindness," he said stiffly, as if the words were dragged out of him.

He had to know any kindness on her part was out of obligation toward Wynona. The thought made her feel rather guilty. He was her neighbor and she should be more enthusiastic about helping him, whether he made her nervous or not.

"Where is your cell phone?" she asked. "You

need some way to contact the outside world."

"Why?"

She frowned. "Because people are concerned about you! You just got out of the hospital a few hours ago. You need pain medicine at regular intervals and you're probably supposed to have ice on that leg or something."

"I'm fine, as long as I can get to the bathroom and the kitchen and I have the remote close at hand."

Such a typical man. She huffed out a breath. "At least think of the people who care about you. Wyn is out of her head with worry, especially since your mother and Katrina aren't in town."

"Why do you think I didn't charge my phone?" he muttered.

She crossed her arms across her chest. She didn't like confrontation or big, dangerous men any more than her daughter did, but Wynona had asked her to watch out for him and she took the charge seriously.

"You're being obstinate. What if you trip over your crutches and hit your head, only this time somebody isn't at the door to make sure you can get up again?"

"That's not going to happen."

"You don't know that. Where is your phone, Sheriff?"

He glowered at her but seemed to accept the inevitable. "Fine," he said with a sigh. "It should be in the pocket of my jacket, which is in the bag they sent home with me from the hospital. I think my deputy said he left it in the bedroom. First door on the left."

The deputy should have made sure his boss had some way to contact the outside world, but she had a feeling it was probably a big enough chore getting Sheriff Bailey home from the hospital without him trying to drive himself and she decided to give the poor guy some slack.

"I'm going to assume the charger is in there, too."

"Yeah. By the bed."

She walked down the hall to the room that had once been Wyn's bedroom. The bedroom still held traces of Wynona in the solid Mission furniture set, but Sheriff Bailey had stamped his own personality on it in the last three months. A Stetson hung on one of the bedposts and instead of mounds of pillows and the beautiful log cabin quilt Wyn's aunts had made her, a no-frills but soft-looking navy duvet covered the bed, made neatly as he had probably left it the morning before. A pile of books waited on the bedside table and a pair of battered cowboy boots stood toe-out next to the closet.

The room smelled masculine and entirely too sexy for her peace of mind, of sage-covered mountains with an undertone of leather and spice.

Except for that brief moment when she had

helped him reposition the pillow, she had never been close enough to Marshall to see if that scent clung to his skin. The idea made her shiver a little before she managed to rein in the wholly inappropriate reaction.

She found the plastic hospital bag on the wide armchair near the windows overlooking the snow-covered pines along the river. Feeling strangely guilty at invading the man's privacy, she opened it. At the top of the pile that appeared to contain mostly clothing, she found another large clear bag with a pair of ripped jeans inside covered in a dried dark substance she realized was blood.

Marshall Bailey's blood.

The stark reminder of his close call sent a tremor through her. He could have been killed if that hit-and-run driver had struck him at a slightly higher rate of speed. The Baileys likely wouldn't have recovered, especially since Wyn's twin brother, Wyatt, had been struck and killed by an out-of-control vehicle while helping a stranded motorist during a winter storm.

The jeans weren't ruined beyond repair. Maybe she could spray stain remover on them and try to mend the rips and tears.

Further searching through the bag finally unearthed the phone. She found the charger next to the bed and carried the phone, charger and bag containing the Levi's back to the sheriff.

While she was gone from the room, he had

pulled the tray close and was working on the dinner roll in a desultory way.

She plugged the charger into the same outlet as the lamp next to the sofa and inserted the other end into his phone. "Here you are. I'll let you turn it on. Now you'll have no excuse not to talk to your family when they call."

"Thanks. I guess."

Andie held out the bag containing the jeans. "Do you mind if I take these? I'd like to see if I can get the stains out and do a little repair work."

"It's not worth the effort. I don't even know why they sent them home. The paramedics had to cut them away to get to my leg."

"You never know. I might be able to fix them."

He shrugged, his eyes wearing that distant look again. He was in pain, she realized, and trying very hard not to show it.

"If you power on your phone and unlock it, I can put my cell number in there so you can reach me in an emergency."

"I won't—" he started to say, but the sentence ended with a sigh as he reached for the phone.

As soon as he turned it on, the phone gave a cacophony of beeps, alerting him to missed texts and messages, but he paid them no attention.

"What's your number?"

She gave it to him and in turn entered his into her own phone.

"Please don't be stubborn. If you need help, call

me. I'm just a few houses away and can be here in under two minutes—and that's even if I have to take time to put on boots and a winter coat."

He likely wouldn't call and both of them knew it.

"Are we almost done?" Will asked from the doorway, clearly tired of having only his sister to talk to in the other room.

"In a moment," she said, then turned back to Marshall. "Do you know Herm and Louise Jacobs, next door?"

Oddly, he gaped at her for a long, drawn-out moment. "Why do you ask?" His voice was tight with suspicion.

"If I'm not around and you need help for some reason, they or their grandson Christopher can be here even faster. I'll put their number in your phone, too, just in case."

"I doubt I'll need it, but . . . thanks."

"Christopher has a skateboard, a big one," Will offered gleefully. "He rides it without even a helmet!"

Her son had a bad case of hero worship when it came to the Jacobses' troubled grandson, wh had come to live with Herm and Louise shortly after Andie and her children arrived in Haven Point. It worried her a little to see how fascinated Will was with the clearly rebellious teenager, but so far Christopher had been patient and even kind to her son.

26

"That's not very safe, is it?" the sheriff said gruffly. "You should always wear a helmet when you're riding a bike or skateboard to protect your head."

"I don't even *have* a skateboard," Will said.

"If you get one," Marshall answered. This time she couldn't miss the clear strain in his voice. The man was at the end of his endurance and probably wanted nothing more than to be alone with his pain.

"We really do need to leave," Andie said quickly. "Is there anything else I can do to help you before we leave?"

He shook his head, then winced a little as if the motion hurt. "You've done more than enough already."

"Try to get some rest, if you can. I'll check in with you tomorrow and also bring something for your lunch."

He didn't exactly look overjoyed at the prospect. "I don't suppose I can say anything to persuade you otherwise, can I?"

"You're a wise man, Sheriff Bailey."

Will giggled. "Where's your gold and Frankenstein?"

Marshall blinked, obviously as baffled as she was, which only made Will giggle more.

"Like in the Baby Jesus story, you know. The wise men brought the gold, Frankenstein and mirth."

She did her best to hide a smile. This year Will had become fascinated with the small carved Nativity set she bought at a thrift store the first year she moved out of her grandfather's cheerless house.

"Oh. Frankincense and myrrh. They were perfumes and oils, I think. When I said Sheriff Bailey was a wise man, I just meant he was smart."

She was a little biased, yes, but she couldn't believe even the most hardened of hearts wouldn't find her son adorable. The sheriff only studied them both with that dour expression.

He was in pain, she reminded herself. If she were in his position, she wouldn't find a four-year-old's chatter amusing, either.

"We'll see you tomorrow," she said again. "Call me, even if it's the middle of the night."

"I will," he said, which she knew was a blatant fib. He would never call her.

She had done all she could, short of moving into his house—kids, pets and all.

She gathered the children part of that equation and ushered them out of the house. Darkness came early this close to the winter solstice, but the Jacobs family's Christmas lights next door gleamed through the snow.

In the short time she'd been inside his house, Andie had forgotten most of her nervousness around Marshall. Perhaps it was his injury that made him feel a little less threatening to her—though she had a feeling that even if he'd suffered *two* broken legs in that accident, the sheriff of Lake Haven County would never be anything less than dangerous.

Chapter TWO

Marsh waited until he heard the door close behind Andrea Montgomery and her children before he allowed himself to grimace and release the breath he hadn't realized he'd been holding.

His entire body hurt like a mother trucker, as if somebody had been pummeling him for the last, oh, twenty-two hours. He couldn't pinpoint a single portion of his anatomy that wasn't throbbing right about now.

Though the surgery to set and pin the multiple fractures in his foot and ankle had taken place in the early hours of the morning, his head still felt foggy from the anesthesia and the pain meds|they had thrust upon him afterward.

Oddly, the leg wasn't as painful as the abrasions on his face and hands where he had scraped pavement on the way down. Some of his pain was probably the inevitable adrenaline crash that always hit after a critical incident.

He drew in a deep breath of air that still smelled like his neighbor, sweet as spring wildflowers on a rain-washed meadow.

He hated that he was now her pity project, thanks to her sense of obligation to his sister. He knew that was the only reason she had come by. Wyn must have blackmailed her into helping him. What other reason could she have for doing it?

Andrea Montgomery didn't like him. He wasn't sure what he'd done to her, but in their few previous interactions she had always seemed cold and unfriendly to him. He would have figured her for the last person to come to his rescue. Few people were strong enough to withstand pressure from Wyn when she was at her most persuasive, though.

He didn't want his neighbor and her kids to come back the next day. Short of locking the door, how could he prevent it?

Less than a day ago, he had been under the wholly misguided impression that he had most facets of his life under control.

He had a family he loved, a widowed mother who had just found happiness again and remarried, a brother he admired and respected, a sister who was now engaged to his best friend, another one who was suddenly passionate about saving the world. He lived in the most beautiful place on earth and he had a position of great responsibility that he had worked very hard to earn.

Yeah, he had some in-house personnel problems in the sheriff's department—the most urgent concern one that involved a significant amount of missing cash in a drug case—but he was dealing with them.

He certainly had a few enemies among the criminal element in his county. Who in law

31

enforcement didn't? Suspects he had investigated and arrested would probably top that list, followed by the people who loved them.

A few powerful people were on that list as well, including Bill Newbold, a wealthy rancher and county commissioner Marsh had had a run-in with a few weeks earlier over a neighbor's claim he was overreaching his water rights.

Marsh could have handled that matter a little more delicately, but he'd never much liked Newbold and figured the man used his political position to line his own pockets. Attempted vehicular homicide, though? He couldn't countenance it.

Maybe he was being too naive.

Marshall would never claim his life was perfect. He had made his share of mistakes—one huge one that was never far from his mind, especially lately. But he never expected to become a target of deadly force, until somebody in a snowy parking lot set out to show him how very wrong he was.

When he closed his eyes, he could still hear the sound of that engine gunning, the tires spinning on slush and gravel.

It wasn't an accident caused by weather and nerves, despite what the investigator with the state police wanted to believe. How could it be? Someone had lured him to an abandoned gas station on the outskirts of Shelter Springs, baiting the trap with the promise of a lead in a long-cold missing persons case he worked when he first started at the Lake Haven Sheriff's Department as a deputy fresh out of the military.

When he arrived, of course no one had been there. Marsh had walked around the dilapidated building to see if he was missing something and that was when he heard the engine gun from behind him. He turned just as the SUV headed straight for him and had barely been able to leap away at the last minute to avoid a direct hit.

He hadn't been quite fast enough and the vehicle had struck his right leg. The combination of the impact and his own attempt to twist away had done a number on his leg. The X-ray looked like somebody had smashed his leg with a hammer, and the grim tally included a compound fracture of his ankle and multiple smaller fractures all the way up to below his knee.

He had been too busy trying not to pass out from the pain and hadn't caught much that would identify the vehicle, except the color—white— and the general make—American-made late-model small SUV.

As for the driver, in the dark and the snow and from Marshall's angle on the ground, he had seen nothing except a dark shape wearing a ski mask. He did have one small piece of evidence he hoped would lead in the right direction, but it was too early to tell.

The state police investigator seemed to think

the anonymous tipster had chickened out at the last minute and tried to drive away but slid into Marshall because of the snowy conditions and had subsequently panicked and raced off into the night.

Marsh wasn't buying it. Why insist on meeting there, in a relatively isolated spot without security cameras or witnesses?

No. Somebody had tried to take him out.

He sat back on the sofa, head pounding and his eyes gritty with exhaustion.

Why?

That was the question he couldn't get out of his head. What the hell was all this about? Who hated him enough to want him gone?

He took a sip of water and shifted on the sofa, fruitlessly searching for a more comfortable spot.

He hated this, sitting here helpless instead of going after the son of a bitch who had done this to him. Worse, he was on mandatory leave for at least three weeks, since Newbold had pushed the other commissioners to insist he take sick leave until the New Year.

They couldn't stop him from investigating on his own. He would make a list and start eliminating suspects, one by one. Cade would help him and so would Ruben Morales, his second in command.

Not right now. He was too damn tired and sore to do much more than sit here and try to find the energy to make it to his bedroom.

His cell phone rang before he could force himself to grab the crutches and get up.

He should have made Andie Montgomery leave it somewhere out of his reach. He thought about ignoring it, but she was right, there were about a hundred missed calls and texts on there. It seemed cowardly to continue ignoring all of them.

He glanced at the readout and saw it was Wynona. With a sigh, he picked it up.

"Hey, Wyn," he said.

"About time you answered your phone! I was just about to pack Pete into the car and drive down there."

"Glad you didn't. We've got a storm moving in fast."

"So do we, but what else am I supposed to do when you won't call me back? For all I knew, you were lying on the floor unconscious somewhere."

How humiliating, that Andrea Montgomery with the lovely eyes had found him after that little spill. Had she called Wyn the moment she left the house to tell her?

"My phone didn't have a charge. Sorry to worry you. I'm not on the floor. I'm currently getting ready to eat what looks like some delicious stew made by your friend."

"Andie stopped by to check on you? Oh, I'm so glad. I didn't like the idea of you in that house alone, just hours after surgery."

"It was totally unnecessary for you to hire

a babysitter for me. I can take care of myself."

"Extenuating circumstances. So tell me what happened. All I know is what I've heard from Cade, bits and pieces I've had to pry out of him."

He would rather she didn't know anything at all, but Wyn always seemed to have her ear to the ground. Until a few months earlier, she had been a police officer herself and had many connections in the local law enforcement community— not to mention that she was engaged to his best friend, who just happened to be the chief of police of Haven Point.

And, yeah, the two of them being together still freaked him out, though they seemed happy enough.

"What have you heard?"

"Something about you heading out to meet a CI and ending up on the wrong side of the CI's grille."

"Yeah. That's about the size of it."

"And the guy behind the wheel just sped off? You didn't get any kind of a look at him that might help identify him?"

"Not really."

He didn't tell her he *was* able to get a partial plate, which was how Ruben, working under the radar, was able to ascertain the vehicle was reported stolen from a Boise box store parking lot two days earlier.

Wyn didn't need to know all the details of the

investigation—at least not until he had something concrete to go on.

"We've got a few leads we're following, but it's early days yet in the investigation."

"*You* shouldn't have *any* leads. You're supposed to be taking it easy."

He glanced around his family room, where he had a feeling he would be spending entirely too much time for the immediate future.

"I couldn't be taking it any more easy than I am right now, unless I were comatose."

"Good. I'm sure that's just what the doctor ordered."

It was, but he also didn't want to admit that to his bossy younger sister.

"What do you need? Gelato from Carmela's? Barbara Serrano's zuppa tuscano? I can have the Helping Hands hook you up with anything that would help you get through the next few days."

More than anything, he wanted to be left alone. Knowing his sister, that was a wish that was doomed from the start.

"I don't need anything. Thanks for worrying about me, but I'm fine, really. I'm managing okay on the crutches. At least I've only fallen once."

"That's not very reassuring," Wyn said. He could almost hear the frown in her voice. "I would still feel better if you would let Andrea check in on you, at least these first few days home from the hospital. I know you're a tough guy, but sometimes even tough guys need a little TLC."

"I appreciate your concern, but it's not necessary, really. I'll be just fine."

"You'd say that even if you had two broken legs, wouldn't you?"

"Can't say. How about we don't break the other one to test your theory, though?"

Wynona snorted. "Sometimes you're so much like Dad, it's freaky."

"I'll take that as a compliment," he answered. He could only try to be half the man John Bailey was. His father had been the best person Marshall knew. He had taught all his sons—and his daughters, come to that—everything they needed to know about being good cops and, more important, how to be decent people.

For a raw, unguarded moment, his heart ached for his father, for lost possibilities, for all the questions he could never ask John now about how to go forward with the rest of his life.

"It is a compliment, mostly. As bad as things were those last few years, the happiest I saw him was that day you won the election last year."

He wasn't sure if his father had even understood that Marshall had decided to run for sheriff after John's good friend announced his retirement. He liked to think so, but his father hadn't spoken a word since surviving a gunshot wound to the brain on the job.

"I'll say this for you, though—you're every bit

as stubborn as our darling father. Seriously, what's the harm in having Andie stop in a few times a day?"

He pictured Andrea with her auburn hair, her big green eyes, that air of fragile loveliness about her that called to a man's deepest protective impulses. The same impulses that had never brought him anything but trouble.

"It was kind of her to bring dinner tonight, but I barely know the woman, Wynnie. She has enough on her plate with those kids of hers to have to worry about checking up on me."

"She assured me she doesn't mind."

"What else is she going to say to you?" he pointed out. "You took a bullet for her."

"Not really. It only grazed me."

"Still. The woman obviously feels a great sense of obligation to you. It doesn't seem fair to emotionally blackmail her into helping out your brother."

"Oh, stop it. You think I don't know what you're trying to do, turning this around to make it seem like I did something wrong by asking her to help me out, since I can't be there?"

"Not wrong. Just not necessary."

"I get that you want to go into hermit mode and keep everyone away while you hunker down and lick your wounds. Cade would do the same thing."

"What's wrong with that?" he muttered.

She sighed. "Face it, my brother, you need help.

You've got a badly broken leg that requires serious pain medication. You live alone and you can't get around well or go to the store or shovel your own driveway. Since you were inconsiderate enough to get hurt when none of the members of your family can step up to help, having Andie stop by a few times a day is the next best thing, short of hiring a CNA to be with you around the clock."

He didn't answer, simply because he couldn't come up with any words to counter her argument. He wanted to think it was the pain medication making his head feel like somebody had stuffed it full of steel wool, but he had a feeling it might have been more than that.

Maybe, just maybe, there was a slim chance his sister was right on this one.

"If the situation had been reversed," she pressed, "you would have insisted on finding one of your friends to check on *me*."

"Right. And who knows?" he said drily. "You might have ended up engaged to one of them."

Laughter rippled through the phone. "Life is crazy, isn't it?"

The last twenty-four hours had been the craziest he had endured in a long time.

"I know you don't want Andie there, but it's only for a few days and it would make me feel better, until I can finish things up here and come back to keep an eye on you. I'll try to speak to my thesis adviser tomorrow and see if I can sneak away early."

"Don't do that." He knew how important Wynona considered this dream of taking her life in a new direction. He wouldn't be able to stomach the guilt if she had trouble with her graduate studies because of him.

"So will you let Andie come back?"

He sighed. Apparently he was no more immune to emotional blackmail than his lovely neighbor. "Fine. She can come back."

"Thanks. Seriously. That's a huge relief to me. Cade says he'll stop in when he can, but you know how crazy things are this time of year."

The sheriff's department was the same. He had a million things to do before the end of the year—and that wasn't counting the investigation into the missing evidence.

Damn Bill Newbold anyway. How was Marsh supposed to endure three weeks of enforced medical leave?

As an elected position, the sheriff of Lake Haven County technically reported to the voting public. The county commission couldn't legally stop him from reporting to work—but the county commission oversaw all county departments and had budgetary control over his department. Newbold was pissed enough right now that Marsh wouldn't put it past the man to do all he could to block the badly needed deputy pay increase

Marsh had been wrangling for since his election.

For the sake of his department, he could roll over for a few weeks, do as much work as possible from home.

"I've got to run," Wynona said. "Pete apparently needs to go out. Are you sure you're all right alone tonight?"

"Perfectly."

"I'll have to take your word on that. Be nice to Andie, okay? You know things haven't been easy for her."

Yeah, he knew. His gut twisted. Detective Robert Warren had sat in the county jail for months after his plea deal and had been transferred to the state penitentiary only a few weeks earlier. Marsh had purposely kept his interactions with the man to a minimum and had made sure Warren had no cause to claim his treatment at the Lake Haven County Jail was anything less than proper and humane, especially considering the sheriff's own personal connection to one of his victims. Wynona.

It was one thing to know in the abstract what Warren had done to Andrea Montgomery. Facts on a report, testimony during his sentencing hearing. It was something else entirely when he thought about that soft, sweet-smelling woman and her cute kids having to live in fear for the better part of a year because she had once trusted the wrong man.

Chapter THREE

"These are absolutely perfect," Andie exclaimed the next day as she looked at the cheery watercolors laid out on her neighbor's kitchen table, a garden of flowers blooming with soft, lovely color to take the edge off the wintry day.

She shook her head in amazement. "We had one short conversation about you designing something for me, that's all, yet you came back with exactly the right concept for my clients."

"Oh, I'm so happy you think something will work!" Louise Jacobs glowed with pleasure. "I've never done anything like this before. Ever. I've always just painted for my own enjoyment, really. It was such a challenge—but a wonderful one."

"I knew you could do it. I have loved the watercolors you sell at Point Made Flowers and Gifts and I had a suspicion my clients in Boise would, too. It's the perfect mood and tone for their natural remedy spa services, exactly what I wanted, and I am certain they're going to love it."

"I hope so."

"Trust me. I've been trying for weeks to capture the right tone and mood for their website redesign and ad campaign, but nothing seemed to feel right. I couldn't get to the heart of it, but you've managed it. You have a gift, my friend."

Louise beamed. "I'm so happy you like them."

Andie saw the possibility of a very successful partnership moving forward. "If you're all right with it, I'll buy each one for the price we talked about."

"Oh, you don't have to pay me anything. I was happy to do it. I should pay you, actually. I needed the distraction and it was so nice to be back in my studio. I haven't been able to pick up my brushes in months. Not since . . ."

Her voice trailed off, eyes bleak with grief. Andie touched her hand. "I'm so sorry, my dear. How are you doing?"

Louise looked down at the bouquet of water-colors for a moment, then offered a strained smile. "I'll be glad when the holidays are over. Everyone told me how hard all the firsts would be. It's so true."

"Yes. It is."

Jason had died in November, the week before Thanksgiving. Andie had no clear idea how she'd made it through that first December. She had been in a fog of shock and disbelief that her perfect world had imploded so wildly.

Last December had been tough in its own way, for reasons she didn't want to think about.

Louise and Herm's only daughter had died just five months earlier. No doubt the wound still felt jagged and raw.

"I wish we didn't have to celebrate the holidays

44

this year, but Herm wants us to go ahead with all our usual traditions, even though none of us has much holiday spirit. He thinks we need to build new traditions with Christopher, now that he's living with us."

Andie looked around the comfortable open-plan house, artfully decorated with greenery, ribbons, candles in slim holders. "It's so warm and cozy in here. I'm sure that's helped him feel more at home."

As if on cue, a thin, gangly boy with shoulder-length dark hair and a semipermanent scowl wandered into the kitchen. Louise's thirteen-year-old grandson stopped short when he spotted the two of them.

"Oh. I didn't know somebody was here."

"Hi, Christopher." Andie smiled at the boy, whose scowl seemed to deepen in response. "No classes at the middle school today?"

His blue-eyed gaze flashed to his grandmother for an instant before turning back to her. "Um, sick day. I think I'm coming down with something."

Judging by his bloodshot eyes and his greenish features, she suspected his sickness might be morning-after regret. Once in a while after a bad day on the job, her husband used to go on a bender and his symptoms were remarkably similar.

"Oh dear. I hope it's nothing serious."

He gave a halfhearted shrug. "Guess we'll see. Nana, what's there to eat?"

Louise pursed her lips, her eyes worried. "I made Scottish shortbread this morning."

He gave a revolted look. "Isn't that like head cheese?"

"That's sweetbread, dear. Shortbread is basically a bar cookie made with butter and sugar. They're in the tin."

"Right here?"

She nodded and he opened the tin. After a moment's consideration, he picked up a couple of them and took a bite from one as he opened the refrigerator and stared inside.

"If you're ready for lunch, I can make you a sandwich or there's leftover chicken noodle soup from last night I could warm up," Louise offered.

He closed the refrigerator door. "This is probably good," he said around the mouthful of cookie. "I'm not that hungry."

"You can't just eat a cookie," Louise exclaimed. "Especially if you're coming down with something."

"I said I wasn't that hungry, okay?" he snapped and abruptly stalked out of the kitchen.

Louise watched him go, eyes glassy with unshed tears. All her pride and excitement about the watercolors and Andie's approval of them seemed to have drained away during the short interaction with her grandson.

"How is *he* doing?" Andie asked gently.

One of those tears slipped out and slid down her

friend's cheek and she brushed it away with an impatient hand. "His mother's dead and his father wants nothing to do with him. He's stuck living in a new town he hates with his boring old grand-parents who have never raised a boy and don't know how to talk to him. He hates school, hates his teachers, hates doing homework. He's made a few friends, but . . ." Her voice trailed off.

"But?"

"I'm not sure they're the nicest young people. They seem to run wild at all hours of the day and night, with no parental supervision that I can see."

Louise seemed so disheartened that Andie couldn't help giving her a little hug.

"He'll make it through this. Please don't worry. Time is the great healer. It's a truism because it's just that—true. That's all he needs. He's got you and Herm, two of the very best people I know. That's far more than many children have in similar circumstances."

Certainly more than Andie had known. Oh, how she wished she could have had someone like Louise in her life, someone sweet and kind and welcoming.

"He's a good boy," Louise said, wiping away another tear. "He's just so *angry* all the time."

Andie remembered that anger after her own mother died, along with confusion and fear and overwhelming grief. Puberty was tough enough, all raging hormones and intensified emotions.

The loss of a parent made that transitional time that much harder, even when the parent hadn't been the best a kid could ask for.

"I'm sorry," Louise said after a moment. "You didn't come here to listen to my problems."

"That's what friends do."

"How are *you* these days?"

She would much rather talk about Louise's problems, any day of the week. She knew what was behind the question. Everyone in Haven Point knew about the incident over the summer when the situation she had tried to escape by moving here from Portland had caught up with her, when she had been held at gunpoint by the man who had raped her the previous year, then stalked her for months.

Andie was doing her best to move beyond her past so she could work toward building a new future with her children here. She knew Louise's question was offered in kindness, but she really didn't want to talk about Rob Warren and the hell he had put her through.

"Everything's great," she said, pinning on a bright smile. "I'm really looking forward to Christmas in Haven Point. I can't imagine a prettier place to spend the holiday. It's perfect."

"It really is, isn't it?" Louise smiled softly. "The lake seems to change colors every day with the shifting winter light."

"It must be fun to paint it this time of year."

"It is." Distracted, Louise looked down at her watercolors and Andie hoped she was thinking about taking her paints out to the water's edge to try capturing that stunning blue.

Andie had taken to carrying her camera on her morning snowshoe walks along the river, catching birds flitting through winter-bare branches, the delicate filigree of ice along the riverbanks, the play of sunlight reflecting on the snow and filtering through the fringy pine boughs.

She had found peace here over the last few months, a calm she had needed desperately.

"I saw in the paper that our neighbor next door had an accident of some kind," Louise said.

Now, there was someone who *didn't* give her peace. Marshall Bailey. "Yes. He was struck by a hit-and-run driver a few days ago and ended up with a badly broken leg."

"Oh, the poor man! Charlene must be having fits!"

"I don't think Marshall wants his mother to know until she and Mike return from their honeymoon."

Louise gave an approving nod. "Good decision. Why give her needless worry?"

"I agree."

"So who's watching over him?"

Andie raised her hand. "Well, I don't know that I'd go as far as to say I'm *watching over him*. Wyn just asked me to check on him a few times a day. I'm heading there after I pick Will up from preschool."

She felt too foolish to add that she wanted her son to come along as a buffer. "It would be helpful if you and Herm would keep an eye on things, too."

"Oh, of course. We would be glad to do that. His mother is one of my dearest friends, though she pulled away a little after poor John had his accident." She paused. "Do you think Marshall would enjoy some of my shortbread? I made plenty."

"I'm sure he would. I can take it to him, if you'd like."

"Thank you! Let me find a container."

She bustled around the kitchen for a moment and ended up producing two tins printed with smiling families of snowmen.

"Here you go. A box for him and one for you and your children, if you'd care for it."

"Oh, thank you! They will love it."

These kind little gestures neighbors did for each other here always warmed her heart. She had enjoyed living in Portland. It was a beautiful, vibrant town filled with interesting people, restaurants, shops. But in all the years she had lived there after striking out on her own, it had never really felt as much like home as Haven Point, even though she and the children had been here less than six months.

She glanced at the whimsical owl clock on the wall. "I should go. Will is going to be done soon from preschool. I don't know where the time went!"

"I'm so glad we had the chance to visit a little. You made me feel a little better."

"I'm glad." She hugged Louise, then slid her friend's lovely collection of watercolors into the portfolio she had provided. "And thank you so much for these. I can't wait to show them to my clients."

"I do hope they like them," Louise said again, her expression anxious.

"How could they not? They're stunning. You really need to have a show, more than just the few you've given Kenzie to hang in the shop. You should think about talking to the owner of that new art gallery that just opened up downtown."

"Me? Oh, I could never do that! I only paint for fun."

"Think about it, my dear." She slid her arms in the sleeves of her coat and headed for the front door. As she neared the stairs, she heard loud, discordant rock music coming from upstairs, then a crash followed by a string of crude vulgarities.

Louise's cheeks turned pink. "That boy! I'm so sorry."

"Don't be sorry on my account, Louise. He's a teenage boy going through a rough time right now. A little creative expression is only to be expected."

51

She hugged her friend one more time, then walked out of her house with the portfolio under one arm and the tins of cookies nestled in the crook of the other.

She took a few steps toward home, then paused and turned back to the house next to Louise's. She could check on Marshall now. Will wouldn't be out of preschool for another half hour.

Why couldn't she stop now, drop off the cookies, check to make sure the man was doing all right and then be on her way?

Yes, he made her nervous and she didn't really want to be alone with him. Or any man, really. Maybe that was all the more reason to push herself into it. While he was big and rough and intimidating, he was also relatively helpless at the moment. This would be a good test for her.

After what had happened the day before, she wasn't in a big rush to surprise him, so she texted quickly as she headed next door.

Can I stop by now?

His answer was so succinct, she had to smile.

Why?

Homemade shortbread, she texted back.

His answer in reply made her smile turn into an actual laugh. Door's open.

Apparently Wyn hadn't been joking about his sweet tooth.

Despite the warning she had just given him, she didn't feel right about just barging in, so she rapped a few times on the door before opening it. "Hello?"

"Back here," he answered, with the same brevity of his texts.

This time she found him on the recliner, with a book open on the table beside him and a rugby match muted on the TV. The worst of the bruises on his face seemed to be fading, she was happy to see, and his color looked better than it had the day before.

"Did you get breakfast?"

He nodded. "I grabbed some toast and coffee, plus a yogurt and banana."

He probably needed groceries and had no way to get to the store. She should have thought of that the night before and at least checked to make sure he had basics. Guilt pinched at her. She was doing a terrible job of filling Wyn's small request to watch over her brother.

"I need to run to the store later today. If you can think of anything that sounds tasty, I'm happy to pick it up for you. Just make a list."

"Homemade shortbread is a good start," he said, a blatant reminder to turn over the goods.

She fought a laugh and set the tin on the table beside him. "Here you go. It might still be warm."

Without hesitation, he opened it and popped one small square into his mouth. He chewed and swallowed with a look of clear appreciation. "Oh, wow. That's delicious."

"I wish I could take credit for making it, but it's a gift from your neighbor next door. Louise Jacobs."

He had just been about to pop a second piece in, but at her words he froze for just a second and returned the cookie to the tin. "You've been to see Louise and Herm?" he said, his tone oddly neutral.

"Only Louise. Herm volunteers once a week, stocking shelves at the library. Apparently retirement didn't completely agree with him and he gets bored during cold weather when he can't fish as much. Louise is a friend of mine and she's doing a little work for me."

"What kind of work?"

She held up the brown portfolio. "I'm a commercial graphic artist—computer graphics, mostly, but photography, sometimes oil on canvas. I needed a watercolor, which isn't exactly my specialty, and Louise was kind enough to work up a few possibilities for me. They're wonderful."

"Oh. I guess I didn't realize she was artistic."

"She considers it more of a hobby, but she's really talented. And not just in making shortbread."

He smiled, but it didn't quite reach his eyes. He looked distracted—whether from pain or something else, she couldn't tell.

"Is there anything I can get you right now?"

"I can't think of anything."

"I'll refill your water bottle while you make a

list of what you'd like me to pick up at the grocery store."

"You don't need to do my shopping."

Good grief, trying to help the man was about as easy as climbing Mount Solace in a blizzard.

"You might as well tell me. If you don't, I'll just look through your kitchen cabinets and see what staples seem to be missing. Who knows what I might come back with?"

He gave a sigh that sounded more resigned than annoyed. "Fine. I'll text you a list of a few things. Does that work?"

"Perfectly. See? You're getting the hang of this whole accepting-help thing."

"I don't believe you're giving me much choice, are you?"

"Not really," she admitted. "I have just enough time to reheat a little more stew or I can probably throw together a sandwich if you would prefer."

He didn't sigh this time, but she could tell he wanted to. "Stew would be fine," he finally said. "Thank you."

"Give me a second."

After dishing some into a bowl and popping it into the microwave, she spent a moment straightening up his mostly clean kitchen while it reheated. She added a couple of the rolls she had brought the evening before and cut up an apple she found in the vegetable drawer of the refrigerator.

"Here you are. Soups and stews are always better the second day, if you ask me."

"Agreed."

"I wasn't snooping—okay, I was snooping a little—and I noticed you didn't have milk or bread and the only other banana looked pretty ripe. I can pick those up for you and whatever else is on your list. And if you think something sounds good for dinner, let me know."

"Stew is fine by me, if there's enough for one more go-round."

She raised an eyebrow. "My stew is remarkable, I will admit, but you can't have it for every meal."

"You're not running a short-order restaurant here. I'm fine with whatever. I've got frozen dinners in the freezer that will do."

"Are you this stubborn with everyone or am I receiving special treatment?"

If she didn't know better, she might have thought the stoic sheriff almost smiled, for a minute there. "My deputies would probably say the former," he answered.

"That makes me feel a little better. I need to run, but make sure you text me your list. I probably won't have a chance to go shopping until after Chloe gets home from school, but we'll bring groceries and dinner around five thirty, if that works. Meanwhile, you've also got leftover pie and Louise Jacobs's shortbread."

"What else could a guy possibly need?"

56

Chapter FOUR

The scent of flowers again lingered in the room after Andrea Montgomery blew out of his house as quickly as she'd come.

He couldn't seem to escape it. He shifted in the recliner, wishing he could find a spot that was comfortable for more than five seconds.

It wasn't only the general discomfort from his smashed-to-smithereens leg or his various other aches and pains that left him edgy and unsettled. Her mention of the Jacobs family next door was even more disconcerting.

He knew Herm and Louise from way back. Louise had been good friends with his mother—in a roundabout way, that friendship had been the catalyst for everything that came after.

When he first moved into Wyn's house here on Riverbend Road in late summer, he had made it a point of going over to say hello to them. It had been the neighborly thing to do, hadn't it?

Since then, he had spoken with them a few times in passing, but he worked long hours and their schedules didn't seem to coincide, plus he didn't really have an obvious excuse for stopping by.

They had bumped into each other a few times at the only grocery store in town—which was one of the main reasons he didn't do his shopping in

Shelter Springs, five miles away, even though the two grocery stores and the box store there were larger and had a far more extensive selection.

He had decided those rare encounters at the little store in Haven Point were worth the disadvantage of having a choice between only two brands of dishwashing detergent.

He needed to figure out a way to do more than say hello in passing. That was the entire reason he was living here in his sister's house instead of his perfectly adequate—and certainly more conveniently located—apartment in Shelter Springs, after all.

In some vague corner of his mind, he had thought maybe he would wait until after the holidays before he burst in and shook their world completely. He glared down at the stupid cast. He could still go talk to Herm and Louise after the holidays, but some idiot in a stolen SUV had added a complication he never would have anticipated.

How could he show up now, in this completely useless state, when he couldn't even go to the grocery store on his own?

Though he wasn't really hungry, he forced himself to take another few bites of Andrea Montgomery's delicious stew. His body needed fuel to heal, and the faster he healed, the faster he could return to work.

He was on his third bite of stew when his phone

buzzed with an incoming text. He set down his spoon and checked the message from Jackie Scott, the assistant he had inherited from the previous sheriff, asking him a question about holiday overtime. He answered her question, which led to two more follow-up texts in quick succession.

Three texts in a row was his personal limit. More than that warranted an actual conversation instead of an endless string of thumbed communications via text or email.

He quickly found her number on his phone and Jackie answered on the first ring.

"You're not supposed to be working, Sheriff. You should be resting."

He didn't bother reminding her she had been the one to text him about overtime.

"I've rested plenty. Just because my leg is broken doesn't mean my brain is. How are things there?"

"Ken Kramer is walking around like he won the lottery since the commission named him acting sheriff. He tried to move into your office, but I wouldn't let him. I told him you left the door locked and I didn't have the key, and if he wanted it, he would have to go there and take it from you."

"I believe I won't hold my breath," he said.

Both of them knew Ken would never do that. On the surface Ken Kramer pretended to be loyal and supportive after Marshall defeated him in the last election, while behind the scenes he whispered and spread rumors. He was the kind of man who was really good at sneaky, underhanded sabotage but didn't have the stones for outright confronta-tion.

He was also a brother-in-law to County Commissioner Newbold. The joys of small-town politics.

"I've also got about a hundred things I need you to sign. I'll try to swing by one day this week."

"Sounds good."

Jackie was hyperefficient, organized and the exact opposite of Ken Kramer. Taking over the job a year ago would have been a nightmare without her on his team to help the transition.

"You should know there are all kinds of rumors flying around about what happened to you. That young reporter from the newspaper called to ask if it was true that you had been airlifted to Boise and were in a coma."

"You didn't tell him the truth, did you? I wouldn't mind sticking with that story, if it meant I didn't have to talk to him for a while."

"You're not that lucky," she answered.

He glanced down at his broken leg. He wouldn't call himself lucky, by any stretch of the imagi-nation.

He and Jackie talked for several more moments about his calendar and meetings he would need to reschedule until the New Year, business details of running a department that employed twenty deputies and ran a jail with up to two dozen inmates.

By the time they ended the call and he hung up, the rest of the stew was cold and the exhaustion pressing on his shoulders reminded him how little sleep he'd been able to find the night before.

He was amazed at how wiped this broken leg had left him.

This wasn't his first major injury. He broke his arm twice during his wild younger days, once skateboarding and another time backcountry snowboarding with friends in the mountains east of Haven Point.

Considering all the crazy things he used to do with his brothers and Cade, it was a wonder he came out of childhood with only those few battle scars.

His mother would freak when she found out he'd been struck by a hit-and-run driver.

Charlene was a fretter, of the highest order. She had always been overprotective, wanting to keep all her children tucked safely under her wing like a hen with her chicks, but she had gone into overdrive after Wyatt's tragic death and then his father's life-altering injury.

The shooting at Andrea's house earlier in the year had only made her worse.

That he was injured on the job as well, while trying to meet a confidential informant, would probably send her over the edge. Good thing Elliot worked in Denver with the FBI or she would be camped out on his doorstep every day, making sure he came home safely from work.

He took one more bite of shortbread from the tin Andrea had brought, which automatically sent his thoughts zooming back to his neighbors next door and the problem he didn't know what to do about.

He was still mulling his options when he drifted to sleep and dreamed of headlights coming toward him in the silvery twilight of a Lake Haven December.

Furtive whispers and the sensation of being watched woke him out of tangled dreams.

"Is he dead?" Marsh heard a nervous little voice ask.

"I don't know," another one answered. "Maybe we should poke him to see."

"You do it," the first voice said.

"No, you."

"Nobody's poking anything," a more mature voice interjected quietly. He opened his eyes a crack and saw Andrea Montgomery walk inside the room with a stack of mail that she set on the table beside him.

Her cheeks were rosy from the cold and she looked pretty and soft and more delicious than all the shortbread in Scotland.

He blinked, wondering where the hell he came up with that thought.

"Leave the poor man alone and let him finish his nap," she said to her children in a low voice.

"I'm not napping," he growled—though he had been doing exactly that. He must have slept all afternoon, like some old geezer in a nursing home with nothing better to do.

"If you weren't napping, why were your eyes closed?" Will Montgomery said, his tone accusatory.

"Just checking for holes in my eyelids," he answered, which had been *his* father's standard answer when one of his kids caught him dozing off in church.

The little girl, whom he had seen only briefly the day before when she slipped in and out of the room like an afternoon shadow, gave a little giggle. The sound seemed to take her by surprise because she quickly clamped her lips together and looked down at the ground.

"Sorry we woke you," Andrea said, her tone brisk. "I have your groceries. I also brought you some chicken casserole and a couple pieces of spice cake."

"I thought you weren't coming until later."

"We have something tonight and I'm not sure how long it will go, so this time worked best."

"It's a party and my friend Ty is going to be there," her son announced. "It's at my mom's friend McKenzie's house. She has a dog who's

63

my friend, too, and her name is Paprika. Only, we call her Rika."

With his mom's auburn hair and a scattering of freckles, the kid was really cute, Marsh had to admit. Too bad he wasn't very good with kids. His uniform had always seemed to make them nervous around him—like the boy's sister was acting.

"I know that dog," he admitted.

Will took a step closer to the recliner. "Rika is *funny*. She licks my hand and it tickles. Guess what? We have a dog, too. We've had her for two whole weeks and her name is Sadie and she's the best dog in the whole world."

"Is that right?"

"She hardly ever pees in the house. Do you have a dog?"

"No. Not right now. I did when I was a kid, though."

One or two dogs were always running through the Bailey house when he was growing up, but he hadn't had one since he left home. It was hard to justify it when he lived alone and worked long hours.

He was much better with dogs than he was with kids, actually.

"We can bring Sadie over if you want, to keep you company while your leg is broked," the boy offered.

The tightness in his throat at the offer was

caused by the pain, he told himself. "That's very nice of you, but I should be okay."

"Are you sure? She's a really nice dog. Just as nice as Young Pete, only not as big. She likes to sit on your lap and watch TV."

"Good thing she's not as big as Pete, then. I don't think I'd have room on this recliner."

The boy giggled, which Marsh had to admit was kind of a sweet sound.

"We had another reason for stopping by," Andrea said with a meaningful look down at the girl, who had moved back to the doorway to be closer to her mother, as if afraid he was going to reach out and whack her with his crutches.

"Chloe?" Andrea said when her daughter only looked at the carpet. "Chloe? Show Sheriff Bailey what you made."

The little girl shook her head vigorously. "You do it," she whispered.

"I'm not the one who made it, honey. You are. You did such a beautiful job on it, too."

Chloe continued to look anywhere in the room but at him, and after a moment her mother sighed.

"Sorry. She's become a little more nervous about people she doesn't know the last few months."

Though he had come onto the scene after the fact, Marshall had read the reports of what happened at Andie's house over the summer. He knew Chloe was an eyewitness to the double shooting at her house, when Wyn and Rob Warren had both been injured.

When he showed up just moments after dispatch called him, Andie had been cradling her daughter close, trying to comfort her.

The tenderness of the image had stuck in his head for a long time—the bruised and bleeding Andrea, who must have been terrified herself, doing her best to calm her child.

He frowned, furious all over again at the man who had caused the whole situation.

Warren had put Andrea and her kids through hell, simply because he refused to accept a simple one-syllable word. *No.*

"Go ahead," Andie encouraged.

"You show him," Chloe said again, her voice whisper soft.

"I'll do it." Will, his tone exasperated, grabbed a paper out of his sister's hand and thrust it at Marsh. "This is for you. It's from Chloe."

An odd mix of emotions tumbled through him as he looked at what was clearly an art project, a wreath cutout made from two pieces of green construction paper that had been sandwiched on either side of a glued-together mosaic of colorful tissue paper pieces.

"Did you make this?" he asked.

After a pause, Chloe nodded. She looked at him now, but her gaze didn't rise above his chest.

"I asked my teacher if I could make two and

66

she said I could," she said, still nearly whispering. "I had to stay inside at recess so I could finish it before Miss Taylor had put away all the art supplies. I didn't mind. Not really. It was snowy and cold out anyway."

Marshall wasn't sure what to say. He almost felt like another SUV had just plowed into him.

Why would she do that for him, a virtual stranger who obviously frightened her?

He cleared his throat, telling himself the thickness there was only thirst. "Thank you. It's beautiful," he answered truthfully.

He considered it a small victory when she met his gaze for about half a second. "It's really pretty when the sun comes through it," she offered, her voice a little louder. "If you want, you can hang it in your window. That's what we did with ours."

"That's a good idea. I think I'll do that."

She nibbled on her bottom lip, something he had seen her mother do the evening before. "Do you want me to hang it for you?" she asked after a minute. "That's why I put a string on it and my mom gave me a hook thing."

Not sure what to say, he glanced at Andie, who was watching the girl with a warm approval that touched him almost as much as the childish artwork. She met his gaze and gave a barely perceptible nod.

"Sure. That would be very kind of you. Thank you."

"Which window should I put it in?" she asked. This time she didn't look away as she waited for his answer.

"How about the middle one? Will that work?"

Her smile flashed like sunlight on snow, then she hurried to the appropriate window. She pulled a suction cup hook from her pocket.

"I want to stick it on! Can I?" her brother asked.

"I guess." She handed the hook to him and Will licked the underside, then stood on tiptoe and reached over his head to push the hook against the window.

"That's not high enough," Chloe complained.

"It's as high as I can go."

"Mama, can you help him make it higher?"

Andrea moved to the window and repositioned the hook, then hung the wreath by the cheerful red yarn holder. "How's that?"

"Good, I think."

Marsh took it as another small victory when Chloe faced him head-on. "Sheriff Marshall? Is that okay?"

"Perfect," he assured her. He tilted his head to admire the way the weak December sunlight slanted into the room just right, filtering through the tissue paper like real stained glass in a cathedral, scattering prisms of colored light around the room.

"It's beautiful," he told the girl again. "I can't help but feel a bit of holiday spirit now."

She smiled at him directly and didn't imme-diately look away. Small steps, he supposed, though he had to wonder why he found such a grand sense of accomplishment in helping her lose her fear of him.

"Hey, you don't have a Christmas tree!" Will said with the same aghast tone a person might use if his buddy's head just rolled off his shoulders onto the floor.

"True enough."

"Why not?"

Andrea sent Marshall an apologetic look before she turned back to her son.

"Honey, we talked about that. Everybody doesn't celebrate Christmas like we do," she said quickly, a sudden pink seeping across her cheeks that didn't come from light rays bending through tissue paper.

"I don't have anything against Christmas," he was quick to assure them. "I've just been pretty busy this year and haven't had time to decorate for the holidays."

The last time he decorated for Christmas, he'd been deployed and he and a bunk mate had made ornaments out of spent cartridges to hang on a scraggly tree.

"And now you have a broken leg and can't do it at all. That's so sad." Chloe's big green eyes filled with compassion and she looked as if she wanted to cry.

"It's fine, really," he assured her. "I don't need much. And now I have a pretty wreath in my window to remind me it's the holidays."

This resulted in a whispered conversation between the two children, with much gesturing, head-shaking and pointing.

Finally, Will nodded and turned back to Marshall. "If you want, Chloe and me can put up your Christmas tree."

He blinked at the unexpected offer and cast a glance at Andie, who looked just as astonished as he felt.

"We put all the ornaments on ours all by ourselves. Only, our mom had to put the high ones on," the boy added. "Then we had to move some ornaments up more because our cat, Mrs. Finnegan, tries to knock them off. She's a rascal."

"You don't have a cat, do you?" Chloe asked, meeting his gaze despite the lingering nervousness that threaded through her voice.

"No. No pets here."

"Okay. Then we can put the ornaments right on the bottom," Will said.

"I can make snowflakes," his sister offered. "And Willie is really good at paper chains."

"I am," the boy said with no trace of false modesty. "I can use scissors all by myself."

Marshall didn't know quite what to say to their magnanimous offer. He hadn't particularly missed having a Christmas tree, though he had loved that ugly little thing in the desert years ago that had somehow made him more homesick than he would have believed.

Most years it had never seemed worth the energy and effort, especially when he always worked extra shifts over the holidays so the guys with families could have more time off with their kids. Anyway, his mother decorated her place like a glitter cannon exploded in there, and Wyn and Katrina always had, too. If he ever felt the need for a little infusion of Christmas spirit, he figured he only needed to stop in at one of their places.

It wasn't worth the trouble now, really. A little holiday cheer wasn't going to be enough to lift him out of the misery of sitting around on his ass for the next few weeks.

"Do you even *have* a Christmas tree? A fake one or a real one?" Will said. "We could go get one, if you don't. I saw, like, a million of them by the store where we buy food for our dog."

"Our mom might have to put it up, like she did ours," Chloe said after a minute. "We don't know how to plug in the lights and stuff."

Andrea, who had been watching this interchange silently, finally spoke. "Kids, let's not get carried away. Sheriff Bailey might not even want a Christmas tree."

He was about to agree with her until he happened to glance at Chloe and Will and saw the eagerness on both of their faces.

They wanted to do something nice for him. It was a sweet and generous offer and it seemed rude to turn that away.

"My sister might have a tree out in the shed," he said after a minute. "But I thought you all were heading to a party."

"Oh yeah," Will said. "I can't believe we forgot the party!"

"Could we do it tomorrow?" Chloe asked.

They both looked at their mother. "I can text Wyn and ask if she's got an artificial tree tucked away somewhere here or if she took it to Boise with her. If she doesn't have one, I'm sure I can find some-body who has an extra they're not using this year."

At this particular juncture of his life, he couldn't contemplate owning *one* Christmas tree, let alone having a spare sitting around.

"As long as Sheriff Bailey doesn't mind."

He had no choice, really, but to shrug. "I guess it would be okay."

"Yay!" Will jumped up and down and Chloe beamed, as if he had just offered to take them to Disneyland instead of merely agreeing to let them do something nice for him.

"We can go home and work on the snowflakes and paper chains tonight before the party and bring them back here tomorrow," the girl offered.

"Thanks."

He supposed that meant he would have to have a couple little kids underfoot for a while the next day. The prospect wasn't as unpleasant as it should have been.

He frowned. He had never much liked kids and couldn't see that changing now, when he was thirty-four years old.

"Maybe *you* could make some snowflakes," Chloe suggested. "You can't do anything else while you have a broken leg."

Andrea tried and failed to hide her wince. "I'm sure Sheriff Bailey has plenty to do without worrying about cutting out paper snowflakes, honey."

Like what? See how many puzzles he could guess right on *Wheel of Fortune* or if he could win Final Jeopardy?

That sounded about as pathetic as he felt right about now, so he opted to keep his mouth shut.

"Your dinner just needs to be popped into the microwave when you're ready," Andrea informed him. "Is there anything else I can do for you before we leave?"

"I think I'm good. You've done more than enough already. I'm not sure the guilt trip Wynona laid on you really required you to decorate my house for the holidays."

She opened her eyes a little wider. Hers were green like Chloe's but the soft green of unfurled leaves in spring. "What guilt trip would that be?" she asked, trying to look innocent.

He was a hardened law enforcement officer and

knew when someone was innocent and when they weren't. "I grew up in the same house with Wyn. I know just how adept she can be at emotional blackmail."

She chewed on her lip, watching her kids as they discussed their decorating plans between them. "If you would rather the children didn't put up a Christmas tree, I can talk to them later and explain things to them. Don't feel obligated, really. They'll be fine. This time of year, they're easily distracted."

Marshall knew that's exactly what he should do—just tell her he didn't want a Christmas tree.

It *had* been really sweet of them to make the offer—especially Chloe, who was obviously still nervous around him. If the little girl was willing to do the work to get over her fear, he couldn't refuse her the opportunity.

"It's fine. I have to stare at these same walls for the next few weeks, so I guess a little holiday spirit would at least brighten the place up for me."

Andrea's relieved smile sent a weird little shaft of warmth through his chest. "That's very kind of you. Thanks. I never want to discourage my children from doing nice things for others, especially when they come up with the idea on their own."

"Glad I could be of service," he said, unable to keep the dry note from his voice.

"Don't worry about the tree," she added. "I'll take care of it."

"Are you sure? I was planning to trudge up the Mount Solace trail in the snow later so I could cut one down."

She made a face. "Ha-ha. I'm sure I can find one."

Andrea glanced out the window, where big, fluffy flakes were beginning to fall like puffs from the cottonwoods along the creek. "Here comes more snow. I heard we're supposed to get several more inches tonight before it warms up later in the week. I worry about you here all by yourself."

He didn't like being the object of anyone's pity. For reasons he couldn't have explained, it bothered him more, coming from her. "I've got a phone. I should be fine."

"Have you arranged with anyone to shovel the walks for you?"

He hadn't thought that far ahead. "No. I'll call around, see if I can find a service to take care of it for me."

"Or you could ask a neighbor boy," she suggested. "Louise and Herm Jacobs have a grandson who probably could use the cash, especially just before the holidays."

He stiffened at the suggestion. "That might work," he said slowly, wondering why he hadn't thought of it himself.

"His name is Christopher. He's got a . . . bit of an attitude, but he's basically a good kid. He's had a rough time of things lately. His mother died this summer, which is why he's living with his grand-parents. Oh, you probably know that already."

"Why would I?" he asked.

She looked briefly confused at his tone, which he just realized sounded abrupt and almost angry. "You're from Haven Point and I know Louise is friends with your mom. You probably knew Christopher's mom, Nicole, their daughter."

For a tense, weird moment, he didn't know how to answer that. "Not well," he finally said. "She was five or six years older than me."

"It's so sad, about her car accident."

She'd had a blood alcohol level of twice the legal limit and had driven head-on into oncoming traffic. The tragedy was the young couple who had died, as well.

"So do you want me to ask Louise about having Christopher keep your walks clear for the next few weeks?" she asked when he didn't respond.

That might be easier. He couldn't imagine picking up the phone and asking for Christopher. He just couldn't do it.

No. This wasn't something he wanted to leave to anyone else. "I'll give her a call."

"Fine. Well, we'll be back tomorrow, bearing snowflakes and paper chains and enough Christmas spirit to power all the boats in the Lights on the Lake parade."

"Can't wait," he answered. Much to his surprise, the words weren't even a lie.

Chapter FIVE

"Oh, I'm so glad you could make it, Andie." McKenzie Shaw Kilpatrick beamed at her as she opened the door to her beautiful lakeside house. "Hazel will be so thrilled."

"Are you kidding? I wouldn't miss it. I've been looking forward to this all week long."

"And hello, Mr. Will and Miss Chloe. Welcome to my home."

Chloe giggled at the dramatic greeting and shook McKenzie's hand solemnly while Will just craned his neck to look behind her.

"Where is Rika?" Will demanded. "I want to give her a great big hug."

"Hey, no fair." Kenzie gave a pretend pout as she bent down to his level. "Where's mine first?"

Will beamed and threw his arms around her neck.

"You give the best hugs of any four-year-old boy I know, sir," Kenzie said. "Let me take your coats, and then you can go find Rika and Hondo. They're hanging out with the kids back in the den."

"Yay! Hondo looks scary, but he's not at all."

"You've got his number, don't you? That guy is nothing but a big old softy."

Until that summer, Will had been terrified of

77

big dogs after he'd been bitten by one in the neighborhood. Thanks to Wynona and her gentle dog, Young Pete, Will had been able to lose his fear and now he embraced all things canine— especially the little Havachon they had rescued from the shelter before Thanksgiving.

"Just head down that hall and you'll find dogs and kids and toys. Maddie Hayward is here and so are Ty and Jazmyn Barrett. I do believe there might be a movie playing, if you want to watch it."

"Can we, Mama?" Chloe asked. Though she wasn't typically nervous around Kenzie, large groups could bring out her anxiety—at least until she found her friends and settled in.

"Sure. You guys have fun. I'll be right here."

Will raced down the hall and Chloe followed at a more subdued pace. She watched them, her heart pinching with worry for her sweet little girl.

"Don't worry. You know Jenna, the high school girl who works for me at the shop after school? I asked her to come out and keep an eye on the kids so the moms can enjoy the party in exchange for my help decorating for her birthday party in January."

McKenzie thought of everything. It was what made her a good businesswoman and a dedicated mayor of Haven Point. "Thank you. I'll still worry, but probably a little less, knowing that.

Call me when the birthday party comes around and I'll help you decorate."

"I just might take you up on that."

"Not that you need my help." She looked around at the entryway, decorated in glittering white, blue and silver. She particularly admired a trio of thick candles spearing up from an elaborate arrangement of twigs, berry picks and pinecones, all spray-painted to match the color theme. "Your house looks beautiful. It should be in a home decor magazine."

"Ben calls it Christmas on crack," she said with a smile.

"Hey. I only said that once."

Both she and Kenzie looked up when Ben Kilpatrick spoke from the doorway. He wore a leather jacket and had car keys in his hand.

"You did," Kenzie said. "But it was memorable."

"I love our house. It's my favorite place in the world," he said. "Hi, Andrea."

He leaned in to give her a quick kiss on the cheek, then stepped quickly away, making her face heat. Ben was always so careful with her, treating her like those delicate ornaments hanging in the front window. It was clear he didn't want to crowd her or make her feel threatened—or maybe he was that way with everyone and she was looking for layered subtext where none existed.

She would have greatly preferred that no one in Haven Point had ever found out what happened to her, but Rob Warren had made that impossible.

"You look lovely tonight, as always," he told her.

"Thank you. I hope we're not chasing you away."

"Not really—though I'd like to think I'm smart enough to duck and run when the Helping Hands are around."

McKenzie gave him a mock scowl. "You love the Helping Hands."

"I do. Everyone knows the Helping Hands are really the heart of Haven Point. Without you, this town would be a cold, sad, cheerless place."

"Don't you forget it."

"You would never let me, darling," he said with a laugh, then kissed her forehead.

"I'm actually heading over to Snow Angel Cove," he told Andie, then pitched his voice lower and looked around as if checking for eaves-droppers. "I'm helping Aidan with a Christmas present. I'd be grateful if you didn't mention anything to Eliza or Maddie. They think I'm heading over to watch a basketball game."

She twisted her fingers as if locking her lips and tossed the pretend key over her shoulder, which earned her one of Ben's rare but devastating smiles.

"Good luck to both of you, then," she said.

"Thanks." He waved at her, then leaned in once more to kiss his wife of only a few months. When he walked out the door, McKenzie's lipstick was smeared and her hair a little rumpled, but that rather dazed smile indicated she didn't really mind.

For one small, selfish moment, envy poked at Andie with sharp, merciless claws, leaving behind a trailing sadness. Oh, she missed that. Jason had been gone for two years and there were times she ached most of all at the loss of those casual little touches. His fingers brushing the back of her neck as he passed by, his arm draped across her while he slept, his hand on her knee as they sat together on the sofa watching a favorite television show.

All those small, tender physical reminders that oiled the sometimes creaky and contrary machinery of a marriage.

Her children gave her hugs and kisses all day, which she adored. She tried to tell herself it was enough. Deep in her heart, on those nights she couldn't sleep because the bed felt too big, she knew it was a lie.

On those nights, she would wrap herself in a blanket, curl up in the window seat and read long into the night to push the loneliness away.

But this was a party and she wasn't going to waste time feeling sorry for herself. "Is the guest of honor here yet?" she asked.

"Yes. Hazel and Eppie were the first ones here. You know how Ronald Brewer is. If they show up ten minutes early, he considers them all late. Everyone's back in the family room."

Andrea continued to look at the various unique

holiday decorations throughout the house as McKenzie led the way, until they reached a sprawling room off the kitchen dominated by glass windows that overlooked the lake.

The room was filled with most of her favorite people in the world. Andie smiled and greeted friends as she headed straight for Hazel Brewer.

Hazel—still trim and fit and always fashionably dressed—beamed a welcome smile at her, which widened when Andie showed her the gift she and the children had made.

"For me? Oh, honey. You shouldn't have. I don't know what it is about all of you who can't read your invitations. It clearly said to make a donation to the library instead of bringing a gift."

Andie added the wrapped present to a small but growing pile on the table next to her. "I know. And I did that. But this is something the children and I made for you. They wanted to do it and I couldn't tell them no, could I? Happy birthday, my dear."

Andie leaned in to kiss Hazel's wrinkled cheek.

"Thank you. Whoever would have thought a grumpy old cuss like me would live to such a ripe old age?"

"I can only say I hope the next eighty are just as amazing."

Hazel made a face. "I'm not sure I have the energy for eight more decades. Maybe just four or five."

"If that's your plan, you better work on finding

yourself another husband," her sister Eppie said. "I don't know if Ronald will be willing to drive you around for another fifty years."

Andie laughed and hugged Eppie, as well. Eppie and Hazel were sisters fourteen months apart who had ended up marrying twin brothers. Andie had learned at her first Helping Hands meeting in McKenzie's storeroom that Hazel's husband had died of cancer two decades earlier. Since then, Eppie's patient and long-suffering husband, Ronald, had taken his wife and her sister everywhere they needed to go.

Andie adored them all. Eppie and Hazel were kind and warm, always full of pithy observations and sly humor—exactly the kind of women she had always wished the grandmother who virtually raised her could have been. Instead, Damaris Packer had been a weak, self-effacing woman who would hardly say boo to a goose, forget about her loud, demanding, opinionated husband.

Andie was afraid she leaned more on her grandmother's side of the personality scale, with a tendency to shrink away from any confrontation. Since coming to Haven Point, she wanted to think she'd learned a thing or two about being strong and capable—in no small measure because of the other women in this room.

"The caterer tells me they've just about finished setting dinner out. Let's eat first and then we can open gifts."

"What's this *we* business?" Hazel said. "It's my birthday, my gifts. I get to open them."

"You mean the gifts you insisted you didn't want?" Eppie said tartly.

"Just wait until *you're* eighty, then you'll see life is too short to waste it pretending you don't like being the center of attention."

Andie heard a muffled cough and looked over at Devin Shaw, who was fighting a grin.

With the skill of a consummate leader, McKenzie ushered the group into her elegant dining room, where a beautiful feast was laid out.

"Wow, this looks fantastic," Julia Winston, the town librarian, exclaimed.

"I can't believe you spent all this money to cater a meal," Linda Fremont grumbled. "Why couldn't we have just done potluck, like we always do?"

"An eightieth birthday requires something special, I believe," McKenzie said. "And anyway, Ben insisted. This is our gift to Hazel but also our gift to the rest of you. And since he's got more money than God, I try not to argue with him when he wants to do something special for my friends."

"Why doesn't Ben have any brothers?" Samantha Fremont complained. The normally effervescent Sam seemed subdued tonight, but then she had been down ever since her best friend—Marshall and Wynona's sister, Katrina—had caught a wild hair after a breakup that summer and took off to see the world.

"Ben is one of a kind," his mother, Lydia, said with a fond smile.

"He is, indeed," McKenzie said. "Don't think about it. Just sit back and enjoy the fabulous food. Serrano's went above and beyond with this one."

The food was, indeed, delicious. Andie was nibbling on a plate of fabulous spinach lasagna when Eliza Caine sank into the chair beside her.

"Hi, Andie. You're just the person I need!"

Andie instantly set down her fork. "Please tell me you're looking for somebody to hold that sweet little boy of yours!"

Eliza laughed. "Well, that wasn't what I meant, but sure."

She carefully handed over tiny Liam Dermot Caine, born just before Thanksgiving. Andie took the bundle-wrapped infant and nestled him in her arms, falling in love all over again with his shock of dark hair like his father's and the big blue eyes she hoped would stay that color.

"Oh, he's precious," she murmured.

"Isn't he?" Eliza beamed.

Liam made a little squawk of a sound and managed to tug his fist out of the bundling so he could suck on the edge of it.

"He loves that fist. I don't know what it is," Eliza said. "It's funny—Maddie did the very same thing."

"When my kids were little, I never wanted to do anything but sit and hold them."

"It's the best part of being a new mom, isn't it? I'm with you on that, but when Aidan's anywhere around, I usually have to arm wrestle him for the chance. He's completely enamored with being a father."

She was charmed to the core at the idea of the sexy genius CEO behind Caine Tech losing his heart to his infant son.

"Aidan and Liam aren't exactly what I wanted to talk to you about, though."

"Oh?"

"I need a favor."

"Sure," Andie said. She was feeling so warm and content right about now with adorable Liam in her arms, she would have agreed to just about anything.

She had the random stray brainstorm that warring parties ought to take note and consider passing around sleepy, cuddly babies during complicated negotiation sessions. It would make the world a much more gentle place.

"It's not a huge favor. You might actually enjoy it. From what I hear, most women would."

"What is it?"

Eliza let out a breath. "Aidan has this younger brother who's coming to town for the holidays," she began.

Cute baby notwithstanding, Andie's stomach

did a crazy somersault, as if she'd just jumped off a ski lift without her skis. She knew what was coming and she didn't want Eliza to go on. Why couldn't she just sit here and hold the baby?

"How nice for Aidan to have family here," she said cautiously. "He comes from a large one, doesn't he?"

"An understatement. He's the third of seven and they're all wonderful. Truly wonderful, though a little overwhelming. It's our year for hosting everyone, but Aidan was worried it would be too much this year, with a new baby and all. It worked out because he's got a sister and a sister-in-law who are both expecting and due next month, so they all decided to stay in Hope's Crossing and will come out this summer."

"Where does the brother fit in?"

"Oh. Jamie. He called last week and asked if he could spend a few days with us, and of course we were thrilled."

"I thought Aidan didn't want his family to overwhelm you."

"This is just Jamie. He and Aidan have always been close and we haven't seen him in a year, since he's been deployed overseas. Jamie is a pilot and he's thinking about getting out of the military and maybe taking a job flying Caine Tech execs around."

"Oh. That would be nice for Aidan, to have his brother working with him." If Andie could keep

Eliza talking, maybe her friend would forget to ask the favor Andie was very much afraid she didn't want to hear.

"It would be great. The thing is, Jamie doesn't know anybody in Haven Point except us and he's used to a pretty active social life."

By that, Andie inferred Aidan's brother was a player. This just kept getting better and better. She wanted to get up and walk to the other side of the room, but she had a feeling Eliza might protest if she kidnapped cute little Liam.

"So here's the thing," Eliza finally said slowly, "I was wondering if you might be interested in showing Jamie around town a little, maybe go to the movies with him or up to the dinner theater in Shelter Springs."

She let out a breath as her somersaulting stomach started rolling with wild abandon. "I, um . . ." she began, then stopped, not sure what to say.

"If you're worried about the kids, Aidan and I would be happy to have Will and Chloe hang out with Maddie at Snow Angel Cove anytime and I know she would love having friends over."

Oh, this was awkward. She treasured her friendship with Aidan *and* Eliza—and his company was her biggest client. How could she possibly refuse in a graceful way?

Yet how could she possibly agree?

"Why me?" she finally said.

Eliza gave a sheepish sort of smile. "I thought it might be good for both of you. Jamie is charming and sweet and very kindhearted. He might seem a little on the shallow side, but he's really not. He's been through a rough time lately and could use a friend, someone different from the kind of girls he usually dates."

He *definitely* sounded like a player—exactly the sort of guy she had always tried to avoid.

"You, on the other hand, can be entirely too serious and you don't take nearly enough time for yourself," Eliza went on. "We thought maybe a few dates with someone sweet and funny and gorgeous like Jamie might be good for you."

"Who is *we?*" she asked. She couldn't imagine Aidan had anything to do with this. If it wasn't a computer screen or his beloved family, Aidan had a hard time focusing.

Eliza's smile was more than sheepish this time. "A few of us. Wyn and McKenzie and Meg," she said, confirming Andie's worst suspicions. "When I mentioned that Jamie was coming to stay for a while and I wanted to set him up with exactly the right person, your name was the first one that came to mind."

"How could I be the right person for *anyone?*" she murmured, unable to meet her friend's gaze. "You know I'm a hot mess."

"Oh, honey," Eliza exclaimed. "You are not. You're *not*."

She squeezed Andie's shoulder. "You've had a terrible time of things, a truly terrible time, none of which was your fault. You deserve to be happy, and I thought—*we* thought—that after everything you've been through, you could use a little fun in your life."

Oh, how she wished she could have come to Haven Point and left her past completely behind her. She drew in a breath, wishing also that she could find a corner somewhere and just hug this sweet, innocent baby until all the ugliness of the world faded into insignificance.

She couldn't. This summer, she had learned that when a person tried to run and hide from her problems, they eventually grew out of control and tried to swallow her whole.

"It's really kind of you to think of me, but . . . I'm not ready yet, you know?"

"Are you sure?"

"Positive."

Eliza studied her for a long moment and finally nodded. "Okay. I get it. Honestly, I do. I completely understand. The last thing I want to do is push you into something. I just love Jamie so much. He's a great guy and I want him to have someone like you in his life. And vice versa, honey. You deserve to be happy."

"I'm happy," she protested. "If you want the truth, I'm in a better place right now than I've been since Jason died."

Things weren't perfect, but she was doing her best to put the past behind her. With Rob Warren now serving prison time, she felt safe for the first time in a year. She and the children were building a new life here, with new friends and activities and challenges.

"That's good to hear," Eliza said. "When you think you're ready to enter the dating world again, you need to let the Helping Hands know."

"Don't you think having everyone try to find me eligible dates is taking the group's name a little too literally? I didn't realize matchmaking services were offered by the Helping Hands."

"Why not? We know just about everybody in town and plenty in Shelter Springs, too. We can tell about the guy who might still be getting over a bad breakup, the one who is a little too comfortable still living with his mother, the whack job you should avoid categorically."

"Wow. You certainly know how to make dating again sound delightful."

Eliza gave a rueful smile. "I'm sorry. That's not my intention. There are some great guys out there, too. Guys like Jamie, who are just waiting for the right woman. I know it's tough to think about. Believe me, I know. After my first husband died, I told myself Maddie and I were fine, just the two of us. We were, for a long time, but that baby in your arms is proof that sometimes life has other plans for us."

The baby in question mewed a little and turned his head to nuzzle at Andie. "I'm afraid he's looking for something I can't deliver right now," she said, aware of a little pang of loss that her days of holding babies of her own were likely over.

"What a little piglet. If I let him, he would nurse twenty-four hours a day. I suppose he is due for some dinner, though."

With regret, Andie pressed a kiss on Liam's forehead, then handed him back to his mother. "Can I get you anything? One of those fabulous-looking desserts Barbara is setting out?"

"A piece of caramel apple pie would be fantastic right about now."

"You got it."

She took Eliza's nearly empty water glass to refill from the fruit-infused supply. She picked out a slice of crumb-topped pie for Eliza and a fork and carried them to her, then returned to the table for herself, studying the other desserts as she tried to decide which indulgence would be most worth the calories.

"You can't lose with Barbara's stacked chocolate cake."

She turned at the voice. "Louise! I didn't know you were coming. I should have thought to ask when I was at your house earlier, and then we could have ridden together."

Now her neighbor mustered a weak smile. "To

be honest, I didn't know whether I would be able to make it until the last minute."

Louise hadn't been to many of the social gatherings for the Helping Hands and the women who participated in the group, at least not in the six months Andie had lived in Haven Point. Andie assumed her life was too chaotic for now, with her daughter's death and the stress and turmoil of her grandson moving in.

"I'm very glad you did. How is Christopher feeling?"

Louise released a heavy sigh. "Right now he's home sulking. I wouldn't let him go hang out with his friends. I told him, if he's too sick for school, he's too sick for friends. That's what my mother always said to me and what I, in turn, always said to *Christopher's* mother. He doesn't agree. We had a huge fight. Slamming doors, swearing, telling me how much he hates it here and hates me most of all. That's why I'm late."

"I'm so sorry," she said, giving Louise an impulsive hug. "That must be so difficult for you."

"I'm fine, really. It's all part of the joy of raising a teenager, right?"

Andie could remember plenty of times when she strongly disagreed with the strict rules at her grandparents' house, but she never would have *dared* slam doors or talk back. She didn't advocate her grandfather's way of handling things, but there had to be a difference between harsh discipline and making sure a child understood there were lovingly considered consequences for misbehavior.

She didn't feel it was her right to give advice to Louise about how to deal with her grandchild, though.

"I need to tell you, your shortbread was a huge hit next door," she said to change the subject. "Sheriff Bailey loved it."

Some of the tightness eased from Louise's features. "Oh, I'm so glad."

"Oh, you've been to see Marshall?" Megan Hamilton turned from picking out a piece of powder-dusted lemon cake. "I heard about his accident. How is he?"

She pictured the sheriff as she had found him earlier that day, rumpled and sleepy and gorgeous. Those dratted butterflies sashayed through her stomach again and she scowled. When would she stop having this ridiculous reaction to him?

"Oh no. Are things that bad?" Megan asked, obviously misinterpreting Andie's expression.

"No. At least I don't think so. He's in pain, but he's doing his best not to show it. Mostly, he's frustrated and annoyed at the inconvenience of having a broken leg, I think."

"That sounds like Marshall," Megan said.

"I don't really know him, so I don't have a baseline to compare to. Wyn just asked me to keep an eye on him, since I live so close. I've stopped in a few times since he came home from the hospital and he seems to be feeling better each time."

"Good. I can't believe someone would just hit him with their car and leave him lying in the snow like that. Who knows how long he would have been there if he hadn't had a cell phone on him?"

An involuntary shiver rippled down her spine, picturing him broken and bleeding in the cold and snow and wind that could be brutal coming off the lake.

"Knowing Marshall, he probably would have patched himself up, dragged himself to the nearest busy road and hitchhiked to the hospital," McKenzie said with a laugh.

Considering the man had a compound fracture, that would have been quite a Herculean feat, though she wouldn't put it past him. Something told her when Marshall put his mind to something, he didn't let too many things stand in his way.

"Marsh is a few years older than me, but he was kind of a legend at HPHS," Megan said, confirming Andie's suspicion. "He played the entire last ten minutes of a state championship football game without telling the coach his shoulder had been dislocated by a bad hit."

"I remember that," Louise said. "Charlene was livid!"

"Marshall was always the strong silent brother," Megan said. "Funny how different they were. Elliot always had his head in a book and didn't have time for most of us, while Wyatt was a big flirt who could talk his way into anything."

At the mention of Wynona's twin brother, Andie felt a twinge of sadness for a man she had never known. When Andie first came to Haven Point, she and Wynona had first bonded over their shared loss. Like Jason, Wyatt Bailey had died helping other people. In Wyatt's case, he had been hit by an out-of-control car during a snowstorm while coming to the aid of other stranded motorists. Andie's husband had drowned while trying to help a man who was trying to commit suicide by jumping off a bridge in Portland. When the man had resisted his efforts and tried to jump anyway, Jason had reached to grab him and had lost his balance and tumbled in, as well.

In another layer of commonality, Wynona's father had also died as the result of injuries sustained on the job, though his injuries hadn't truly claimed his life until two years after a shoot-out with a robbery suspect. John Bailey had suffered a severe brain injury, however, and spent the last two years of his life in a nursing home.

Marshall had endured those losses, too, she suddenly realized. Like Wynona, he had lost his brother and his father, both in the line of duty. It was a connecting thread between them and she couldn't believe it hadn't occurred to her until now.

Now he joined the ranks of lawmen injured on the job. She didn't like thinking about it.

"Who do you think ran him down?" Louise asked. "Herm and I think it must have been tourists who didn't know the area and maybe thought they hit a dog or something. No one from around here would do such a thing, would they?"

"I could think of a few miscreants from Sulfur Hollow who would probably love to get even with a Bailey. They likely wouldn't even care which one," Megan said, her expression dark. "Any of the Lairds would top the list."

"There are all those newcomers in town, too, that we don't know a thing about," Linda Fremont put in from her side of the table. "Not to mention all the people in Shelter Springs. It makes my blood run cold."

Andie didn't want to think about it. Picturing him injured and alone in a snowy parking lot made her stomach hurt. It was entirely too similar to the dark days before Jason's body was eventually found downriver from Portland.

"Knowing Marsh Bailey, he won't rest until he finds who did this to him," Megan said.

"Whoever did it, our Andie is very sweet to watch over him," Louise said.

She wanted to tell them Wynona hadn't given

her much choice, but she didn't want to sound resentful. She wasn't. She was happy to help, she just wished the man didn't make her so nervous.

"I haven't done much, only brought dinner a few times." She paused, remembering her conversation with him before she left earlier. "I don't want to speak out of turn," she said to Louise, "but there's a chance Marshall might be calling to see if Christopher would be interested in earning a few bucks by shoveling his snow while he's laid up."

"That's out of the question," Louise said firmly.

Her vehemence took Andie by surprise and for a moment she didn't know what to say. "All right," she finally said. "I'll tell him. I'm sure he won't have trouble finding someone else."

"Oh, Christopher will be happy to shovel the walks, I'll make sure of it, but he certainly won't let Marshall pay him for it. He'll do it for free, as a favor to a neighbor," Louise said firmly.

Megan snorted. "Good luck convincing any teenager to be so magnanimous."

"He'll do it if he wants to eat at my table," Louise said. "Christopher needs to learn that thinking about others is necessary and important to grow up as a decent adult. I'm afraid the boy hasn't had the greatest examples in this department. I loved my daughter, but she could be very self-absorbed. His father is ten times worse—

the man can't even be bothered to visit his own son!"

"I'm sorry. That must be very painful for Christopher," Andie said, her voice soft with compassion.

"Being in pain doesn't give him a free pass in this world," Louise said. "He still needs to learn how to care for others. From now until spring, I'll make sure he shovels Sheriff Bailey's walks when he's doing ours and he won't need a dime for it."

She had a feeling Marshall would insist on paying Christopher anyway, but the two of them could hash it out between them.

Chapter SIX

"Basically what you're saying is you have absolutely no leads, even though you've got the stolen vehicle."

"I wish to hell I had better news to report." Ruben Morales looked apologetic and frustrated at the same time. "The state crime lab has gone over and over the thing and they can't find so much as a stray hair strand. Everything was wiped down, even the mirror buttons and the turn signals. We couldn't even find the *owner's* fingerprints anywhere."

Marshall mulled the chilling implications of the information. "So we were right. This wasn't just some joyriding kid, out to make trouble for a stray cop."

"Exactly. What kid would be smart enough to clear evidence from somewhere obscure like the seat adjustment bar?"

"So that's a clue right there. Either this is somebody who watches every single forensic crime show on TV or someone who knows his way around the system."

"Which you suspected from the beginning."

Marshall shifted in the damn recliner, trying in vain to get comfortable. It seemed harder than ever, especially with this grim conclusion sitting in his gut like a hunk of bad meat.

The decided lack of evidence seemed to point to a perpetrator with advanced law enforcement knowledge. Someone smart enough to scout locations without cameras and then clever enough to lure him there by tantalizing him with a lead on a case they knew he couldn't ignore.

It was becoming harder and harder to avoid the conclusion that someone in his own department had deliberately come at him with deadly force.

He had enemies within his own house. It was tougher to swallow than the giant horse-pill-sized antibiotics the doc gave him. He didn't want to believe it, but the mounting evidence was becoming inescapable.

"What's the scuttlebutt in the break room about the incident?"

Ruben hesitated, a shadow shifting across his features. "For the most part, everyone is concerned about you and angry that the perp drove away and left you there."

He didn't miss the careful wording. *"For the most part.* What about the rest?"

Again, Morales hesitated. Marshall knew he had put his deputy in a difficult position, asking him to investigate his coworkers. The Lake Haven Sheriff's Department was too small for a dedicated internal affairs department. Usually, they would call in the state police to investigate cases of wrongdoing in the department. Marshall had, in fact, been preparing to bring in state police investigators to look into the missing funds.

Something was sour in his department, something that had been going on longer than he had been in office.

After a long moment, Ruben finally spoke. "I can't help notice that certain parties clam up whenever the conversation swings around to you and your injuries."

"Let me guess. Wall and Kramer."

"You don't seem particularly surprised."

"Who would be? They haven't exactly been quiet about some of the changes I've tried to implement over the last year."

Both deputies had worked in the department for years. Ken Kramer, in fact, had run against him in the general election the previous year. Both Ken Kramer and his longtime friend Curtis Wall had made no secret they thought Marshall won the election because of his family name and not his own qualifications.

John Bailey had been well liked and respected by nearly everyone, save for a few lawbreakers in certain segments of the population. Before Marshall's father, Marshall's grandfather had served as chief of police of Haven Point for many years and his great-grandfather before that.

For the Baileys, being in law enforcement was a proud legacy, almost a family tradition.

Marshall wanted to think he had earned the office because the voting public believed he was the best man for the job. He had promised new ideas and a commitment to making sure every representative of the sheriff's department carried out his duties with integrity, honesty and transparency.

So much for that.

Somebody was stealing money from inside his department, at least two of his deputies practiced open insubordination, a county commissioner wanted his badge and somebody hated him enough they were willing to run him down.

He hadn't done a very good job of keeping his election commitments.

"What about dash cam? Anything there?"

"The guy has on a balaclava, so we can't see anything. For all we know, it could have been Frosty the freaking Snowman driving the car."

"I'm beginning to think he might be our prime suspect. Who else could have melted away like that?"

"There's got to be something we're missing," Ruben said. "But I can't think what it might be. Whoever did it was extremely lucky or extremely smart or both."

Lucky, smart and vicious. It wasn't a good combination. "For now, just keep an eye out and I'll continue looking into the missing funds from here."

"You got it. Nobody can be that lucky or that smart forever."

The doorbell rang before Marshall could answer and Ruben raised an eyebrow. "You expecting somebody?"

"Not that I know about."

The distinct sound of the door opening a moment later sent Ruben into instant protective mode, his hand sliding to his sidearm and his muscles tense and alert, ready to pounce.

"Sheriff Bailey?" a woman's voice called out. "It's me, Andie Montgomery."

Ruben shot him a quick look, eyebrows raised, and Marshall gestured for him to stand down.

"In the den," he answered her, before adding in a lower voice to his deputy, "She's my neighbor. Wyn blackmailed her into helping me out for a few days. I can't manage to convince her I don't need help."

His gaze slid to the cheery little wreath hanging in his window that filtered the morning sunlight in splotches of color. Every time he caught sight of it, he remembered the quiet, nervous little girl staying in from recess to make it for him.

Andie came into the room carrying a large wicker basket that contained something warm, at least judging by the steam curling from it. Her cheeks were pink and she looked bright and fresh in a light-blue-and-white parka and matching knit cap.

"I made cinnamon rolls this morning for a friend and thought you might like some. They're still warm and—" She stopped short when she spotted Ruben there in his brown sheriff's department uniform.

"I'm sorry to interrupt."

"We were basically done," Marshall said. Ruben's visit had been a big waste of time anyway, since all they had was a whole lot of nothing.

"I was just leaving. It's almost time for my shift."

For reasons he didn't want to identify, Marshall was strangely reluctant to introduce them. "Andrea Montgomery, this is one of my deputies, Ruben Morales," he finally said. "He lives just on the other side of Snow Angel Cove. Ruben, this is my neighbor. Andrea Montgomery."

The deputy smiled warmly and Marshall realized where his protectiveness came from. Ruben was a good friend and a great officer, but he was a big favorite with women, handsome and smooth, and could charm even the coolest customer.

"Mrs. Montgomery, it's really great to see you again, and under much better circumstances," he said.

Andie blinked, clearly trying to place when she might have met the man previously to warrant that "again." Haven Point was a pretty small town.

If a person stuck around long enough, eventually she would run into everyone.

Marsh could tell the moment she remembered meeting Ruben. Her smile slid away and she tensed almost imperceptibly.

"You were one of the deputies who responded to the incident at my house this summer," she said flatly.

"I wasn't far away, on my way back to Haven Point after my shift, when Chief Emmett's call went out of an officer down. I pulled up just behind the sheriff."

Until that moment, Marshall hadn't even remembered Ruben had been there. He mostly remembered charging into Andie's house and finding Wynona on the ground with Cade hovering over her, the handcuffed perp bleeding and cursing in the corner and Andie looking pale as death as she held her trembling daughter.

He'd been in law enforcement of some kind or another since he turned eighteen years old and enlisted in the military. He had seen mass shootings, bank robberies, horrific assaults. All of them impacted him in some form or another, whether he wanted to admit it or not.

But some calls stick with a guy.

That warm June night seemed burned into his brain. How could it not be, when his sister and his best friend had been involved?

It was more than that, though. He hadn't been

able to forget the sight of the lovely, fragile Andie —her features pale as death in stark contrast to the blood and bruises from Warren's attack—pushing away the medics so she could comfort her frightened children.

"I'm sure I didn't have the chance to say it that night," she said now, "but thank you for responding so promptly and for all you might have done to help put Rob Warren in prison."

"It was my pleasure, ma'am. It truly was."

Ruben was definitely putting out the vibe now, beaming that charmer of a smile at Andie. Why wouldn't he, especially when she looked soft and pretty and smelled like warm cinnamon rolls?

"Thank you," she said, blushing a little.

"It's really neighborly of you to watch over Sheriff Bailey here. Marsh and I have been friends since school and I'm sure the ornery cuss can't be an easy patient."

She sent Marshall a look under her eyelashes and awareness seemed to spark and shiver between them.

"I'm not a nurse or anything like it," she assured Ruben quickly, looking away. "I'm only a concerned neighbor who was asked to check on him throughout the day, only until his mother and sister return to town."

Marshall frowned. He should be glad. He didn't want her here, as he had made plain, so why did it bother him that she sounded so eager to

107

hand him off to his family, like he were some kind of charity case.

"How are you and your kids settling into Haven Point?" Ruben asked.

She smiled, losing a little of her initial nervousness. "We love it here already. I'm looking forward to the holidays. You said you knew, er, Marshall in school. So you must be from this area."

"Born and bred, a couple generations back. My father is a veterinarian in town."

"Oh! Dr. Morales. Of course. He is the *nicest* man. We adopted a dog from the shelter last month and he has been so helpful through the whole process."

"Glad to hear it. He's a good guy," Ruben agreed. "What kind of dog and how's it going?"

Andie's features lit up. "Sadie is a Havachon and she's wonderful."

"Ah. Part Havanese and part bichon frise. And all cute."

She thawed several more degrees and gave him an approving smile. "You know your dog breeds."

The deputy shrugged modestly. "I grew up helping my dad in the clinic and naturally picked up a few things here and there."

"Would you care for a cinnamon roll? If the sheriff doesn't mind, anyway."

What if he *did* mind, very much? What if he wanted Ruben to take his charming smile and his easy conversation and get the hell out of here?

"Go ahead," he said, feeling crotchety and sore and about a hundred years old, even though Ruben was only a year or so younger than he was. "You can take it with you. Don't you need to go report in?"

Ruben glanced at his watch. "Yeah, you're probably right."

Andie pulled out a yeasty roll the size of a salad plate and drizzled with frosting from the wicker basket and transferred it to a paper plate that she also pulled out of the basket, and then she handed it over to Ruben. "Here you go."

Ruben's smile was as warm and gooey as the frosting. "Thank you so much. Wow, this looks fantastic. I didn't have time for breakfast this morning, so this and a cup of coffee will be perfect."

"I'm glad."

Marshall wasn't. He wanted his cinnamon roll back and he wanted his deputy to focus on the job, not on flirting with pretty widows.

"Get back to me if you find out anything new," he said.

"You got it, boss. See you both later."

Andie smiled and waved, but Marshall could muster only a curt nod.

"I hope he didn't leave on my account," Andie said, setting down her basket on a nearby table.

On the contrary. Ruben had stayed about five

minutes longer than he should have, on her account. "No. We were basically done when you showed up."

"He's investigating the hit-and run?" she asked as she pulled another plate from the basket and set a second cinnamon roll on it.

"Yeah. No leads yet."

"That must be driving you crazy."

About as crazy as she was driving him, taunting him with pastries she had yet to actually deliver. "I'm not happy about it."

"I can only imagine. You're still convinced it wasn't an accident?"

"I think I know when somebody tries to take me out."

A look of distress shifted across her features, making him regret his harsh words. She didn't need to know all the details of the noninvestigation.

"Did you have a reason for stopping by this morning? Besides the cinnamon rolls, which I appreciate," he added pointedly.

She seemed to collect herself and handed over the plate at last. "Sorry. Yes. I did. I finally had a chance to talk to Wyn and she told me she has a tree in the shed."

His taste buds were too busy savoring the delicious cinnamon roll—which, oddly, had a frosting that held notes of maple—to do more than gaze blankly at her while he chewed.

"A Christmas tree," she clarified. "Remember? My kids are coming over later today to help you decorate it."

Oh. Right. Her children seemed convinced he needed only a Christmas tree to make everything all better. He swallowed another bite of cinnamon roll, thinking he would have to figure out a way to lift weights sitting down if he wanted to burn off all the goodies he wasn't very good at resisting when he was cranky and sore.

"I thought I would try to set the tree up and test the lights before the kids get home this afternoon and start hounding me about coming over," she went on.

He wanted to tell her again that he didn't need or want any more holiday cheer. The little colored wreath was more than enough. He really didn't have anything against Christmas. When he was a kid, he'd been no different from other boys, giddy with excitement from before Thanksgiving until December 26. Over the years, that excitement had started to fade, then to atrophy and then finally to seep away.

Christmas for law enforcement officers invariably meant domestic disputes, when every emotion was heightened, every family problem exacerbated.

"Are you still okay with them coming over?" Andie said when he didn't immediately answer.

"What am I supposed to say to that? At this

point, I don't know how to talk you out of it."

"I'm not the one who needs persuading. Chloe and Will are both very excited to do this for you and they would be gravely disappointed if you changed your mind. Chloe got up early this morning to cut out about two dozen more snowflakes before she left for school, and Will insisted on making paper chains all morning. At this point, I think your paper chain garland would stretch from here to Shelter Springs."

She gave a rueful smile and he was struck by how lovely she was. She had the most beautiful skin he'd ever seen, creamy and clear. His fingers suddenly itched to touch it, to glide across her jawline, just to see if it could possibly be as soft as it looked.

His reaction appalled him. He had no business being attracted to her. A soft, warm, nurturing sort of woman like Andrea Montgomery deserved far better than someone like him, someone too focused, too set in his ways to make room for family.

Besides what she needed and deserved, he was *not* in the market for another busybody, interfering woman, not when he had a mother and two younger sisters who filled that role with gusto.

"My walks were cleared this morning," he said, suddenly achy from more than his damn broken leg.

She blinked a little at what she must have seen

as a complete non sequitur. "Oh. I didn't even register they were clear until you mentioned it! That's great."

"Did you talk to Louise or Herm about having Christopher shovel my snow after I expressly told you I would take care of it?"

Her smile slid away at his curt tone. "I saw Louise at the party last night and might have suggested it to her."

"I said I would handle it, didn't I?"

"Yes," she said slowly.

"I might not be particularly mobile yet, but I can still use a damn telephone."

He didn't miss the way her shoulders tensed, as if bracing against a blow. The reaction made him feel even worse about himself, if that were possible.

"I was only trying to help. *Thank you* would typically be the polite thing to say in this situation."

Guilt, regret and self-disgust turned his tone even more harsh. "I didn't ask for your help, if you remember. Between you and Wynona, I wasn't given much choice."

"*If I remember?* How could I forget? You've been so very gracious about accepting help and have been reminding me constantly that you don't want me here."

"Then why haven't you clued in and stayed away?"

The hurt flaring in her eyes burned through his gut like a hot poker.

"Fine," she said tightly. "I'll call Louise and tell her I spoke out of turn when I asked if Christopher could help you with your snow. Is that what you want?"

He didn't need her to hate him. He just needed her not to *like* him. "You don't have to call Louise," he said gruffly. "I hobbled out to the porch and spoke with Christopher. We've made an arrangement between us."

"You offered to pay him."

"That's usually how these things work."

"His grandmother wanted him to learn how to provide service to others. She said his mother couldn't be bothered to teach Christopher that basic lesson and that his father is even more selfish."

She could have no idea how her words gouged, mostly because they were true.

He didn't want to talk about this anymore. "I'm not a damn charity case," he growled. "I told the boy I'd pay him to clear my sidewalk and he agreed. End of story. At least somebody in this town listens to what I want."

Her eyes were the same wintry green as the evergreens just below the tree line on the nearby mountains. "I'm sorry I've been such an annoyance," she said stiffly. "You want me to stay away, fine. I will stay away—after my children decorate your Christmas tree. You said they could and I don't want to hurt or disappoint them. Where is the key to the shed so I can find the Christmas tree?"

Marshall flinched. He wanted to tell her he was sorry for being such a bastard, to admit that, despite what he'd said, he was grateful for her help and touched that her children were being so kind to him when he certainly didn't deserve it.

He *really* wanted to tug her into his lap and kiss away her glower, which he knew was as impossible as him getting up and marching across the house to find what she wanted.

"Kitchen, top drawer left of the sink," he finally said. "You can't miss it. It's on a blue carabiner and marked *shed*."

"Thank you."

She said the words in a tone as barbed as fishhooks, then turned and marched from the room, leaving behind that spring wildflower scent.

He frowned after her, feeling even more like a bastard, if that were possible.

She had done nothing to deserve his foul temper except try to make life a little easier for him. It wasn't her fault he was frustrated and sore and beginning to long for things he knew he couldn't have.

Chapter SEVEN

Andie quickly found the carabiner with the shed key hooked to it and hurried out to Wyn's beautiful stone patio that bordered the Hell's Fury River.

In summer, this was a lovely, tranquil spot where one could sit and listen to the river and enjoy the view of the mountains beyond.

The snow hadn't been cleared here. Because the patio faced north and was shaded by the house and the bordering trees, it seemed as if each wintry storm that had hit since before Thanksgiving had left a few inches behind that never had a chance to melt in the sunshine.

Even though she wore boots, it was still a struggle to crunch across the foot-deep snow to the garden shed. She didn't mind. The exertion took her mind off the emotions roiling through her.

When she reached the shed, she paused to catch her breath. Deep belly breathing had been a big part of her therapy this summer and she still found it immensely useful.

She closed her eyes and focused on expanding and contracting her diaphragm while she listened to the river's song and the scrape and rustle of tree branches in the brisk wind, heavy with the promise of more snow.

When she opened her eyes a few moments later, she felt much more centered. At least she no longer wanted to scoop up a bucket of this crusty weeks-old snow and dump it on a certain frustrating sheriff.

She didn't lose her temper very often. Growing up in the household her grandfather ruled with harsh words that hit much harder than iron fists had taught her young to learn how to contain any excessive emotions. She had always rather prided herself on her self-control, her ability to pause and think before she responded instinctively to a given situation with anger and words she couldn't take back.

For the first time in a long while, she had almost let that control slip away and had come dangerously close to giving Marshall Bailey a big, angry piece of her mind.

Did he seriously think she had nothing better to do than traipse back and forth between their houses, making up excuses to drop in on him?

Remembered hurt sliced through her again, a hurt she didn't understand. He hadn't exactly made it a secret that he didn't want her help. She supposed she had thought—hoped—that perhaps they were becoming friends.

She had to ask herself why his words seemed to cut so deeply. Did she really care what the sheriff thought of her? She barely knew the man. Until a few days ago, she would have said he made her nervous and uncomfortable. He had always seemed a cold, hard man.

Somehow she had convinced herself there was something more beneath the surface. She thought she had seen glimpses of kindness, a vulnerability she never would have suspected until she spent a little time here.

She was a fool.

He was exactly as he appeared—humorless and ungrateful and arrogant.

If it wouldn't break her children's hearts completely, she would march back inside, toss the shed key on his lap—broken leg and all—and tell him just where he could stuff the Christmas tree she was on her way to find.

The temper she had just tried to cool in the December air flared all over again, with an intensity she found more than a little disquieting.

When was the last time she had been truly angry?

For the last two years, she had been living in a kind of limbo. She had grieved for Jason until she was sick with it, but about four months after his death, she had forced herself to shove down the worst of her grief so she could focus on caring for her children.

That raw sense of loss had always been there inside of her, just muffled as if she had wrapped it in layer after layer of cotton batting.

She had finally been coming to terms with the grief when Rob Warren had destroyed everything in one terrible night when his obsession spiraled out of control and he refused to take no for an answer.

She pushed away the dark memories. She was so much more than what had happened to her. It was a small chapter out of her life, not the central, defining theme. She refused to let his actions dictate her choices going forward or the sort of life she wanted to provide for her children.

A few stray snowflakes fluttered down, landing on her cheeks, and she lifted her face to them, trying to focus on the pure beauty of her surroundings and the calming sound of the river. Eventually, it worked its inevitable magic on her spirit. When she felt the tension and anger begin to ease, she went to work unlocking the shed and flipped on the light.

The shed was constructed from the same stone as the house and the patio. The cold, dusty interior was filled with boxes, gardening tools, a couple of kayaks and a bike that looked older than she was.

She found the Christmas tree at once, clearly marked in a red bag. A few matching boxes around it held ornaments, just as Wyn had told her.

"Use whatever you want," Wyn had said when Andie called her the night before. "I can't even remember what I have there, to be honest. So much has happened this year—last Christmas seems like one big blur."

Wynona's father had died in January after contracting pneumonia at the care center where he had lived for several years after his brain injury, Andie remembered. A year ago, her friend had been a police officer on the Haven Point Police Department, working for Cade Emmett.

Now Wyn was finishing the last few credits she needed for her master's of social work and she and Cade were engaged.

The two of them were so sweet together. Andie knew Wyn had loved him most of her life and Cade looked at Wyn like she was everything he had ever wanted in a lifetime of birthdays and Christmases combined.

At the party the night before, she had told Eliza Caine she wasn't ready to date again, but here in the quiet solitude of this dusty, cold shed, she could admit the truth.

Jason had been a good man. From the moment they met when she was studying art in Portland and he was a rookie cop, their love had seemed so natural. Inevitable, even. He hadn't been the perfect husband and she certainly hadn't been the perfect wife, but they had been happy together.

She yearned for that connection again, even though it terrified her.

Should she call Eliza and tell her she had changed her mind about going out with Aidan's brother? Eliza would be thrilled, Andie knew.

The idea of dating again completely terrified her. Figuring out what to wear. Trying to make conversation. Wondering what her date thought of her—if he would call her for a second date, if she should let him kiss her, if her breath smelled minty fresh or like the onions on her salad.

She shivered from more than the cold, musty air inside the shed. She could hardly even bear thinking about it.

Maybe that was the very reason she needed to do it, to get past this mental block. Once she went on her first date, she would probably not have so much angst the second time.

Why was she even thinking about this? She wasn't going to call Eliza. Let someone like Samantha Fremont entertain Aidan's brother and show him around town. She had enough to do—but at least that list wouldn't include watching over Wynona's brother.

She grabbed the bag containing the tree and wrestled it out the small door of the shed, then returned for the boxes of ornaments.

It took two trips to carry everything back across the snow. On the second trip, she spotted movement from the small porch. When she looked up from navigating the path, she spotted Marshall Bailey standing in the open doorway on his crutches. Even hunched slightly to use the crutches, he seemed tall and imposing. She had a feeling that was more from his personality than his physical posture.

She frowned as she headed up the steps. Thinking about dating again made her break out in a cold sweat, but at least it had distracted her from her annoyance at a certain sheriff.

"You shouldn't be out here," she said, her voice cool. "It hasn't been cleared and isn't safe for someone using crutches."

A muscle clenched in his jaw. "You were taking a long time. I thought maybe something happened to you—that you slipped on the ice or something."

He was concerned about her. The unexpected softness sent a little bubble of warmth flaring to life in her chest, though she knew it was silly. Her own ridiculous reaction made her more honest than she might have been otherwise.

"I needed a little time to cool down," she admitted.

He studied her for a moment, his expression unreadable, then he sighed. "I owe you an apology. That was the other reason I came looking for you."

An apology? Now, *that* was unexpected. "Let me get these things inside, and then you can apologize to your heart's content."

For a moment, she thought he might smile, but he merely nodded. "I guess you need me to get out of your way."

On so many levels, she thought. "That would help."

He pivoted on the crutches—not an easy undertaking—and swung his way back into the kitchen. Andie picked up the tree and carried it through the doorway and into the living room before she returned to the porch for the boxes of ornaments.

"Guess you found what you needed."

"Wyn had a tree and some ornaments, right where she told me they would be. I locked it again and here's this." She pulled the key from the pocket of her coat and set it back in the drawer.

"And now, I believe you were about to offer me an apology."

He leaned back against the small island in the kitchen, the black orthopedic boot outstretched in front of him, and studied her with that same unreadable look. "You already may have figured this out," he finally said, "but I'm not very good at being needy."

"Yes. I believe I've noticed," she murmured.

"This damn broken leg is bringing out the worst in me, I'm afraid. It's tough for a guy like me to be dependent on others, but that's no excuse for me to be mean about it, especially when you've been nothing but generous and helpful. I'm very sorry I took my bad mood out on you. I'll try not to let it happen again. I can't make any promises, but I'll do my best."

Andie blinked as the last vestiges of her temper fizzled to nothing but embers. As far as apologies went, that one sounded sincere and heartfelt. She had a feeling apologies weren't any easier for a man like Marshall Bailey than accepting help, yet he had done it with a graciousness that completely disarmed her.

"Thank you. Very nicely done. I accept your apology."

He looked slightly amused. "Thanks. I guess."

She looked around the kitchen, remembering other times she had sat here with his sister and talked for long hours. "Did Wyn ever tell you how she and I became friends?" she asked suddenly.

He shook his head. "Knowing her, I don't imagine she gave you much choice in the matter."

"True enough." She smiled a little, remembering the events of early in the summer and how Wynona had pushed her way into her life.

"I came to Haven Point with one goal in mind. I just wanted my children to be safe, comfortable and happy and I planned to keep to myself as much as possible."

He raised an eyebrow at that, no doubt because it had to be obvious to him how that particular objective had gone down in flames.

"The first day I moved here, I met your sister. And, you're right—she didn't give me any other choice. The kids and I were exploring the neighborhood a little and headed across the bridge and along the Mount Solace trail when I sprained my ankle."

"That's a weird coincidence."

She gestured to his boot. "I didn't break anything. It wasn't really serious, just painful. But there I was, sprawled out on the trail and trying to catch my breath while trying to comfort my frightened kids when your sister and Young Pete came down the trail in the other direction."

"It's always been one of her favorite evening walks."

"And mine. When she found me, Wyn insisted on helping me all the way home, even though I told her firmly that I didn't need or want her help. After . . . everything we left behind in Portland, the last thing I wanted was a busybody police officer pushing herself into my business."

His jaw tightened almost imperceptibly before he met her gaze. "Wyn has always been good at doing what she wants, no matter what anybody says. You should have known her twin. She and Wyatt were definitely cut from the same cloth."

The clear affection in his voice made her a little sad, both for his loss and for the siblings she had never had.

"Not only did she all but carry me home that day, but the next day she showed up with enough meals for two weeks, provided by the Haven Point Helping Hands."

"Again, sounds like Wyn." His mouth softened into an almost-smile that lightened his austere features. If he ever gave a full-on smile, the man would be devastating.

"She didn't stop there. She spent the entire next day helping me unpack boxes while I was stuck on the sofa doing nothing. It was very hard for me to watch, but I learned something important that day."

"Not to stumble on the Mount Solace trail when Wynona Bailey is around?"

That was nearly a joke. She smiled, even as she shook her head. "That was one of the luckiest days of my life. I cherish my friendship with your sister, something I might not have had if I had continued in my isolationist stubbornness. No, what I learned that day is that none of us who shares this planet can claim to be completely independent. We need each other, plain and simple. The trick is accepting it's a zero-sum equation. Sometimes you're on one side of that equation, giving help. That's the side most of us are most comfortable with, I think. It makes us feel magnanimous and generous, like we're good people. But just as we have to be willing to help others, circumstances sometimes place us on the other side of the scale. The needy side. Those are the times we also must learn how to accept help when it's graciously offered, as hard as it is."

"Point taken."

"I know you don't like accepting help and I completely understand that, believe me. We all

126

like to think we have the strength to handle whatever life throws at us by ourselves. It's not about strength or fortitude or independence. Maybe this is simply my way of giving back to Wyn for all she has done for me and my children, by helping her grouchy wounded bear of a brother while he's going through a rough few days."

He gave a rough-sounding laugh. "Wounded bear? Is that what I am?"

"Close enough. You want to hunker down in your cave by yourself and lick your wounds. I get it. But my particular cubs want to make that cave a little more cheerful and I can't think that's a bad thing. I want to teach them the same lesson Louise is trying to teach her grandson. Decent human beings help each other when they can."

He paused, looking uncomfortable. "I am grateful for that, even when I don't always act like it and when I'm lousy at admitting it."

She had to smile again. "Don't worry. It gets easier."

"I doubt we'll get to that point. It's only a matter of time before everything is back to normal."

He had a few miles to go before then, but she didn't bother mentioning it. "You probably need to sit down, don't you?"

"I'm supposed to be moving around. It actually feels good to be on my feet. Or foot, anyway."

She shouldn't be noticing the way his shrug

rippled the loose T-shirt he wore or how his hands looked big and capable on the crutches.

She swallowed and gestured to the Christmas tree. "I should probably set this up and check the lights. Wyn told me it was only a year old so should work fine, but I would rather be sure of that before Will and Chloe hang all their decorations. It's easier to do earlier, rather than later."

"I'm sorry I can't help you."

"Zero-sum, remember?" She carried the tree into the den, aware of him hobbling down the hall behind her.

As she worked to pull the pieces of the tree out of the bag and set them in the correct order, he stood beside the sofa flexing his toe. How was it possible that he could look so virile and manly when his face was still scraped and battered and he wore something that wouldn't look out of place at the gym?

She thought of that wounded bear comparison. Marshall Bailey was more like a big, gorgeous mountain lion, sleek and strong and muscular.

Something else she probably shouldn't notice.

"How is the leg feeling today?" she asked to distract herself.

"Fine. Like the rest of me. More than ready to go back to work."

"When do you think that will happen?"

His features twisted with annoyance. "Technically I'm supposed to take sick leave until after the New Year."

"That's only a few weeks, at least."

It was obvious by his expression that seemed like a lifetime to him. Something told her Marsh was not a man who liked being on the sidelines very much.

"I've still got a few investigations spinning and I can work a few angles at home. I'm also going to dig into some of the county's cold cases from before my time."

He was obviously very dedicated to his job. That should be all the reminder she needed to ignore her growing attraction to him.

She refused to be involved with another law enforcement officer. It was as simple as that.

Some women had the fortitude to be married to LEOs or men in the military. They could handle the long shifts, the dark moods that could steal over them after a horrible day, the constant awareness of the danger they willingly walked into.

Since Jason's death, Andie had come to accept that she did not possess that necessary gene. If she ever married again—which was a very big and nebulous if, since she apparently couldn't bring herself to even think about the dating world—she wanted a man who was safe, stable, steady.

She could never let herself care about someone willing to risk his life and his future and all those he loved for a stranger who might not even want to be helped.

Not that Marshall Bailey was asking her to care about him, she reminded herself. This particular mountain lion apparently was a solitary beast.

"I'm also following a few leads into whoever did this to me," Marshall said, interrupting her thoughts.

She pulled the last segment of the tree out of the bag and set it into place. "You said Deputy Morales is working on the case for you?"

"Yeah, as far as that goes. He's not making much progress."

"That must be terribly frustrating."

"You could say that. It's like the perp disappeared into thin air. Or jumped into Lake Haven."

"You don't really suspect that, do you?"

"No. He's out there somewhere." He finally slid into the recliner, setting the crutches next to him. "Several leads would indicate it's someone who knows me. Someone close."

"Wow. That's got to be tough. What sort of leads?" she asked, genuinely interested.

"For one thing, he knew just what bait to dangle in front of me in order to lure me out to a deserted gas station parking lot. Every cop has that one case he can't shake and mine is a missing mother of two named Jessica Foster. Not many people even remember the case, but whoever called me offered a lead, after all this time, and I jumped at it like catfish on stink bait."

"What other evidence would lead you in that direction?"

"More like the lack of evidence. Your average criminal makes mistakes. It's the nature of the game. They talk about what they did to the wrong people, they create an alibi that's full of holes, they call attention to themselves. In this case, the fact that we can't find anything substantive would lead me to believe he's either lucky or knowledgeable."

"You're leaning toward knowledgeable."

"Yeah. But you don't want to hear this. I'm probably boring you to tears."

"Not at all," she assured him. "Jason would often go over cases with me, at least the ones he could talk about. He used to tell me a pair of fresh eyes always offered a new perspective and I enjoyed being helpful. Once, he solved a string of jewelry store heists after following up on one of my suggestions. It was a great feeling, you know? One of the things I really miss about being married."

That wasn't the *only* thing she missed about being married, of course. At the thought, a hollow, achy yearning shivered to life. She wanted a man to kiss her. Not just a man. *This* one. The surly, rumpled, sexy sheriff of Lake Haven County.

Heat washed over her and she knew she must

be blushing violently. She ducked her head, hoping he didn't notice and inevitably start to wonder where her thoughts had drifted to spark such a fiery blush.

She swallowed hard and plugged in the Christmas tree. The room immediately seemed brighter as the tree came to life.

"Looks like everything lights up just the way it's supposed to," she managed. And by everything, she meant . . . *everything*.

"Good to know," he murmured. She flashed him a look, grateful he couldn't possibly read her mind.

She had to get out of here, now, before she did something completely foolish. "I guess my work here is done, then, at least for now. The kids and I will be back this afternoon. I'll bring dinner, if that's okay."

For an instant, he opened his mouth as if to protest but closed it again. "It's not necessary, but I will do my best to accept your help graciously."

So he *had* been listening. She picked up her coat and wrapped her scarf around her neck.

"I look forward to seeing that," she said with a smile.

She walked out of the house, more than a little uneasy at the bubble of anticipation fizzing through her.

Chapter EIGHT

"This is going to be the best Christmas tree *ever*. Maybe even prettier than ours," Will declared, his breath coming out in puffs that lingered in the cold as he carried the box of trimmings down the street.

"No way. No tree is prettier than ours," Chloe argued, their little dog, Sadie, trotting in front of her. "We have the best tree in town."

"It's beautiful, but I'm not sure it's the *best*," Andie said mildly.

Her daughter narrowed her gaze. "Why not? What's wrong with it?"

"Nothing. I said it was beautiful, didn't I? It's just that everyone thinks his or her Christmas tree is the best one in town. They're all beautiful in their own way. I'm sure Sheriff Bailey will love the tree you decorate for him."

She actually wasn't sure of any such thing. He had only agreed to let them spread a little Christmas cheer because he didn't want to disappoint the children. She just hoped his forbearance would last through the evening.

Sadie sniffed at a mailbox, her little tail wagging like crazy. That was the other thing she hoped Marshall would be tolerant about. The children had begged to be allowed to bring Sadie along with them on their visit to Sheriff Bailey's.

"She can help us decorate the tree," Chloe said. "Remember how much fun she had when we decorated *our* tree?"

As Andie remembered it, the little dog had mostly enjoyed the excitement of the children. Sadie had thrived since they adopted her from the shelter.

At first, Andie had worried the little Havachon would struggle with a couple of noisy children, since her previous home had been as the adored pet of an elderly woman who passed away with no relatives willing to take in the dog.

Instead, Sadie had proved the sweetest of dogs, with the perfect temperament. She didn't yip or snarl. She could calmly sit beside Chloe when she had to practice reading aloud, then play and wrestle with Will when called upon.

They all adored her, after mere weeks of having her in their home, and the children wanted to take her everywhere. In this particular instance, Andie probably should have said no, but she hadn't had the heart for it, especially since Sadie had been alone most of the day while Andie ran errands and had meetings with a couple of executives she worked with at Caine Tech.

The dog needed exercise and company. Surely Marshall wouldn't object too strenuously to an unexpected guest, would he?

To give him a little warning, she texted him

they were on the way along with her dog. He still hadn't answered by the time they reached the stone house beside the river, so she knocked a couple of times before pushing open the door.

"Marshall? Can we come in? It's Andrea Montgomery."

"And Will and Chloe and our dog named Sadie," her son sang out, and she couldn't help but smile at this sweet boy with so much love to give.

Silence met her greeting for just a minute before he answered. "Yeah," he said, his voice sounding a little rough and sleepy. "I'm back here."

It was the kind of bedroom voice a man would use when he first rolled over in the morning. *Hey, babe. Come over here.*

Her skin erupted in goose bumps and she was very grateful he was in another room and couldn't see them—not that he would be able to see many goose bumps beneath her coat.

Sadie sniffed at everything, her tail wagging like crazy, as Andie led the way back to the den. They found him in the recliner, obviously just waking up from dozing. His dark, wavy hair was a bit messy, his eyes still blinking away sleep, and a mystery novel was spine-up on the arm of the chair.

"Hi, Sheriff Bailey! Hi!" Will said. "We're here to put the ornaments on your Christmas tree! Aren't you so glad?"

"So glad," he murmured. Though she gave him

135

a close look, Andie couldn't detect a trace of sarcasm.

"This is our dog, Sadie." Will pointed to the animal in question. "She's four years old, like me. Only, for a dog four years old is all growed up. She's gonna help us decorate your tree."

"How generous of her."

"I know. And wait until you see all the snowflakes Chloe made. There's, like, a billion of them."

"Not quite," Chloe said quickly, as if she didn't want to be arrested for colluding to deceive an officer of the law.

"I'm glad it's not a billion," he said. "That kind of snowflake number would probably break your scissors, never mind your fingers."

Chloe offered up her shy smile at his gentle teasing, which Marshall seemed to take to heart.

Will stood close to the sheriff and gazed down at his boot. "Does your leg hurt a lot today?" Will asked.

"Every day it's feeling better," he said, which she wasn't sure was completely the truth.

"Will they have to cut it off?" Chloe asked. "My friend Janie said her grandpa had a sore that wouldn't get better and they had to cut off his foot and now he has a fake one that he can pull on and off."

Marshall looked alarmed. "Nobody's cutting anything off."

"Whew." Will dramatically plopped onto the sofa in relief.

The sheriff appeared to be more awake now. Andie supposed a subtle threat of amputation could do that to a man. He eyed the little dog, but Andie couldn't tell if his expression was one of interest or annoyance.

They were on borrowed time, she knew. He had said they could decorate the tree, but she knew he wasn't looking forward to the activity and would probably use any excuse he could find to curtail it.

"Kids, we have work to do. Let's get to it, shall we? I'm sure Sheriff Bailey can't wait to enjoy the results."

He gave her a steady look, that expressive eyebrow raised. What would it take to make the man laugh? She was far more curious about that than she ought to be.

"I'll go get the stepladder I saw in the hall closet," she said.

"Okay," Chloe said. "But remember, you can only hang the top of the garland. We have to put on all the rest."

The children had insisted this was their idea, their project, and she wasn't to take over. She hoped that was more a measure of their desire to do something nice on their own than an indication that she hovered too much.

She found the small ladder—just right for

decorating the top of the tree—and carried it back to the den, where she found Will holding the garland up for Marshall to admire.

"It wasn't that hard. I made one in preschool before, only that time my teacher helped me cut out the paper and use the glue. This time my mom did it." Will glanced at her, then back at Marshall. "She uses a *lot* more glue than my teacher did. We had to glue and glue and glue."

Marshall shot her a curious look, probably wondering why she and her children were going to so much trouble to decorate a tree he likely wouldn't even turn on after they left. Her reasons had far more to do with her children than him. That was what she told herself, anyway.

"I'm climbing up the ladder," she announced. "Once I get up there, hand me your garland."

She set the stepladder next to the tree and started up.

"Careful," Marshall said. "That ladder's not the steadiest in the world."

Warmth spilled through her, sweet and comforting, though she knew it was ridiculous. He was probably more concerned about the ladder than her.

"I'm fairly certain I'll be okay. I'm only three feet off the ground," she pointed out.

"You never know," he said. "What if an earthquake hits while you're up there? You could still fall and crack your head open."

"Mom, be careful," Chloe said, eyes wide.

"I'm not going to fall," she assured her daughter. "And there's not going to be an earthquake. Isn't that right, Sheriff Bailey?"

"Probably not," he admitted. Amusement sparked in his eyes, but he still didn't smile. He caught her looking and the amusement slid away, replaced by something glittery that made her stomach jump, and she quickly turned her attention back to the paper loop garland.

She stuck the end loop on the topmost branch of the tree, then began spiraling it carefully around the tree.

When she glanced over again, Will had picked up Sadie and was holding her up for Marshall to admire.

"Yes, she does look like a good dog," he said, apparently in response to something Will had said. "I haven't met every dog in town so I can't say for sure, but I would guess she's *one* of the best. How about that?"

Will said something she couldn't hear and Marshall's mouth quirked a little. He looked inordinately handsome, even with the fading scrapes and bruises on his features—like some kind of sexy MMA fighter who had just won a tough round.

Those nerves jumped in her stomach again. She seriously had to knock it off.

"How's this so far?" She directed the question to the room in general.

Chloe, busy sorting her snowflake ornaments by size, looked up. "That's good. I can do the rest, just like you showed me when we decorated our tree."

"Come and grab this end, then," Andie said. "Will, you had better help. It's a two-kid job, I think."

Her son unceremoniously dropped the little dog onto Marshall's lap and headed toward the tree. The sheriff winced a little and repositioned the dog, though he didn't seem inclined to set her back on the floor. Instead, he earned Sadie's undying devotion by scratching her between the ears in that particular spot she loved.

Andie pulled the stepladder away while her children worked together to hang the garland the final three feet to the ground. When they finished, it wasn't designer-perfect and sagged on one side, but she thought it looked beautiful, especially because of the sincere effort behind it.

"Great job," she exclaimed. "Don't you agree, Sheriff?"

"Sure thing. I've never had a tree with such a nice garland."

She suspected he spoke truth, likely because he'd never had a tree with *any* garland.

"Okay. Now can we hang the ornaments?" Will demanded.

"Yes," Andie answered. "But make sure you don't only hang the snowflakes you made. Mix it up a little with some of the ornaments Wyn already had. They're in those boxes by the tree."

"But we can do *mostly* snowflakes, right?" Chloe asked.

"Ask Sheriff Bailey."

"Sheriff Bailey, can we do mostly snowflakes?"

"I love snowflakes. And you know, you don't have to call me Sheriff Bailey. You can call me Marsh or Marshall."

"Like Marshmallow?" Will said with a giggle.

"Just like," he said, and Andie wanted to roll her eyes. The man was about as similar to a marshmallow as this plastic Christmas tree was to a soaring Douglas fir.

After she ascertained the children were carefully hanging the ornaments and weren't likely to knock over the tree, she turned to Marshall.

"If you're here to keep an eye on things, I'll go put your dessert in the oven, then."

"What is it?" he asked, not bothering to hide his avid interest. She fought a smile at this further evidence of his sweet tooth.

"Wait and see. Maybe you can identify it by the scents once it starts cooking."

"You won't even give me a hint? That's just cruel, to tease like that."

141

"Anticipation makes everything better. Haven't you learned that lesson yet?"

"Or sometimes just makes a guy ache with hunger."

Her heart rate kicked up a notch at his low words. They *were* talking about dessert, weren't they? She hadn't flirted with a man in a long time and felt completely out of her depth.

She could only think it was a good thing she was heading to the kitchen, where she could think about sticking her head in the refrigerator for a minute.

Anticipation makes everything better. Haven't you learned that lesson yet?

Marshall gave an inward groan at the question. It could make things better—or it could make him miserable. Right now, he was anticipating kissing Andrea Montgomery, but it didn't make him feel at all better, simply because he knew it wasn't likely to ever happen.

He glanced up from his thoughts in time to see her children stealthily trying to move the step-ladder to another area without attracting his attention.

"Are you guys supposed to be using that?" he asked.

Both children gave him guilty looks.

"No," Will finally admitted.

"But we have to hang some of the ornaments

142

higher or your tree will look funny," Chloe protested. "I thought I could lift Will up and he could hang them, but he's too heavy."

"Maybe I can lift *you* up," Will suggested to his older sister.

"Nobody needs to lift anybody," Marsh said, reaching for his crutches. "I'm pretty tall and can probably reach the top."

"You have a broked leg, though," Will reminded him, as if Marshall could forget for a second.

"Yeah, but my arms are fine."

He maneuvered out of the chair, cursing the blasted crutches, then swung over to the tree. "What do you need me to do?"

"You can only help us with the top branches, and then maybe you could go out while we finish."

Go out where? He wasn't exactly up for a ten-mile hike here. "Sure. Hand me an ornament. Where do you want it?"

"Right up by the top," Chloe said. She handed him one of her paper snowflakes, lacy and so delicate he was afraid he would rip it, then pointed at a spot on the tree.

Holding the snowflake in one hand, he maneuvered closer on the crutches, then reached to the top branches to hang it where she indicated.

"How's that?"

"Good. Now this one."

She handed him what looked like an ornament out of Wyn's collection next, a glittery white kneeling reindeer that Chloe proclaimed adorable.

For the next few minutes, the children alternated between having him hang paper snowflakes and pulling new treasures out of Wyn's ornament collection for him.

Marshall did his best to comply with their wishes. If he were asked a week ago to make a list of activities he might have expected to be doing at any point in his immediate future, decorating a Christmas tree with a couple of cute red-haired kids never would have made the cut. Much to his surprise, he found it quite enjoyable, though.

In between decorating the tree, the children talked to him about their schools, a funny trick their dog could do, a Christmas song Will had learned in preschool.

It wasn't a bad way to spend an evening—and almost enough to make a guy forget all about the throbbing pain in his leg.

"Are you ready for another one?" Chloe asked him.

He considered it a great honor that she didn't seem terrified of him anymore, though she was a bossy little thing once she lost her nervousness.

He shifted position on the stupid crutches. "Sure. Lay it on me."

She handed him another snowflake to go with the veritable blizzard he had already hung on the tree. "We're running out of room here, kid."

She narrowed her gaze and studied the tree,

then pointed to a spot just to his left and up a bit. "Right there. I think it can fit there."

He complied with her wishes.

"Okay, Will and me can reach all the rest," she said. "You go out now."

"Why can't I just sit back down and close my eyes?"

"This will be the second-best tree in Haven Point, after ours," Will declared. "You wait and see."

"And you can't see it until it's done. We want it to be a surprise," Chloe said.

Marshall wanted to ask how the tree could possibly be any sort of surprise when he had personally hung at least a third of the ornaments. He didn't have the heart to spoil their fun—and he was undeniably touched that these generous children wanted to bring a little brightness into his life. What was the harm in playing along with them?

"I guess I *could* use a drink of water."

"We'll call you and our mom to come in and see it when we're all done," Chloe said.

"Fine. I guess I'll go see what's smelling so good in the kitchen."

He made his careful way down the hall to the kitchen, which smelled of apples and cinnamon and cloves. There, he found Andie with her back to him, bending over to add something to the bottom rack of the dishwasher.

Yeah, he had a broken leg and an assortment of other aches and pains, but he was still a guy. He couldn't have prevented his gaze from drifting to her shapely curves any more than he could stop the Hell's Fury runoff in springtime.

His body stirred with awareness—which had the potential to be more than a little embarrassing, considering he wore loose, soft basketball shorts.

With her auburn hair piled on top of her head in a messy updo, she looked soft and pretty and he had an insane urge to press his mouth to the back of her neck just below her hairline.

He blinked away the impulse and moved farther into the room as she stood up. Her dog spied him first and gave a tiny, excited *woof,* which alerted Andie. She whirled and for an instant he could swear heat flared between them before she seemed to collect herself.

"Oh! You startled me!"

"Not sure how. No one could say I'm exactly stealthy on these things." He gestured to the crutches.

Appealing color bloomed on her cheeks. "I guess my mind was somewhere else. Sorry. Are they about done in there?"

"I've been banished from the room while they put the finishing touches on."

"You're a good sport, Sheriff Bailey."

That was something not very many people

would have said about him, but he wasn't about to argue with her. "I said this earlier and I meant it. Please call me Marsh or Marshall. Once you've decorated a man's Christmas tree, you should be allowed to call him by his first name."

Her color seemed to heighten. "Fine. Marshall."

The way she said his name in her soft alto voice sent a funny little shiver down his spine. Probably some kind of nerve receptor misfiring, he told himself, even as he tried to rid his brain of imagining her using that voice in the bedroom.

She cleared her throat. "I know you weren't crazy about having my kids decorate a tree for you. It means a lot to me that you let them do it anyway."

He didn't deserve her gratitude. He *hadn't* wanted them to decorate a tree and had agreed only because he hadn't had the heart to turn down the offer. He didn't bother telling her it likely would be a chore for him to remember to even plug in the lights throughout the remainder of the holiday season—not to mention, taking the thing down once Christmas was over.

"Something smells good in here," he said.

"Oh. That. It's an apple brown Betty. I thought it would go well with that vanilla ice cream you had in your freezer. It should be done in ten minutes or so, and then I'll see if I can hurry the kids along so we can get out of your way. I promised you we wouldn't take long."

He had been a complete jerk to her earlier, but she still had been willing to overlook it and was making him something she thought he might enjoy.

Her words and the reminder of his own behavior made him feel about six inches tall. His jaw worked. "You probably already figured this out, but I'm an ass sometimes."

She flashed him a look that said she didn't completely disagree. "You're in pain and hate being laid up. I get it."

"That's not a valid excuse."

"Honestly, Marshall, you apologized very sweetly earlier and you've more than made up for it this evening by being so kind to my children."

"Kind? They're the ones who wanted to do a nice thing for me. It's not some huge sacrifice for me to let them, though I'm still not quite sure why they're going to so much trouble for some cranky neighbor they barely know."

"I can't answer that for sure, but . . ." She hesitated. "I don't know how much Will remembers his dad or really understands what happened to him, but Chloe does. She knows her dad was a police officer who died in the line of duty. You're in law enforcement and were *injured* in the line of duty. I have to think maybe she's made some kind of connection there between the two of you."

"Between her dad and me." He wasn't sure how to feel about that.

"She adored her dad and used to love leaving little gifts for him all the time. A bracelet she made out of string, a picture she colored, cookies she saved from her own snack and packed in a little bag to tuck into his lunch the next day. That kind of thing. Since she can't give Jason those little gifts now, maybe somehow she feels like doing something nice for another police officer is the next best thing."

His throat felt tight and achy and he couldn't seem to find any words.

"That's about the sweetest thing I've ever heard," he finally said, his voice raspy. "Now I really *do* feel like an ass."

She smiled. "Or maybe she just wanted to cut out a bunch of snowflakes and you were the lucky recipient. Who knows? She's six."

It would be entirely too easy to lose his heart to this whole family. The lovely, deceptively fragile-looking mom, the cute chatterbox of a four-year-old boy and the sweet girl who saved her own treats and tucked them away to give to her police officer father.

"That's nice," he finally said. "Law enforcement isn't always very popular these days."

"Yet you do it anyway. Why is that?"

Sometimes he wondered that himself. He shrugged. "It's kind of a Bailey family tradition."

"I know. Your father, your grandfather, your brothers. Wyn has told me as much."

That was part of it, but not the whole picture. "It's all I've ever wanted," he said. "My dad was my hero. I guess I'm a lot like Chloe in that way. I used to watch him leave the house in his uniform day after day and think he was better than Superman or Batman."

Her features softened. "Everyone tells me what a good man he was. You must miss him a lot."

"Hard not to," he admitted.

The ache was always there; it just hit him harder at certain moments.

He pictured John Bailey and the last difficult years of his life. Deep guilt always threaded through that image like some kind of foul, twisted creek.

He might have been able to prevent those tough final years. If he had stepped up and confronted his father in the months before he was shot about his suspicions that John Bailey wasn't behaving like himself, his father might still be alive.

Instead, he had let his love and respect for the man color his own judgment as a fellow law enforcement officer.

His father hadn't been fit to serve. Something had been very wrong. Marsh had begun to suspect it but had said nothing, wanting to believe he was imagining things, that his father was simply tired or stressed or overworked.

Only after the fact, he had confronted Cade

about what really happened that night and his best friend reluctantly confirmed his suspicions.

John had begun to show signs of early-onset senility.

Both he and his best friend felt responsible for not identifying it and taking steps to remove John from the force.

"This is probably going to sound strange," Andie said, breaking into his thoughts, "but I'm a little jealous that you had such a good example. I can only wish I had a dad like John Bailey, even if it meant I had to suffer the pain of losing him one day."

"Your father wasn't a good man?"

She shrugged. "Who knows? He wasn't in my life. I don't know if my mother even knew his last name. When I asked her about him once, she told me she thought his first name was Kevin and he had a cute Irish accent. That's it, probably because she was too high to remember the rest."

Her words revealed volumes about her childhood. She seemed so put-together, so loving and kind, he never would have guessed she came from a rough background.

"You were raised by an addict?" he asked carefully.

The sudden regret in her eyes told him she had disclosed more than she intended. "Not really," she said. "My mother got clean when she found out she was pregnant with me, moved home with her parents and stayed away from drugs until I was about five, when she relapsed. She was in and out of rehab after that and I stayed with my grandparents."

He didn't miss her flat, guarded tone when she spoke of her grandparents, so unlike the open affection she showed to her children. "You never had to do the foster care route?"

"No. I guess I was lucky in some respects. Living with my grandparents might not have been ideal, but at least I had a secure home."

Might not have been ideal. What kind of pain did those words conceal? He felt a rush of compassion for her at the same time he was deeply grateful for his own childhood—fishing trips with his brothers and Cade, hiking the mountains around here, swimming in Lake Haven.

In many respects, he had enjoyed an ideal, rosy, Norman Rockwell sort of childhood.

This inevitably drew his thoughts to Christopher next door, angry and hurting and lost, whose childhood was vastly different. His chest ached for both the boy and Andie.

"I don't know why I told you that," she said a moment later. "You seem to be excellent at getting me to confess things I rarely talk about. I guess that's what makes you a good police officer."

"Why don't you talk about your childhood?"

She picked up a cloth and used it to wipe down

the countertops. The smell of lemon dish detergent mingled with the apples and spices from the oven.

"What's the point?" she said after a moment. "It's the past and I can't change it. It wasn't horrible, anyway. I was never physically abused or starved or locked in a closet or any of the ugly things you can encounter in your line of work. It just wasn't a very loving place for a child to thrive or feel secure."

"I'm sorry. Every child deserves to feel loved."

"I agree. I promised myself when I left home at seventeen that I wouldn't look back. I don't very often. I also vowed that I wouldn't for one moment ever give my children a reason to feel unwanted or unimportant."

Again, all she didn't say about her childhood seemed to expand to fill the kitchen. His heart twisted with compassion—and admiration that she had come from that and then had suffered great loss and trauma in her own life yet still struggled so valiantly to make a beautiful world for her children.

"You're a very good mother," he said quietly.

She gave a laugh that sounded self-conscious. "Here's a news flash for you, Marshall. No mother ever thinks she's good at her job. We do our best. That's all."

He couldn't help thinking of Charlene, who had been a very loving—if somewhat smothering—

parent. He loved her dearly and didn't tell her that often enough.

"I'm sure those happy kids in the other room would tell you what a good job you're doing."

As if on cue, Chloe and Will rushed into the room, their faces bright with excitement.

"Okay. I think we're all done," Chloe said. She looked like she could hardly contain her enthusiasm.

"Come see!" Will ordered, reaching for his hand to tug him toward the living room.

When the boy's fingers slipped between his, Marsh felt a weird jolt in his chest.

"William Jason Montgomery, be careful," Andie exclaimed. "You don't want to knock over Sheriff Bailey."

"Sorry," the kid said, pulling his hand away quickly. Marsh wanted to tell both of them it was fine, but he decided it was probably better not to say anything.

He followed the kids back to the den. They had turned all the lights off and only the tree was illuminated, glowing bright and cheerful.

"Oh, kids," Andie breathed. "It's beautiful!"

He had to agree. As far as Christmas trees went, it wasn't exactly a professionally designed job. Some of the ornaments were clustered in bunches and there were a few uneven spots, but it was clear the two kids had taken great care to hang the ornaments.

It touched him to the core that they had done such a kind thing for him.

"Your mom is right," he said gruffly. "That is, without a doubt, the prettiest tree I've ever had."

"Really?" Chloe looked as thrilled as if he had told her Santa Claus lived upstairs.

"Honest. It looks like a different room in here. I can't help but catch a little Christmas spirit, with such a beautiful tree."

The children grinned at each other and at their mother, who gave him a bright smile that hit him like a sunbeam in July.

"Thanks a lot for going to all this trouble for me," he said, his voice gruff. "I feel really honored, especially since you made so many of the decorations yourself."

"It was fun. I'm glad you like it," Chloe said.

"Yeah, because if you didn't, we would have to take all the ornaments off and that would be a lot of work and I'm already starving," Will said.

Andie brushed a hand across her son's head. "Let's clean up the bag and the boxes now and leave Sheriff Bailey to enjoy his tree in solitude."

That's what he wanted, right? For everyone to leave him alone so he didn't have to work so hard to be nice.

Right now, it somehow didn't seem at all appealing.

"You don't have to rush off," he said on

impulse. "Why don't you stay for dinner? I was thinking pizza sounded good. We could order from Serrano's—and we've got apple brown Betty and ice cream for dessert."

"Pizza and ice cream!" Will exclaimed.

"Can we?" Chloe implored her mother.

Andie looked caught off guard at the invitation. "I think we've bothered Sheriff Bailey enough for the evening."

It was an obvious reference to his words of earlier in the day, the ones he suddenly would have given just about anything to take back.

"But he invited us!" Will pouted.

"I did. And I meant it. Think of it as my way of repaying you for all the trouble you just went to."

"Please?" Chloe entreated.

Andie looked down at her children, then at him with an expression that managed to mingle puzzlement and suspicion. She was probably wondering how he could flip so abruptly from telling her basically to stay away to inviting them for dinner.

If she figured it out, he would like to know the same thing.

"Serrano's pizza is delicious and I haven't figured out any other plans for our dinner," she finally said. "I suppose that would be okay, if you're sure."

"Positive. To be honest, I get tired of eating by

myself. My own dinner conversation is pretty boring."

This made Chloe giggle but was nothing less than the truth. He spent a great deal of his free time in solitude. Unless he was grabbing lunch with Cade or one of his deputies or having family dinners at his mother's, most of his meals were spent at his desk or in front of the television set on low for background noise while he worked on reports.

He had always thought that a perfectly acceptable state of affairs, but suddenly it seemed a pretty isolated way to live.

Chapter NINE

Whoever would have guessed the serious, gruff sheriff of Lake Haven County was lonely?

Andie sat across from Marshall Bailey at Wynona's kitchen table and finished her final bite of the basil-and-mozzarella goodness that was Barbara Serrano's margherita pizza, trying to figure out the man who seemed to be more layered than some of Barbara's famous tiramisu.

Even before he was injured, Marshall Bailey had come across to her as stiff and unapproachable, a hard, solemn, dangerous man who didn't have time for things like children and little dogs and silly women who seemed to become increasingly flustered around him.

As early as that morning, she would have been convinced he was fiercely proud, the type of man who refused to rely on anyone else. He hated needing help; he'd said so himself. Yet as she listened to him interact with her children over pizza and crusty bread sticks, she was forced to reevaluate her perception.

So many adults claimed they liked children, but they quickly tired of them. Marshall seemed patient at their endless questions and genuinely interested in their opinions.

He was even cute to Sadie. Andie had caught

him more than once reaching down to pet her. The dog, in turn, seemed enamored and had plopped beside his chair on the opposite side from his broken leg.

Andie didn't want to be attracted to him, but it was becoming increasingly difficult to deny.

After dinner, she and the children cleaned up while Marshall took a call from one of his deputies in the den. When she served up dessert on a plate and carried it in, she found him looking pensive, lit only by the lamp beside the recliner and the glowing Christmas tree.

"Thanks. It looks delicious. I'm a sucker for dessert."

"I believe I've noticed," she said. "The kitchen is clean. I put the rest of the pizza in the refrigerator for you to heat up tomorrow. The kids and I are going to take off, unless you need something else."

"No. I'm good. Thanks again for everything." He hesitated and she had the distinct impression he wanted to say something else. Finally he sighed.

"This is awkward, but I need a favor and I don't know who else to ask."

She did her best to hide her shock. Had he come so far in one evening that he could not only tolerate someone helping him but actually *ask* for it?

"Of course," she said quickly. "Whatever you need."

The words hovered between them, for some strange reason. She hadn't meant anything sexual, of course, but when she heard the echo of them, she felt her face heat. What *did* he need? And why did her mind immediately go there?

After a charged moment, he cleared his throat. "I've got to take care of a few things I left hanging at the sheriff's office in Shelter Springs tomorrow and I'm not cleared to drive. I could probably manage it with my left foot on the gas, but I guess that's not the example I should be setting for my department, let alone the community at large."

"You need a ride," she said.

He looked distinctly uncomfortable. "Yeah. If you can manage it. If not, there's a taxi service in Shelter Springs. I can call them out here."

"I thought you were ordered to take time off until after the holidays."

"I was, but I'm in the middle of a couple of investigations and I don't want to lose momentum. Some of the secured files are on my computer at work and I can't access them from the network, only in person. And it has to be me."

His jaw tightened. "Not to mention, if somebody in my department did this to me, I want them to see I'm still fighting."

He was a stubborn man. She found it surprisingly attractive.

"What time?" she asked.

"We typically have a weekly briefing at ten every Thursday. If you could run me in on time for that, I was thinking I could catch a ride back later when the shift is over."

That would mean hours of him sitting at his desk in an uncomfortable chair when he was still only a few short days out of surgery. She didn't think that would be good for him.

"Or what about this?" she proposed, thinking quickly. "I have some Christmas shopping I've been meaning to do in Shelter Springs. I could drop you off at the sheriff's department and take care of my shopping while I'm in town, then pick you up and bring you back here a few hours later."

He frowned. "I don't want to take up your whole morning."

"You wouldn't be," she assured him. "This will be a good excuse for me to wrap up some errands. Really, you'd be doing me a favor."

He somehow managed to look grateful and uncomfortable at once. "I'll pay for your gas and time."

"You will not," she exclaimed. "I have things of my own to take care of in Shelter Springs. It's no trouble at all to drop you off while I'm there. Since I've come to Haven Point, I've learned these are the things neighbors do for each other."

"I have a feeling I won't win an argument with you over this."

"Smart man." She smiled, but it slid away when she thought for a crazy moment that he was staring at her mouth.

"You said the briefing starts at ten," she said, trying to pretend she wasn't suddenly flustered. "I can pick you up at nine thirty—or earlier, if you need it."

"Nine thirty works." He didn't look particularly thrilled about it. "Somehow when this is all over, I'll figure out a way to pay you back."

"Not necessary," she said, her voice soft. "My debt to your family is larger than I can ever repay."

He looked as if he wanted to reply, but the children came in arguing about who was the better elf, Buddy or Hermey, the elf with dreams of dentistry from *Rudolph the Red-Nosed Reindeer*.

"I'd better go before this breaks down into open warfare," she said. "Kids, grab Sadie. And what do you say to Sheriff Bailey?"

She was gratified when Chloe and Will instantly stopped arguing and came to Marshall's recliner.

"Thank you for the pizza, Sheriff Marshall," Chloe said.

"It was super-duper delicious," Will added.

To Andie's surprise, her son threw his arms around Marshall and hugged as much as he could reach. The sheriff looked more than a little nonplussed but patted the boy's back.

"Thank *you* both for doing such a good job at Christmas decorating."

As she said her own goodbyes and ushered her kids out the door, Andie was rather horrified by how badly she wanted to do the same thing—just throw her arms around the man and hug him.

She knew the impulse was completely ridiculous, and so was the excitement fluttering through her at the prospect of seeing him again the next day.

The anticipation didn't abate overnight, as she had hoped.

The entire time she prepared breakfast for Chloe and Will, signed permission slips, found boots and hats and mittens, she was aware of it bubbling just under the surface. She did her best to ignore it, to tell herself she was being ridiculous, but all her internal lecturing didn't seem to matter.

The day was cold but gloriously beautiful as she pulled into Marsh's driveway, the snow a startling white against the brilliant blue sky and the dark pines along Riverbend Road. The driveway and sidewalks had been cleared of the few inches of snow dropped by the storm during the night. At least he wouldn't have that worry to contend with, though ice would always be a treacherous concern for a man on crutches in the wintertime.

He opened the door before she reached it, as if he had been waiting there for her. Andie almost lost her own footing and it was all she could do not to gawk at the jarring change in him.

For days, she had seen him wearing only T-shirts and basketball shorts or sweats over his orthopedic boot, but now he wore a pressed shirt and tie, blazer and slacks. His hair was neatly combed and he was clean-shaven, without the usual dark beard stubble that, in combination with his assorted scrapes and bruises, gave him the look of a wounded, disreputable pirate.

She should have been ready for it. He was the sheriff of Lake Haven County, after all. He certainly couldn't go to a briefing of his deputies wearing a Broncos T-shirt.

She drew in a breath, trying her best to gather her thoughts, which had scattered like snow geese. "Hello. I'm sorry I'm late."

"You're not. We said nine thirty. It's just a few minutes past that."

"I got hung up at Will's preschool. They're having a Christmas party next week and I'm supposed to take cupcakes, but I didn't know how many or what kind. Plus, there's a girl with gluten allergies, so I needed to ask if I should bring something she could eat and the mom who is organizing the party was busy talking to another one of the mothers who is on the game committee and I didn't want to be rude and break into their conversation and . . ."

She stopped, mortified when she realized he'd taken on a slightly glazed look. "Sorry. I'm rambling. It's a bad habit of mine when I'm nervous."

He gave her a curious look. "Why are you nervous?"

Rats. Had she really just said that? Running off at the mouth and spilling inner thoughts she absolutely shouldn't were apparently *also* bad habits of hers when she was nervous.

She certainly couldn't tell the man he left her tongue-tied and jittery, like a junior high school girl with a crush on the cutest boy in school.

"It's not every day I chauffeur the local sheriff to work," she improvised quickly. "Maybe I'm worried you'll find fault with my driving. Are you allowed to give me a ticket when you're a passenger in my vehicle?"

"Don't worry. I'm not officially on duty."

"Well, that's a relief." She managed a smile, though she still felt completely ridiculous. "Are you ready to go?"

"I think so."

That was a stupid question. Would he be waiting at the door for her if he wasn't?

"What can I do to help?"

"I just need a little room to maneuver these things."

"Of course." She stepped to the side as he reached to pick up a brown leather laptop case hanging on the doorknob.

"I'll grab your bag," she said.

Though he looked as if he would like to argue, he handed it to her and she again told herself to ignore the little current of electricity that passed between them.

He had only a few outside steps to maneuver the crutches off the porch, but she couldn't help hovering, muscles tensed and ready to spring into action if he stumbled.

He handled the steps as if he'd been doing it for a long time, which again made her feel foolish. He easily made his way to the car and opened the passenger door before she could reach around and do it for him.

"I can set those in the back," she offered, gesturing to the crutches. He handed them over and she slid them and the laptop case into the backseat on top of the children's boosters.

"Thank you again for doing this," he said after she walked around the vehicle and slid into the driver's seat.

"It's no problem," she said. She couldn't let it be. The actual driving time between their neighborhood on Riverbend Road and the sheriff's office and jail in Shelter Springs couldn't be more than fifteen minutes. Certainly she could handle thirty total minutes in the man's company, no matter how nervous he made her.

Always a careful driver, aware she usually had children to protect in the backseat, she drove more cautiously than usual, pausing at stop signs a second or two longer than she would under normal circumstances and signaling well in advance of her turns.

She hadn't lied when she said driving with him made her nervous, even though she knew it was silly.

Haven Point rarely had much traffic and she reached the town limits without delay and took off around the lake and north toward Shelter Springs.

The beautiful blue waters and soaring, snow-covered mountain range on the other side managed to soothe some of her nerves. Conversely, the man beside her seemed to grow more tense with each passing mile.

"Are you okay?" she finally asked, wondering if he found the seat position or angle uncom-fortable for his leg.

"I hate this so damn much," he muttered.

He wasn't talking about her seat or her driving, she suddenly sensed. Depending on someone else for something as basic as his own transportation couldn't be easy for a man like Marshall.

Poor guy.

She had a feeling he was going to be driving his own vehicle long before his doctors advised it wise.

"You're already getting around better than you did a few days ago," she pointed out. "Soon enough, these few weeks will just be a bad memory."

He didn't look at all convinced. After a few more minutes, he glanced in the backseat at the empty boosters.

"No Will today? I thought he would be along for the ride. I guess you said he had preschool."

Her son and his sweet personality and constant chatter would have provided a very welcome buffer right about now. "Yes, and a playdate afterward with a friend that we arranged earlier in the week. I told you the timing was good for me."

Ty Barrett had quickly become Will's best friend after they moved to Haven Point. The two of them were always begging to play at each other's houses.

"I guess you probably wouldn't drag him along Christmas shopping anyway."

"He's not crazy about shopping for anything," she said. "Speaking of shopping, it occurred to me this morning that you might need some help with your own Christmas presents. Is there anything I can pick up for you while I'm in town?"

"Thanks, but online shopping has been my friend this year. I would have been sunk, otherwise. I'm envisioning a constant parade of deliveries between now and Christmas."

"You know, there's a good reason they warn

people not to make major purchases while under the influence of narcotics."

His low, amused laugh rang through the car and she nearly swerved into a mile marker post.

He laughed.

Marshall Bailey actually laughed.

The sound of it rippled down her spine like he had just trailed his fingers along the skin just above her neckline.

She swallowed, hands tightening on the steering wheel, and her gaze focused on the road. She was going to drive both of them into the icy waters of Lake Haven if she didn't maintain a little control here.

"What a beautiful day," he said after a moment. "I can't even tell you how good it is to be out of the house. I feel like I've been trapped inside for weeks."

Yes. She probably was safe talking about the weather and their stunning surroundings. "I love this drive along the lakeshore between Haven Point and Shelter Springs. It has to be one of the prettiest roads in the world."

"I've always enjoyed it, too."

"I guess that's a good thing, since you have to drive it every day now that you live in Haven Point."

"True enough."

"Do you think you will stay in Haven Point after Wyn finishes school and moves back?" she asked.

"Haven't decided yet. Wyn's going to want her house back eventually, I suppose."

"Don't you think they'll move into Cade's house when they get married, since it's bigger?"

If she hadn't shifted her gaze to glance in her mirror on his side of the vehicle, she might have missed his slight grimace.

"What's the matter? You don't like the idea of the two of them together?"

"He's my best friend. She makes him happy, and vice versa. Why would I have a problem with that?" he asked, but she thought she still heard an edge in his voice.

It must be a little weird for him, but as far as she could tell, he had never been anything but supportive of his sister's relationship with Cade.

"What was it like growing up in Haven Point?" she asked, taking pity on his discomfort to change the subject. "It must have been amazing."

"Amazing? I don't know about that, but it was a good place to grow up, at least for me. That probably had more to do with my particular family than our geographic location."

"I could see that. Your family is wonderful."

"Despite the idyllic setting, everything here isn't perfect, you know. Like any town, Haven Point has its share of trouble. Even as a kid I knew that. When your dad is the chief of police, you can't help but know a little about the darker side, though he tried to keep it from us as much as he could."

"I suppose that's true of every town."

"No doubt. The boat factory, which was the biggest employer, had struggled to stay profitable for a long time in a changing economy. Various layoffs hit the town hard over the years. You probably know that Ben Kilpatrick had to finally close shop after he inherited the company, which left a lot of people out of work. It's been nice to watch all the towns around the lake come back to life since Caine Tech moved in."

McKenzie had told her a great deal about the ill-fated history of the wooden boat factory owned by her husband's family and her and Ben's efforts to move in a Caine Tech facility to take its place and bring jobs and commerce back to the struggling lakeside town. As someone trying to rebuild her own life, she found Haven Point's efforts to reinvigorate itself fascinating.

"What about you?" he asked her. "You told me a little about your home life but not where you grew up. Portland?"

She shook her head. "Eugene. My grandfather was a professor at the university there."

She had always found it ironic—and rather frightening—that her grandfather could have been so beloved on campus yet so harsh and dictatorial at home.

"I graduated from high school a year early and moved to Portland as soon as I could in order to go to art school. My grandfather wasn't at all happy about it, but I took out loans and earned scholarships and basically told him to go to hell."

He made a disbelieving sound. "Did you? Somehow I can't quite picture that."

"Why?"

He appeared to choose his words carefully. "You're a very nice person. You've been nothing but kind to me, even when I've been an ass. Somehow I can't see you telling *anyone* to go to hell."

She did consider herself nice, but that wasn't the same as weak.

He wasn't completely wrong, she had to admit. She hated the frightened shadow of herself who had first come to Haven Point. She wanted to be strong and confident again, the woman she had been before Jason died and the world crashed in—and especially the woman she had been before she allowed Rob Warren to climb inside her head and torment her for months.

"You might be surprised," she told Marshall. "I might look like your average suburban mom now, but there was a time when I was an art school rebel. Henna tattoos, purple hair, emo black clothes and all. I even smoked a joint once at a party. Oh, wait. I probably shouldn't have told you that. Are you going to arrest me now, Sheriff?"

He gave a rough, amused sound that did crazy things to her nerve endings. When she glanced over, she found he wasn't quite smiling, but almost.

"You went to art school in Portland. Isn't that part of the required curriculum?"

This time she was the one who laughed. "If it was, I failed that part of my education miserably. It made me sick, if you want the truth, just like a certain former president I won't name, so I never tried it again. I guess now you know my guilty secret."

He knew other things about her, she remembered. Dark, horrible things that the whole town knew had happened to her.

"Anyway," she said quickly, "a year later I met a handsome rookie cop at the coffee shop where I waitressed so I could make ends meet. Somehow he saw past my attitude and kept coming back for more of the restaurant's lousy coffee. Eventually he asked me out and the rest is history."

It was sad history, yes, but lately she'd begun to think about Jason without the crushing pain of loss.

She had lost the husband she loved, yet she couldn't regret any of it. Pain and all, that fairy tale that ended so sadly had produced two amazing children who filled her world with joy and light and purpose.

"And now here you are creating a new history for your children."

His words and the quiet understanding in them sent goose bumps rippling over her skin. Yes. That was exactly what she was doing—trying to give Chloe and Will the warm, happy life she hadn't known herself, in a town that had embraced them all.

"It's worked out better than I ever could have hoped," she said softly. "It was pure chance I picked Haven Point when things became intolerable in Portland. I was in desperate need of a refuge, and what better place than a town that had *haven* in the name?"

He was silent for a long time. When she glanced over, she saw his features looked stony, cold. Dangerous.

When he finally spoke, his voice was as hard as his features. "I wish I'd torn that bastard Rob Warren to pieces during the months he stayed at my jail."

She gave him a shocked look for just an instant, then turned her attention back to the road, blinking rapidly, and Marshall saw her fingers tighten on the steering wheel.

"It must have been tough for you, trying to be courteous to the man who shot your sister," she said.

He hadn't been thinking of his sister just now, though he supposed he should have been. "He messed with a Bailey, which was a big mistake," he acknowledged. "What he did to you—a fellow cop's widow? That's unforgivable, in my book."

Every time he thought about what had happened

to the kind, compassionate woman behind the wheel of her SUV, Marshall wanted to pound something.

He hated thinking someone had taken advantage of her sorrow, her neediness, and forced himself on her.

She had been violently raped by a man she had trusted, her husband's partner and a man she had relied on in the first difficult months after Jason Montgomery gave his life trying to rescue someone else.

Rob Warren was a narcissistic sociopath who had masqueraded as one of the good guys for too damn long. The only solace Marshall could find in the whole thing was remembering that ex-cops rarely fared well in prison.

Yeah, he had no right to feel so protective of her, but he couldn't seem to help it.

"You have no idea how tough it was for me to treat him as anything but the garbage he is," he said. "I had to limit my interactions with him. In the few months he was an inmate at the jail, my deputies figured out early that Warren is really good at manipulating other people's emotions and goading them into saying and doing things they would rather not. We had to keep him segregated from the other inmates or risk a full-on riot."

Her hands tightened on the steering wheel. "It's a beautiful day. I would really rather not talk about him."

"You're right. I'm sorry. I shouldn't have brought it up."

"I wasn't thrilled about the plea deal he accepted, but at least he's in prison now, where he belongs. I have decided I won't give him the satisfaction of wasting another moment of my life thinking about him."

"That sounds like an excellent plan," he said.

She was much tougher than she appeared on the surface, with a deep, unexpected core of strength. Not only was he fiercely attracted to her, but he admired her far more than he wanted to admit.

"Am I going the right way?" she asked.

"Yes. Turn onto Center Street and head up the hill."

Shelter Springs was a nice town, with charms of its own, but the downtown wasn't quite as quaint and picturesque as Haven Point.

"Turn in there," he said, pointing to the square, bland complex of buildings that held the county offices.

She obeyed and pulled into the parking lot.

"You can park there," he said, gesturing to an empty spot a few stalls down the row.

"Why? I can just drop you at the door, then pull into the space so I can carry in your laptop."

"I don't need your help."

She frowned. "You are a stubborn man, Sheriff Bailey."

"I believe you've mentioned that."

"What can you possibly gain by forcing your-self to go an extra thirty feet on your crutches through a possibly icy parking lot, especially when there's no good reason?"

He didn't want to have to explain himself to her, but he supposed she deserved it after she had gone to all the trouble of bringing him to work.

"There is a good chance somebody inside that building tried to run me down five days ago. By now, they probably know I suspect an inside job, no matter what the idiots at the state police say. It's important, under the circumstances, that I appear at my department from a position of confidence and strength. I appreciate the ride and your help, but I need to carry in my own bag. The crutches are bad enough. If I could lose them, I would in a heartbeat."

The look she gave him was not without sym-pathy, though it was mingled with a healthy dose of exasperation. "I'm glad you've at least got enough sense to know you need the crutches."

"I'm stubborn. I'm not completely stupid."

She didn't look convinced as she pulled into the space he indicated. "I could carry the laptop up to the door for you and just not come inside. That way you won't reveal a hint of weakness."

"I'll be fine," he said. Right now he was more concerned about not revealing how touched he was by her concern for him, even though he knew he shouldn't be.

After she parked, she slid out of the driver's side and walked around the vehicle to pull the damn crutches and the bag in question out of the back seat, then she hovered close to make sure he could pull himself out of the seat and up onto his good leg and the crutches—not as easy a task as it should have been.

When he was on his feet, she handed him the bag and he slung it, messenger-style, around his neck and under one arm.

"Are you sure you're all right?"

"Positive. No problem."

He would be a little off balance, carrying the bulky laptop bag, but he could handle it.

"When do you need me to come back?"

"Should we say two hours? That should be long enough for the staff briefing and to download the files I need from the secured server. Is that enough time for you to finish your shopping here in town?"

"I only have a few small items. I'll be back here just before noon, then." She paused. "Good luck. Be careful."

He nodded and made his way across the parking lot, careful to watch for speeding vehicles that might come at him out of nowhere. It likely would be a long time before he could comfortably walk across a parking lot without remembering head-lights zooming toward him out of the darkness.

Chapter TEN

He was just as watchful when he walked into the building, this time to gauge the reaction of his personnel to his presence.

As he might have expected, everyone acted shocked to see him and eager to talk about his injuries and the accident. Though he wanted to deflect each inquiry—talking about himself had never been his favorite thing—he was compelled by the circumstances to sift through each conversation for any clues he might find pertinent to the investigation.

As far as he could tell, the concern of most of his deputies seemed genuine. The two exceptions were Ken Kramer, of course, and Curtis Wall. Though they, like everyone, expressed sympathy, the smirks they both wore and the insincerity of their tones indicated something else.

The most upset person in the office seemed to be Jackie Scott. His administrative assistant couldn't even talk to him without her eyes welling up with tears.

"You're just so brave about this," she said, sniffling, as he tried to go over the agenda for the briefing with her.

"I wouldn't say that. It was scary as hell and

I won't deny it. But I'm here and I'm fine, for the most part. The leg will heal."

When it looked as if she would start crying again, he did his best to deflect her attention. "More important, how are *you?*" he asked. She really did look a wreck.

Though she was only in her early forties and was usually groomed to perfection, right now she looked much older, with dark circles under her eyes and her usual professional hairstyle looking ragged and unkempt.

"Fine," she answered quickly. He didn't need to be a detective to know she was lying.

"What's going on? Is it Jeremy?"

Jackie had walked a tough road the last few years since her investment banker husband walked out on her and their teenage son to take up with a cocktail waitress from Coeur d'Alene.

Her son had taken his father's defection hard and Jeremy had tangled with the law more than once over the past two years.

If circumstances had been different, he would have liked to confide in her about Christopher and ask her advice. With everything she had going on, he couldn't do it.

"Everything's fine," she said, which he was smart enough to know was clearly a lie. "You don't need to worry about me. You need to focus on getting better, that's all."

"And finding the bastard who did this."

Her smile looked wobbly. "That, too. Are you . . . any closer to finding answers?"

He pondered what to tell her, then decided on the truth. She might be able to help more than he'd considered.

"Close the door, Jackie."

Looking wary, she complied, then sat down in the visitor's chair across from his desk.

"I need you to tell me the truth."

Her mouth sagged for a moment. "About . . . about what?"

"What's been going on around here the last few days?"

She looked somewhat surprised at the question. "Everyone's worried about you, if that's what you mean. And I've had a devil of a time keeping Ken out of this office. He seems to think because the county commission named him acting sheriff, he can completely take over, but I reminded him you will be back before he knows it. Other than that, everything seems to be normal. Why?"

"Have any of the other deputies been acting suspiciously?"

She stared. "You think it was someone from the department who did this to you?"

"I wish I could rule it out as a possibility."

"I'm sure that can't be true." Her eyes were wide, her mouth slack. "Nobody here would hurt you. Why would they?"

"Maybe I'm in someone's way. You said yourself Ken has been pushing to get into the office. It could be a power play."

Her hands shook as she brushed them down her thighs. "Oh, I wish you hadn't said that. I hate thinking someone I work with every day—someone I joke with in the break room—might be capable of something so . . . cold-blooded."

"I don't have anything concrete, only suspicions at this point. I would just ask you to keep an ear to the ground. Let me know if you hear any whispering in that break room that might point in a particular direction."

"I will. I sure will, Sheriff Bailey."

He hated adding another layer of stress to her already heavy burden. But if he wanted to figure out what was going on, he would have to gather those he trusted around him.

"Thank you. I don't know what I would do without you, Jackie. Seriously. You keep the whole department running smoothly."

She sniffled, her eyes suspiciously red. "Thank you," she said, barely above a whisper. "I love my job. I don't know where I would have been without it after . . . after Bobby left. This job and Jeremy are all I have."

Her depressed tone left him worried for her. Jackie was a dedicated, loyal employee. He had inherited her from the previous sheriff and she had done all she could to make his transition in the office as painless as possible.

"You need more than just this job," he advised. "I've never asked. Do you belong to any clubs or anything?"

"Clubs?" She gave him a blank look.

"I don't know. Clubs, church groups, social circles. A friend of mine in Haven Point belongs to a group whose entire objective is to help people in need around town. Maybe you could find something like that here in Shelter Springs. Or if there isn't one, maybe you could start it."

"I don't know if I would have anything to offer something like that. Who would even want me?"

Had he really been so blind that he hadn't realized his assistant seemed to be on the brink of a serious depression?

"Sure you do," he answered, even though he really didn't have time to cheerlead her right now, with everything else he had going on. "You've got plenty to offer. You're warm and kind and you genuinely want to help people. You're the most organized person I know and one of the most honest."

Now her eyes did well up with tears. He shifted, uncomfortable from more than just his blasted leg. He was more than a little relieved when a knock sounded at the door.

"I asked everybody to come in here for the briefing," Marshall explained. "I figured it was easier than me trying to hobble down the hall. Can you bring a few more chairs in?"

"Of course. Whatever you need."

He should have tried harder to help her these last few months and he felt guilty that he hadn't. He didn't want to think anything good could come out of his injury, but if it left him a little more aware of those around him and what they might be going through, he supposed it couldn't be all bad.

"Are you going to be okay?"

"Eventually," she said with a sad smile.

The door opened and a couple of his deputies came in for the briefing before he had a chance to address her again.

By the time the hour-long meeting was over, his leg ached like a son of a bitch and his head wasn't much better.

At least he had a little more clarity that the sheriff's department was indeed a house divided. Ken Kramer took every opportunity to challenge Marsh's leadership, with sly remarks and subtle opposition. He was joined by Curtis, as if they were joined at the hip. Could the two of them together have planned the hit-and-run? Both knew he had worked the Foster case and still dug into it whenever possible.

He didn't want to think he was going to have to clean house, but the conclusion was becoming inevitable.

He asked Ruben to stay behind after the meeting

to update him on the state of the investigation—which had come to a standstill, apparently.

"I'm getting nowhere. I'm sorry, Marsh."

After he gave his report, Marshall had to agree. In five days, all they had was a stolen vehicle with no identifying forensics.

When he finished giving his report and they talked strategy going forward, Ruben gave him a careful look. "Need me to give you a ride back to Haven Point?"

He was trying hard enough to return integrity and honor to the office that he didn't want any appearance of wrongdoing.

"You're on duty. I've got a friend picking me up."

That was the second time that morning he had referred to Andrea Montgomery as his friend. It was something of a shock to realize it was nothing less than the truth. He was coming to care about her, entirely too much.

"Listen, I know you've already taken on far more than I should ask, but I need another favor."

"You got it," Ruben said instantly.

"My plan is to be back before Christmas, but if I'm not, can you look out for Jackie?"

Ruben frowned. "Our Jackie? Why? What's up?"

The department knew about her divorce and a select few knew Jeremy struggled with drugs and petty crime and had been in and out of rehab. "She's going through a rough time right now. You know how tough the holidays can be, especially when you've got family trouble."

"Oh yeah. They don't call it the hell-idays for nothing."

"She seems upset. Maybe even clinically depressed. If I were here all day, every day, I could probably wriggle it out of her and make sure she gets help. Or maybe not, since I gather she's trying to put on a happy face on my account. Just keep an eye out, offer a listening ear."

"You got it." Ruben rose. "Anything else?"

"You've done more than enough. When I'm back, I plan to make you take some of those vacation days you've been accruing."

"Can't wait." The deputy headed for the door, but when he opened it, he nearly bumped into the soft, pretty woman standing on the other side.

"Oh. Sorry."

Marsh felt a hard little kick in his chest at the sight of Andie, cheeks pink from the cold and a cute little powder blue scarf twisted around her neck.

"I'm the one who's sorry," Ruben said. "Should have been watching where I was going. Are you all right, ma'am?"

"I'm fine, Deputy Morales. How are you?"

"Please. Call me Ruben. You must be the sheriff's ride."

Before his eyes, he saw Ruben again start putting out the vibe, smiling down at Andie like she was some delicious piece of Christmas candy he couldn't wait to pop into his mouth.

She seemed oblivious. "I am," she said. "It was no trouble, though. I needed to come into Shelter Springs anyway."

"I hope the sheriff knows how lucky he is to have such a nice neighbor. We're all very grateful to you for the good care you're taking of him."

Andie shot a glance in his direction and he was almost certain he saw color climb her cheeks again. "He hasn't let me do much. I was rather amazed he allowed me to drive him here today at all instead of climbing behind the wheel himself, using one of his crutches to hit the gas."

Ruben's laugh was full and rich and as annoying as hell. "You know him well."

Again, she darted a quick, sidelong look at Marshall but said nothing.

"Aren't you supposed to be out on patrol?" Marshall said, with no subtlety whatsoever, when Ruben seemed content to stand there the rest of the day gazing down at the lovely widow.

"Yeah. You're right." His smile was filled with appreciative warmth. "I hope I see you around again."

"Good to see you, Ruben. Be careful out there."

He waved and took off and Andie moved farther into Marsh's office.

"You could have texted me you were in the parking lot. I would have come out."

"Or better still, I could have just honked the horn, like a teenage boy picking up a date," she said drily.

"That would have worked, too."

She rolled her eyes as he pulled himself up on the crutches and started gathering his laptop and the other things he wanted to take home.

"I know you said you didn't want to look weak in front of your deputies, but I thought if you *did* need something carried out, you would prefer my help over having to ask someone from your staff."

She was right, he realized. He couldn't do something as simple as carrying a lousy box of files on his own.

He hated this helplessness. He was going to be on the crutches for several more weeks and he didn't know how the hell he was going to survive it.

"I guess you've got a point," he said gruffly.

One thing he liked about Andrea Montgomery, she didn't gloat. She simply smiled. "What do you need me to carry, then?"

He gestured to the cardboard box. "Just that box on top of the pile. I figured I would go through some of the department's coldest cases while I've got time on my hands."

"That sounds interesting."

"A little more challenging for my brain than soap operas and game shows, anyway."

"Are you ready, then?"

"Just need my jacket."

"I'll grab it for you." She moved to the coatrack, where he'd hung his blazer. She pulled it off the hanger, then carried it back to him. When she handed it to him, he tried not to notice the soft, flowery scent of her.

"Thanks."

Trying to balance on the crutches while slipping his arms through the sleeves of a jacket was tricky. Again to her credit, Andie didn't step in to help, she simply waited until he was done, then slipped the laptop bag over her shoulder and scooped up the box of files.

"Anything else?"

"That should do it. Let's go."

He found this excruciating.

Andie could tell by the sheriff's body language how much he hated having to depend on her for anything, even something as inconsequential as carrying a box of files. His mouth was set in a hard line and he moved swiftly through the office, stopping only briefly to speak with a couple of deputies who seemed to be comparing notes over a map of the county.

She had complete sympathy for him. When she sprained her ankle earlier in the summer, she had been astonished at how difficult every single thing became, from grocery shopping to fixing her hair to going out to the mailbox.

She walked slowly, matching her pace to his. When they finally reached her SUV, that mouth was set even tighter, with lines radiating out. She shifted the box to one hand so she could open the passenger door for him, then quickly set the files and the laptop bag in the backseat while he maneuvered his way inside.

While she knew it was dangerous to spend more time with him, she also sensed he wasn't eager to return to the enclosed space of his home. Fresh air and sunshine could only be beneficial.

"Why don't we grab a bite to eat while we're out?" she suggested after starting the engine but before she backed out of the parking space. "We can grab something to-go here in Shelter Springs and then have lunch at one of the scenic pullouts between here and Haven Point, overlooking the lake and the Redemptions."

He looked startled at the suggestion but quickly warmed to it. "That sounds really nice, actually."

"Any favorite places in Shelter Springs? I'll admit, I'm not very familiar with the culinary offerings."

He mulled the question for only a moment. "There's a great sandwich shop a couple blocks from here. Ali's. He's a fresh sandwich genius and he has a drive-up window. I usually stop at least once or twice a week."

"That sounds perfect. Just tell me how to get there."

After he pointed her in the right direction, she pulled up to the window. Ali himself took their order and greeted Marshall like an old friend.

"What happened to you, Sheriff?" he exclaimed across Andie when he spotted the crutches and the orthopedic boot. His friendly, weathered face wrinkled with concern.

"It's a long story. Once I'm back at work, I'll try to stop in and tell you all about it."

"At least you've got a beautiful woman to take care of you, right? Hello, my new friend. I'm Ali Bhattacharya."

Andie was completely charmed by the man, who looked to be in his early seventies. "Hello, Mr. Bhattacharya."

"My new friends call me Ali. Or darling. Whatever you prefer."

"Stop flirting, Ali," Marshall growled. "We just need a couple of sandwiches."

"Always so serious, this one. No time for fun *or* beautiful women. Fine. What do you want?"

"I'll have a club with your spicy mayo and a water." He turned to her. "What about you?"

"Turkey. No cheese. Also water."

"You got it. Two minutes flat."

Mr. Bhattacharya bustled away and returned in the promised time with two bags overflowing with food. "Here you go. I threw in some of the orange nankhatai biscuits my friend the sheriff likes."

"Thank you," she said. She tried to hand him her debit card, but he shook his head.

"No, no. On the house."

"You know I can't take free food from you, Ali," Marshall said. "It's against department rules."

"You did not take any free food. It is a gift for your beautiful woman, as I am sure she has earned it and more, having to take care of a grouch like you."

Andie couldn't help but laugh. "He obviously knows you well," she said. "Thank you for the lunch," she added to Ali. "I will pay you twice the next time."

The man's booming laugh followed them as she pulled forward and out of the drive-up.

"That was fun."

"Ali is a character," Marshall said. "He came to Shelter Springs twenty years ago after his wife and only son died in a car accident in India and has been here ever since. He's always been very kind to everyone at the sheriff's department."

She had a feeling by their brief interaction that the man was particularly fond of Marshall.

"Where would you like to eat?" she asked.

"Your idea of one of the lakeside pullouts was a good one."

Traffic in Shelter Springs was light as she drove through town on the way back to Haven Point. Not long after, she found the perfect spot, a picnic area with a lovely view. The road crew had cleared the snow off the small stretch of pavement, though Lake Haven in the wintertime wasn't exactly picnic-friendly.

She parked overlooking the lake and for a moment she simply enjoyed the view.

Lake Haven was beautiful in the summer, when the evergreen forests were green and lush, but the winter was simply stunning, especially the vivid contrast between the lake's unearthly blue and the sparkling white of the new snow.

They ate in silence in the car for a moment, both absorbed by the food and the peaceful surroundings.

"You're right. Ali is a genius. This is delicious."

"I was more hungry than I realized."

She had to smile at that. "You sound like Will. He'll insist he's not hungry, that he couldn't eat a bite, but as soon as I put food in front of him, he wolfs it down like he hasn't had a meal in days."

"He's a funny kid."

"I think so."

He took another bite and washed it down with his water. "This was a good idea. Lunch with a view, I mean."

"I'm glad. Anytime you need to go for a drive, let me know. Even fifteen or twenty minutes can give your spirits a lift."

"That's kind of you to offer, but I'm sure you've got enough to do, with Christmas just around the corner."

The sunshine beamed in through the windshield and she fought the urge to stretch out in it like their shy new cat. "Not really. I will still have to wrap the few things I bought today, but other than that, everything's basically done. It had better be, since I started in September."

"You really get into this whole holiday thing, don't you? The presents, the decorating, the baking. All of it."

She shrugged, a little embarrassed. "I just want my children to enjoy the magic, especially this year in a new house and new town. The last few haven't been the greatest, so I vowed this year I would give them the joy-filled, meaningful Christmas I always wanted, no matter what."

He looked out at the water. "I guess that's what makes good parents," he said after a moment. "You have to be willing to sacrifice whatever it takes to do what's best for your children."

She thought she heard a low undertone of sadness in his voice, just a hint, but it was enough for her to take a closer look. In profile, his features were hard, set, his mouth a firm line. She had noticed that reaction before when they talked about children and she wondered at it.

"The challenge is figuring out what that is. What's best for your children, I mean. And our idea of what's best for them isn't always what they want or need."

His jaw tightened. "How do you figure it out?

How do you make those tough calls, especially when what *you* might want and what they might *need* aren't the same thing?"

It seemed an odd question from a single man with no family, but the intensity of it warranted an honest answer.

"The moment I gave birth to Chloe, what I wanted in the moment no longer mattered. It couldn't be the driving force of my life any longer. She was. She became the most important thing, then Will after her. Every choice I make as a parent, I have to ask myself if this will help them grow up to be kind, compassionate, decent human beings who contribute to society."

"No pressure, right?"

"Parenting is all about pressure—and most of the time I feel like I'm making things up as I go along."

He seemed to absorb that and grew pensive again, gazing once more at the water and a small flock of Canada geese skimming past.

Vague impressions she had gathered throughout the last week seemed to coalesce in her mind as she sifted through his words.

She decided to take a wild guess that still somehow seemed right on the mark. "Is your child a boy or a girl?" she asked.

Marshall swiveled to stare at her, his mouth agape and shock flaring in blue eyes that appeared the same shade as that stunning lake.

"*What?* Why would you ask that?"

He didn't immediately tell her he had neither, she couldn't help but notice. "It was just a guess. I'm right, though, aren't I?"

He turned back to the water, his features stony. She could feel the tension rippling off him just like the water behind that small group of geese and regret pinched at her.

On impulse, she reached out and touched his arm, a gesture of apology and comfort. "You don't have to answer. I'm sorry. That was intrusive and rude."

His gaze shifted to her hand on the arm of his blazer. When he looked up, his eyes were murky with turmoil. Indecision? Regret? She couldn't tell.

"I have a son," he finally said, his voice hesitant. "He's thirteen now and has no idea I'm his father."

Chapter ELEVEN

She held her breath, struck by not only his words but the pain she clearly sensed behind them.

He had a son. Thirteen years old.

A son who didn't know Marshall was his father. He was a serious man who took his responsibilities very seriously. He took cold cases home with him to study while on sick leave for a broken leg! She couldn't imagine that he would have refused to take responsibility for a child.

"How long have you known about your . . . son? Did his mother not tell you she was pregnant?" It was the only explanation that made sense.

He had the distinct look of a man who regretted opening his mouth. "I wish I could take that easy way out. I knew. She—the mother—contacted me when she was six months along and told me about the baby but claimed she didn't think it was mine. In the same breath she asked me to sign away all paternal rights, just in case."

"And you agreed?"

He flashed her a look as if searching for condemnation, but she purposely kept her features as bland as her voice.

She wasn't naive or stupid. She knew about extenuating circumstances, about one-night stands and relationships that didn't work out.

At the same time, she had been a child of a single mother, never given the chance to know anything about her own father. A little corner of her heart would always ache from the loss.

"I didn't want to. I refused the first and second time. We could wait until a DNA test to make any decisions, I said."

"You didn't wait?"

He sighed. "It felt like an impossible situation. I was twenty-one years old and deployed in Iraq. All the communication between us was via email when I could manage it and a few hurried satellite phone conversations. She happened to be a few weeks away from marrying a man who thought the baby was *his*. Apparently they were engaged when we were . . . together, which I swear I didn't know. She thought the baby was his, too, but if there was a chance, even a slim one, she wanted me to sign away any future rights before they were married. She wanted everything neat and clean. That's just how she was."

If the woman wanted neat and clean, maybe she shouldn't have slept with one man when she was engaged to another, Andie thought caustically.

"She didn't come out and say it, but I knew she didn't want me showing up one day after I got back to the States and messing up her happy little family."

What kind of woman would pressure a man serving his country in dangerous conditions to give up rights to a child he might have helped create?

"She and I, uh, didn't really have a relationship. Just a quick fling. I was stationed in San Diego and a couple buddies and I went out one night. In one of those weird coincidences, I happened to bump into her at a bar. She was from Lake Haven, though several years older than me. I'll admit, I was a little homesick and nervous about shipping out and we just . . . hooked up for a crazy long weekend. It wasn't anything serious and we both knew it. Hell, it obviously wasn't serious, since she never got around to telling me about her rich, important fiancé until six months later."

Andie was beginning to seriously dislike the woman.

"I figured I'd never see her again, you know? Unless we happened to bump into each other at Lake Haven Days, anyway."

"And then she found out she was pregnant."

"Right. Her fiancé apparently was thrilled because he and his first wife had infertility issues. He'd been told, uh, that he didn't have very strong swimmers."

"And that's why the woman felt she needed to have you sign away rights."

"Right. Just in case. It was a tough decision. Tougher than I might have expected." The lines around his mouth seemed to deepen. "But what did I have to offer a kid right then? I still felt like a kid myself, in a lot of ways. I was twenty-one, single and halfway across the world. The guy she was marrying had money and lots of it. He was older and had already raised a couple of adopted kids. I figured my son—she knew it was a boy by then—needed parents who were married and stable, not some military police officer living paycheck to paycheck. He was probably much better at being a dad than I could be anyway."

She had to disagree on that point. She had seen his patience with her children and thought he had the potential to be an excellent father, given the chance.

"I still refused the first few times. I just couldn't bring myself to do it. She kept after me and I finally decided I didn't have much choice. The chance that the baby could be mine anyway didn't seem very compelling, so I figured, why not."

He watched the Canada geese take flight in a rush, their wings brushing the water with their takeoff. "Worst decision of my life."

His voice was thick, raw, and the pain in it made her chest ache.

"Why do you say that?"

"Three years later, the two of them were divorced. I didn't know until recently that she spent the last decade hopping from guy to guy, neglecting the child I threw away, until she died earlier this year."

"Oh no."

"Right. Meanwhile, the man my son thinks was his father basically abandoned him after the divorce. I don't know, maybe the guy suspected the kid wasn't his, but as a result, my son is now left with no one."

She frowned as the story seemed to ring oddly familiar. Her mind tried to sort through the bits and pieces, but she couldn't figure out quite why.

"The poor boy. Can you step up now and be a father to him?"

"How? I have no legal rights and the only proof I have that we were together is the document she had me sign. He has no idea I even exist and I can't figure out how to approach his gra—guardians."

He stumbled over the last word and as she caught his slip and tried to make sense of it, all those stray pieces clicked into place. Of course! She leaned back in her seat, the rest of her lunch completely forgotten as she tried to absorb the stunning truth.

So much of his behavior made sense now and she couldn't believe she hadn't seen it before. She released a breath and spoke before she really thought through the implications.

"Christopher Page is your son."

Her words seemed to echo through the SUV, bouncing off the roof, the windows, the floor mats.
Christopher Page is your son.

For so many years he had held the secret close, knowing he might have a son out there somewhere but trying not to think too often about it.

It felt so strange to hear someone else say it aloud for the first time ever.

Over those years, he had still hung on to the idea that the baby couldn't have been his. He and Nikki Jacobs Page spent one wild weekend together and had used protection.

A few years earlier, on a whim, he had tried to look her up on social media. It hadn't been easy—which he found out later was probably because she married twice more and changed her name multiple times.

Louise Jacobs had been his ticket in. When Louise finally joined social media and became friends with his mother, he had been able to slip through the back door to track Nikki from his mother's page to her mother's to her own social media profile.

What he found had made him sick. More than a decade after that wild weekend they spent together, Nikki Jacobs Page Alexander Guyman had seemed as immature and self-absorbed as ever. She hadn't posted a single picture of her son and rarely mentioned him.

And then about a year ago, Louise had put up a picture of her grandson and his heart had stopped.

Christopher Page is your son.

He stared at Andrea now, not sure how to respond.

"Who said anything about Christopher?" he finally said, stalling for time.

Her sideways look told him plainly not to bother dissembling. "It wasn't very tough to connect the dots. His grandmother is my good friend. I know his mother died this summer and he fits the age frame you're talking about. His parents were divorced when he was young and Louise told me his father has nothing to do with him."

She paused, her gaze sharpening. "Christopher is the reason you moved to Haven Point from Shelter Springs after Wyn left for school, isn't he?"

There was no point in denying it when he had done everything but draw her a picture. He didn't want the whole world to know—the boy in question didn't even know—but he sensed he could count on Andrea to be discreet.

In some little corner of his mind, he was actually relieved that someone else knew the truth. He didn't have to carry this secret by himself any longer.

She didn't seem condemning or judgmental, only concerned. That was almost more of a relief.

"When Wyn told me she was going to rent her house out while she was in Boise working on her master's, I knew I couldn't pass up the chance to move into the house next door to him. It seemed the perfect opportunity to make a connection."

"Have you?"

"So far it hasn't worked out the way I planned. I don't quite know how to barge in and say, *Hey, guess, what? I'm your father.*"

"You seem so sure of that. How can you be, without a DNA test?"

"Except for the dark hair, he's the spitting image of Wynona's twin, Wyatt, who died five years ago. To tell you the truth, I can't believe no one else in my family has picked up on it yet, now that Christopher is living in Haven Point. I guess everyone has been too busy planning weddings to notice."

He couldn't imagine what his mother would say when the truth came out. Would she be understanding of the choices he had made or would she be disappointed in him for not initially stepping up to take responsibility for his child?

"You've been living beside them for months and you still haven't told them?"

"He's so angry and hurting right now. At this point, I'm not sure how he will react when he finds out about one more person who walked away from him."

"You're here now, though, unlike his mother and the man he thinks is his father. You moved to Haven Point to be closer to him. That ought to give you a few points."

"Or tip the scale toward creepy stalker."

She smiled a little and tucked a loose strand of hair behind her ear. Sunlight danced in and out of the tree branches. As he watched the random play of light on her features, he felt a little jolt in his chest.

"I think you should tell Herm and Louise first and let them work with you to figure out how best to let Christopher know the truth."

He instinctively rejected that idea. "No. Not yet. They have enough to deal with right now without me throwing another complication at them."

"I can't agree. You must know how they're struggling to reach him. They would probably welcome all the help they can find."

Not his help. What would the boy gain from the unexpected appearance in his life of a father who showed up out of the blue, one who had never claimed to even like kids? "I doubt Christopher will be thrilled to find out the father who signed away all rights to him just happens to be the sheriff of Lake Haven County."

"You don't know that," she argued. "I really think you should tell Louise and Herm."

"I don't want him to know yet. This is my decision. My problem. I'll deal with it in my own way."

"When? Christopher moved here in August and you haven't done anything yet."

The reminder of his own inaction gnawed at him. He could give a hundred excuses. The trouble in the ranks at work. His own guilt over signing away his rights, coupled with his natural caution. Christopher's obvious unhappiness, living in Haven Point.

"I do not want him to know yet. I have to ask you not to say anything."

She looked offended. "Of course I won't."

Despite her words, he could picture her thinking, in some misguided way, that she was doing the right thing by telling Louise or Christopher. Ali's delicious sandwich seemed to congeal in his gut.

"I gave in and let you help me after the accident because I didn't have a choice," he said curtly. "I let you bring food and decorate my tree and fuss over me like I'm five years old."

"I have not," she said, looking offended.

"I never wanted you pushing your way into my life, but you did it anyway. I told you I would talk to his grandparents about shoveling and you went ahead and did that, too. Don't get it into your head you can do the same thing where Christopher is concerned. I need you to stand down. This is my problem and I have to deal with it my own way."

She stiffened, hurt flaring in her eyes before she looked away from him.

"Your call, Sheriff." Her voice was stiff, cool,

and he instantly wanted to apologize. "Are you finished?"

What else did she want him to say? "For now."

"I meant with your lunch, so I can take you home."

Now he felt like an ass *and* stupid, too. "Yeah. I'm done."

She stuffed the remains of her sandwich—most of it uneaten—into one of the bags Ali had given them, then pulled back onto the road without another word.

The rest of the way, she drove in silence, her features remote. He didn't know what to say. He wasn't wrong, but perhaps he could have worded things a little more diplomatically.

Why did she always bring out the worst in him? he wondered as she drove around the lake. He could pinpoint at least part of the reason— he was fiercely attracted to her and the futility of it left him sour and out of sorts.

Most women liked him. He could even be charming when he set his mind to it.

With Andie he had been cranky and sour, like a dyspeptic old man with gout.

She hadn't done anything to deserve it—rather, she had been nothing but kind to him, even though she had never wanted to help him in the first place. She had just spent two hours chauffeuring him to Shelter Springs and back, and instead of showing his appreciation, he repaid her by lashing out and basically accusing her of being a busy-body.

He could have tried to conceal the truth when she guessed correctly that Christopher was his son, yet he had made the choice to confide in her.

It was completely unfair of him, then, to blast her in return.

"Do you need to go anywhere else while you're out?" she asked, her voice still cool, as they reached the town limits of Haven Point. "I can spare another hour before Chloe gets home from school when we need to drive up to Evergreen Springs to pick up Will."

Her determined politeness made him feel even worse. "I don't think so. You've done enough."

The moment he said the words, he knew they sounded wrong, hostile. He sighed. "That didn't come out the way I planned. Nothing I say does around you."

"I'm sorry."

She said the last word as a half question and he had to shake his head. "Why are *you* apologizing? I'm the one who's sorry. I just spent the last ten minutes trying to figure out why I'm such an ass around you."

She didn't argue with his assertion—but then, he hadn't expected her to. She merely gave him a steady look. "What brilliant conclusion did you draw?"

He couldn't very well tell her his impossible attraction to her was clouding his normal courtesy.

"No brilliance here. Just a man who's forced to apologize once more for taking out his bad mood on you."

She turned onto Riverbend Road but didn't speak until she pulled into Wyn's driveway and turned off the engine.

"When my babies were teething, I always found it sad and funny at the same time how they would always tug at their ears. The ears might have hurt, too, I don't know, but maybe they couldn't quite figure out exactly how to fix the pain they were in, so they reached out to the closest tangible object."

"You're comparing me to a teething baby?"

"I'm saying you've got a lot on your plate. Someone tried to kill you, possibly a person who works for you. Your injuries have forced you to be in a dependent position, which you hate. And you're struggling to deal with the very real problem of how to reveal yourself to a son who doesn't know you exist. It's enough to make anyone cranky."

"Whatever the reason, it's my behavior that matters and it's been lousy, especially to you. I am grateful for all you've done, even if I'm not doing a very good job of communicating that. I'm very sorry."

The smile she gave him was much warmer. Somehow it left him feeling like he'd just been sucker punched.

"Apology accepted," she said.

They gazed at each other for a moment. She was the first to look away and he didn't think he imagined the little rosy flush on her cheeks.

She couldn't possibly be attracted to him, too. It would make no sense, considering how he had consistently acted toward her.

"You're too forgiving," he said. "You shouldn't tolerate anybody treating you poorly. You deserve better."

"Good advice. I'll try to keep that in mind, the next time I'm blackmailed by a friend into watching over her injured brother."

Despite everything, he couldn't help laughing at her tart tone, which earned him a surprised look.

"What's the matter?" he asked. "Do I have something in my teeth?"

"You should laugh more often."

"I laugh," he protested. "I just haven't found that many things funny lately—until you and your kids came along, anyway, and reminded me the world doesn't have to be so serious all the time."

"Oh," she exclaimed softly. "That is the nicest thing I've ever heard you say."

"See? I'm not always the biggest ass in town."

"Not always," she murmured.

The moment seemed to stretch between them, soft and sweet as a summer afternoon. She melled like summer, too, of wildflowers and sunbeams and a gentle breeze blowing through meadow grass.

In contrast to the winter landscape outside the vehicle windows, she was irresistible.

He gazed at her for just a moment and then he couldn't resist leaning forward and stealing a little taste. The instant just before their mouths met, he knew it was a colossal mistake, but he could no more have prevented himself from moving forward that last half inch than he could stop the ice floes on the Hell's Fury.

Her mouth was soft, sweet, delicious. She tasted of orange and cardamom from Ali's cookies, a taste he had a feeling he would forever associate with her.

For just an instant she froze, green eyes wide and startled, and then her lashes fluttered down and she gave herself up to the kiss.

Chapter TWELVE

For just an instant when Marshall kissed her so unexpectedly, she panicked. Her last time in a man's arms had not been by choice and the memory of it slithered in, dark and ugly.

And then, suddenly, this man, this moment pushed it away.

The scent of him—soap and laundry soap and a unique mix of cedar and sage and *him*—mingled with the leather from the vehicle upholstery and the cinnamon-and-clove air freshener she'd hung after Thanksgiving. Just like that, she was back in the present, being kissed by the very sexy, very intriguing Marshall Bailey, the tough, stubborn sheriff of Lake Haven County.

She closed her eyes and let the sensations shiver through her, silvery and bright and wonderful. How could she possibly have forgotten the delicious magic of a slow, sensual kiss? The kick in her heart rate, the tingle in her fingertips, the delicious, sensuous churn of her blood.

Oh. She could do this all day.

Whoever would have guessed that the sometimes dour and taciturn sheriff could kiss so eloquently?

He kissed with the same seriousness he brought to everything else, focused only on tasting her, exploring her mouth. Andie savored it as myriad sensations consumed her.

She wanted to be closer to him and she instinctively moved to press her body to his but banged her hip into the console instead. A little startled gasp escaped her and he froze, his gaze catching hers. His eyes were beautiful, she thought idly, a vivid blue flecked with gold and rimmed by unfairly long eyelashes.

She saw a dazed arousal there, heavy-lidded and sensual, that made her insides thrum with need as if he had pressed his mouth to the curve of her breast. She leaned forward for more of those delicious kisses, but just before her mouth could slide against his, he growled an expletive that seemed to shock both of them.

"What?" she demanded.

Yes, it had been a while for her, but surely she hadn't completely forgotten how to kiss, had she?

He didn't answer, but he didn't have to. She suddenly recognized the subtle shift in his expression, the brief instant of pity followed by self-disgust, and she knew.

He suddenly remembered who she was, what had happened to her. It was as clear as a road sign on his features. This had nothing to do with the two of them. His reaction was based on what happened to her a year ago.

He was seeing her not as an attractive woman

with needs and desires, but as a victim. The poor, pathetic widow who had been unable to fight off her late husband's partner and then had been too frightened and weak to report the attack.

Except for that first initial burst, she had been too busy enjoying every second of that kiss to be nervous. She had wanted only to close her eyes and enjoy all those delicious sensations.

She didn't quite understand how panic could flare through her *now,* when he wasn't even touching her.

Marshall swore again and raked a hand through his hair. "I'm sorry. That . . . shouldn't have happened."

He was *sorry*. She was still soft and warm and gooey inside and he was *sorry* he had kissed her. Her throat suddenly felt ridiculously tight and she leaned farther back in her seat.

Oh, how she hated Rob Warren for ruining something else beautiful and right in her life.

"It's no big deal. You kissed me. I enjoyed it. End of story."

For a moment, he looked uncertain, as if he wasn't quite sure how to reply to her casual response.

"I . . . should have been more considerate, under the circumstances. I don't know, maybe I should have given you a little warning or something. I wasn't thinking."

"That's the second-nicest thing you've ever

said to me," she said with complete honesty. "A woman likes knowing a man loses his head a little around her."

Too bad he had found it again so soon.

She didn't want to have some awkward conversation where he apologized again or asked if she needed to go into counseling or something, simply because of an unexpected but not at all unwelcome kiss.

"I should be going," she said briskly, determined to change the subject. "Sadie is probably more than ready to go out again and the kids will be home soon."

Trying to act casual and unaffected, she opened the door and climbed out. The December breeze off the river quickly cooled cheeks she feared were bright red. When she handed him his crutches from the backseat, he frowned, looking as if he wanted to say more, but she didn't give him the chance.

"If you'll wait here, I can carry the box of files and your laptop and then come back to spot you on your way in."

As she might have expected, he didn't seem to favor that idea much. By the time she unlocked the door with her key, he had maneuvered his way out of the vehicle and was halfway up the sidewalk.

Stubborn man.

She set the box and computer inside, then

returned to the porch to watch him move with his inherent grace. She didn't need to worry about him. He seemed to be much more comfortable on the crutches every day.

"I forgot the rest of your sandwich and your special cookies from Ali."

Without waiting for him to answer, she returned to her vehicle, found the bag, then carried it into the house.

She found him in the kitchen filling a cup of water. The afternoon sunlight streamed in through the original stained glass transom on the kitchen window, creating a kaleidoscope on the polished wood floor with splotches of swirling, intense color.

He looked solemn again, no trace of a smile. His obvious regret at kissing her stung, but she decided she wouldn't let it bother her.

"Here you go," she said, holding up the bag. "You've got half a sandwich left, which might be tasty for dinner."

"Thanks," he said.

She opened the refrigerator and found room for it. "Do you need anything else?" she asked, pointing to the refrigerator's well-stocked shelves. "I'll probably be running to the grocery store tonight or tomorrow. They're saying a big storm is coming early next week and I need to be sure I've got all I need for Christmas dinner."

Though she could still read turmoil in his

expression over their kiss, he apparently decided to let it go, much to her relief.

"If I think of anything, I'll let you know."

"I'm keeping my fingers crossed the storm doesn't come early and interfere with the Lights on the Lake festival this weekend. My kids have been looking forward to it since we moved here."

He nodded. "That's always a fun holiday tradition for people in both Haven Point and Shelter Springs—unless you're in law enforcement. Then you spend the whole time directing traffic and handling crowd control."

"This year you can just sit on the sidelines and let your deputies and the Haven Point Police Department handle it."

"Oh yeah. Won't that be fun?" he said, his tone dry. "In case you didn't know this about me, I'm not particularly good at sitting on the sidelines."

She doubted anyone in town would be surprised by that. "You could always ask Mayor Kilpatrick to cancel this year."

"Ha-ha."

She mustered a smile in response. "I'm sure the celebration will survive without you. This year, you could possibly just try to enjoy it."

"Maybe."

He didn't look at all convinced, but she decided to let it drop. If he wanted to stay home and brood, that was his own business.

"I had better go. Do you need anything else before I take off?"

For a brief instant, something hot and intense flared in his eyes, stirring an immediate answering response in her. For one wild moment she let herself imagine how things could be between them. That kiss had given her only a sampling, but it had been addictive enough. Given the chance, she had no doubt Marshall would bring that serious intensity of his into the bedroom, coupled with scrupulous attention to detail and that underlying sweetness.

She really tried not to moan aloud.

"I think I'm good," he said.

Oh, she had no doubt about that—but realized he was only answering her inquiry about doing anything else for him.

"Have a good afternoon and evening, then." She was quite proud of her casual, unaffected tone. "I'll see you later."

She turned to leave, but his outstretched hand stopped her.

"Andie, I have to tell you again that I'm sorry about what just happened."

She caught her breath, wishing she had hurried out the door just a little faster to avoid this awkwardness.

"Fine. You said that. Can we just drop it now?"

"You need to know, I don't usually kiss women out of the blue like that. I should have been more . . . sensitive, under the circum-stances."

He had obviously been stewing about this since they left the car. She *didn't* want to talk about it, but short of rudely walking away, she didn't know how to avoid it.

"I hate to point out the obvious, but you have a broken leg. If I hadn't wanted you to kiss me, I could have walked out at any point and you wouldn't have been able to do much to stop me."

"I'm bigger than you are. I could have over-powered you."

"But you didn't. Nor would you."

"How would you know that?" he asked, with obvious skepticism.

"I just do. Gut instinct. I wanted you to kiss me, Marshall. I'm glad you did. I enjoyed every moment of it."

"Did you?" He looked a little taken aback but not entirely displeased.

She didn't want to have this conversation with him, but now that they had started, she decided to be completely honest.

"I will not let one terrible night out of my life dictate how I live the rest of it. I will *not* let something that happened to me against my will take control over my sensuality and my desire."

As she spoke the words, she felt a tiny spark inside her, a little echo of the confidence and

219

self-assurance that seemed to have been hibernating somewhere deep down.

"I wanted you to kiss me. I'm glad you did," she repeated. "If circumstances were different between us, I might even want to do more than kiss you. When your injuries heal, anyway. You're a very attractive man, and what's more, I like you. I didn't expect to a few days ago, but you've kind of grown on me."

He gave a surprised-sounding laugh. "That's blunt enough."

"I just want to be clear you did nothing wrong in kissing me. I kissed you right back, remember?" She paused. "If anything, I'm grateful to you."

"Grateful. That's a first."

"Oh, I doubt that," she murmured, suddenly certain he likely knew his way around the rest of a woman's body as well as he had demonstrated around her mouth.

That heat flared in his eyes again and she wondered how she had ever thought him cold and hard.

Her face flared with answering heat and she cleared her throat. "It's not in my plan anytime soon, but eventually I probably will start dating again—which means the whole kissing thing would be looming over me the entire time. Now it's out of the way, thanks to you, so I won't be so nervous the next time I kiss a man."

For some reason, he didn't look at all thrilled about the idea of that. Before he could answer, though, the doorbell rang and a woman's voice called out.

"Marshall? Darling? Are you there? Do you know there's a strange car in your driveway?"

Andie's gaze slid to his. She recognized that voice—and judging by his expression, he did, as well.

"Speaking of dating again, it sounds like your mother is home from her honeymoon."

Chapter THIRTEEN

"Marshall?" Charlene called again.

"Did you lock the door behind you?" he asked Andie, a hopeful note to his voice.

She shook her head and he sighed. "In the kitchen, Mom."

"Oh, your tree looks beautiful! So charming!" his mother called from the entryway. "I bet it's stunning with the lights on. Did Wynona come back to decorate it for you?"

Before he had a chance to answer, Charlene Bailey née Bailey—who had just married her late husband's brother—came into the kitchen.

She was round and tanned, blue eyes like his, glowing with happiness. She stopped short when she spotted them together, surprise flaring in her eyes.

Andie knew all about mother's intuition. It had come in handy more times than she could count with her own children. Could Marshall's mother sense that the two of them had been locked in an embrace a few short moments earlier?

"Here you are," she exclaimed. "And with Andrea, too. Hello, my dear. This is a lovely surprise!"

Charlene had been nothing but kind to her the last few months. Despite Andie's worries, the

Bailey matriarch didn't seem to blame Andie for her part in the incident that had culminated with Wynona being shot by Rob Warren while trying to protect Andie and her children.

Whenever she was around her friend's mother, Andie was always aware just under the surface that she and Charlene shared a bond, the grim sisterhood of those who had lost loved ones in the line of duty.

She hated they had that bond in common, that the sweet Charlene had suffered not only the loss of her husband but also one of her sons.

That didn't mean the woman was necessarily quick to forgive those children still walking the earth for their perceived mistakes. After that first moment of shock and greeting, Charlene marched over to Marshall and smacked his arm.

"Ow. What was that for?"

"Trust me, son, you're getting off easy. That's not half of what I'd like to do to you—and to your brother and sisters, too. Why didn't anyone tell me you'd been hurt? Look at you! Oh, Marshall. What have you done?"

Andie couldn't help being charmed when the ears of the big, brusque sheriff started to turn red.

"Nothing," he mumbled. "It's just a broken leg, Mom. I'm doing better."

She imagined he was grateful the bruises and scrapes on his face had mostly faded. At least his mother had been spared the worst of those.

"Imagine my shock and horror when we came back into town this afternoon and found the rumor mill burning up with gossip about *my son*."

Andie winced. Honeymoon or not, Wyn should have told her mother. She couldn't imagine hearing that kind of information about one of her children by accident.

"Who knows? If I hadn't stopped for groceries right after we pulled into town, I still might not know. Just my luck, the first person I bumped into in the produce section while I was buying bananas was Linda Fremont."

Andie winced again. Linda was the *last* person in town she would choose to tell her bad news. She loved the woman's daughter Samantha, but Linda was fatalistic in the extreme.

"As you can imagine, she had an earful for me. According to Linda, you were all but at death's door, in a coma on life support. I thought I was going to pass out, I'll tell you that much. If your uncle hadn't been there, I might have. Lucky for us, McKenzie Kilpatrick came along just then and heard every word Linda said. The mayor set me straight, but still. You were hit by a car and have a broken leg! And you didn't say a word to me! I'd like to horsewhip the lot of you."

"You were on your honeymoon, Mom. And I was fine, really. Wyn was on the fence about telling you, but I told her not to bother you."

Charlene's glower looked remarkably like her son's. "Why on earth would you do that? I'm your mother. I have the right to know when one of my babies is hurt."

Her "baby"—a tall, hard, dangerous lawman who was well over six feet tall—grimaced. "What you had the right to was an uninterrupted honeymoon. You and Uncle Mike both deserved it. I was fine and there was nothing you could do about the situation anyway."

She looked as if she wanted to strenuously disagree, but after taking a moment to collect herself, she gave her son a steady look. "I cannot understand why you, Elliot and the girls had to keep me in the dark and I certainly don't agree with it. I'll have a thing or two to say to them, you can be sure, but what's done is done, I suppose. The important thing is, I'm here now, ready to take care of you."

She took off her coat and hung it on a kitchen chair, looking for all the world as if she wanted to move right in. Andie fought a laugh at the panicked look on Marshall's face.

Apparently the tough, dangerous sheriff of Lake Haven County was intimidated by his round, sweet mother. She found it rather adorable.

"You don't have to fuss over me, Mom. I promise. The accident was nearly a week ago and the leg hardly even hurts anymore."

Andie was quite sure that was a bold-faced lie.

She'd seen the winces he tried to hide, those white lines around his mouth when he was trying to soldier through the pain. He had been up and moving all day. Though he would rather be tortured than admit it, she could see he needed nothing so much as to sit down.

She didn't feel it was her place to point that out, however. If he wanted to fib to his mother, it wasn't her business.

"I'm getting around now without too much trouble and I even went back into the office today."

"How? You can't drive, surely."

He inclined his head in Andie's direction. "Andrea kindly agreed to drive me and then hung around in Shelter Springs for a few hours so she could bring me back here."

Charlene's eyes widened at that particular piece of information and she sent Andie an appraising look she found nothing less than ominous.

"Why, that's very neighborly of you, my dear."

Neighborly. That was one word for it. Her mind flashed back to the heated embrace they'd shared mere minutes earlier and she had to fight a shiver.

"It was nothing. I was more than happy to help."

"She's been a lifesaver, actually," Marshall shocked her by saying. "With Katrina gone and Wyn busy with school, Wynona persuaded Andrea to help me out. She's done a wonderful job. I couldn't ask for more."

He aimed a smile in Andie's direction, brimming with so much affection she might have fallen over without the kitchen counter at her back.

"I don't know what I would have done without her," he said, with a warmth in his voice she had never heard there.

After a pause pregnant with shocked speculation, Charlene looked at Andie with an expression of pure delight.

"Oh, I'm so happy to hear that. Thank you so much for watching out for my boy."

What was happening here? She did her best to gather her tangled thoughts.

"Um, you're welcome."

"As you can see," Marsh went on, "I'm in very capable hands. Really, I'm fine. Andie has been amazing. There is absolutely no reason you can't climb back in your car and trot back to your new husband. Now that you're back, the two of you can get to work creating a life together. Have you finally decided where you're going to live?"

Though an obvious ploy to change the subject, Charlene followed the temporary detour. "We haven't made a final decision. We do know we're selling both houses and buying something together. It will be a new start for both of us. Who knows? Maybe we'll build. Mike has that property on the other side of Redemption Bay that would be a lovely spot for a new house."

"That is a nice place."

"We've decided we'll live in my house for now, since it has more space for all of us to get together. Which reminds me, I'm planning Christmas Eve. This is the first year in forever you haven't been working, so you've got no excuses."

She turned to Andie. "You know, my dear, we would be absolutely delighted to have you and your children join us. I don't have any grandchildren yet, but I usually invite friends over who do, so your children would have others to play with."

His mother was under the very mistaken impression there was more between them than one ill-fated kiss, but that didn't make the invitation any less appealing. Wyn was Andie's dearest friend in Haven Point. It would be lovely to spend Christmas Eve dinner with her and her family.

"Thank you," she said sincerely. "I'll think about it."

"I do hope you come, but if you have already made plans, we completely understand."

"We haven't. This is our first holiday in Haven Point and the children and I are building our own traditions together."

"You really must make my Christmas party one of them. It's always great fun—though don't ask Marshall here about it, since he's missed the last dozen or so working double shifts. One might almost think he doesn't like Christmas."

He shrugged. "Mom, you know how it goes in

law enforcement. Somebody has to work during the holidays. If I'm working, that means one of my deputies can be home with his kids."

Oh, he was a hard man to resist. Every time she thought she had, he managed to sneak in and topple a few more barriers.

He was a police officer, she reminded herself sternly. Yes, he might be a compassionate one to his fellow officers, but that didn't make his job any less dangerous.

He had been hit by a car less than a week ago because of his job. He could have died that night. She couldn't afford to forget that.

She had vowed she would never let herself care for another police officer. She couldn't endure the agony of waiting by the door, wondering if this was the day he wouldn't come home.

"I need to go," she said abruptly. "I'm sorry. I need to let my dog out and do a few more things before my kids are done with school."

She did need to leave, but she had also noticed those lines of pain had returned around his mouth. He would rather yank his fingernails out than admit to his mother he needed to sit down.

"Oh, I'm parked behind you in the driveway," Charlene said. "Let me move my SUV to the front, then I'll come back in."

"Mom, you don't need to stay, I promise. Right now, I just want to grab a beer and watch a basketball game. I'm sure Uncle Mike needs help packing up what he needs to take to the house. If you're not there directing him, he might just load up that terrible tweed sofa he's got in the living room."

Charlene looked torn between her maternal duty and the challenges of creating a new home with a longtime bachelor. She shuddered slightly, then sighed. "Fine. Since you obviously don't want me around, I'll go where I *am* wanted."

She gave a small, private smile that made Andie want to laugh—and made Marshall shudder this time, though it was barely perceptible.

His mother deserved every bit of happiness she had found, this new chance at a happy ending. From what Wynona had told Andie, Charlene had spent more than two decades as a devoted police chief's wife and then tirelessly visited him in the nursing home every day of his final two years.

Andie, for one, was delighted to see her enjoying this new phase of her life.

"I'll call to check on you later tonight and stop by again tomorrow morning," Charlene assured her son.

"Again, not necessary. Andie has things covered."

"I'm so glad." Charlene looked torn between her own need to step in and coddle her son and her obvious delight that someone else was allegedly doing it.

"We'll talk tonight," she promised. She kissed

her son's cheek, then enfolded Andie in a warm hug that smelled of lavender and vanilla.

"Thank you for watching over my boy. I hope he hasn't been a terrible bear."

"Not terrible," Andie temporized with a sidelong look at Marshall.

"I'm sure I'll see you both very soon," she said, then hurried out of the room humming a Christmas song.

Andie waited until she was certain the door closed behind his mother before she turned and faced him.

"You just threw me under the bus," she accused.

He focused on a spot above her head. "I don't know what you're talking about."

"Oh. Not true! You purposely gave your mother the idea there was something . . . romantic between us."

"We did just kiss," he pointed out.

She narrowed her gaze. "One kiss does *not* make a relationship."

"I love my mom. She's wonderful, really she is, but she can be overwhelming. If you let her, she'll sweep in and try to take over everything in your life. She has always fussed over us, but just typical mom stuff. Those maternal instincts seemed to go into overdrive after Wyatt died and then became even worse after Dad was shot. She thinks it's her life's work to worry and fret over us."

"Sounds like normal mom behavior."

Andie didn't want to tell him how jealous she was over it. She couldn't remember if her own mother had worried and fretted over her those few years she was sober. If she had, it hadn't lasted long—and her grandmother had been too busy trying to keep Andie's grandfather happy to have much room left for a sad little girl.

"It might be normal," he said, "but I could easily see her feeling like she has to abandon her husband of less than two weeks so she can move into my spare bedroom and make sure I don't fall on my way to the bathroom in the middle of the night."

It wasn't completely impossible, judging from what Wynona had told her about their mother's tendency to go into overdrive.

"You're using me as a ploy to keep your mother at bay," she said slowly. "I don't believe I've ever been a mom-beard before."

He made a face. "If she thinks you're here fussing over me, she's less likely to feel inclined to do it herself."

In a weird, convoluted way, his logic made sense. She was even a little amused, despite the terrifying implications.

"You forgot one tiny little detail in your deviousness."

"What's that?"

"Eventually she's going to figure out you misled

her. What are you going to do when she figures out there's nothing between us but the few hundred feet that separate our houses?"

He didn't say anything for several breaths, only gazed at her with an odd expression that made her mind race with possibilities.

"By then, I'll be well on the road to recovery and won't need *anybody's* help."

He couldn't wait to be free of *all* of them. She had a feeling she was only slightly less annoying than his mother.

The realization shouldn't have the power to sting.

Chapter FOURTEEN

He was becoming really tired of his own company.

By the next evening, he fully understood the definition of cabin fever. He wasn't quite at the point where he was going to start writing *edrum* on the walls of Wynona's house like something out of a Stephen King novel, but the strain was beginning to weigh on him.

He was even beginning to have a little sympathy for the inmates at the county jail. He had never really understood how much he valued the ability to come and go as he pleased—to just hop in the car and go visit a friend or simply grab a beer if he wanted at the Mad Dog Brewery or one of the taverns in Shelter Springs.

He stood at the window watching a few fluffy flakes gleam in the porch light as they fluttered down. Nothing moved out there except the snowflakes and he was grimly aware that he hadn't actually seen another human being all day, barring the two-dimensional kind on TV.

Cade had called that afternoon and promised to come over after his shift to play cards and shoot the breeze, but the Haven Point police chief—and his best friend and prospective brother-in-law—had called an hour ago to beg off, with the excuse that a long-haul truck driver trying to take a shortcut had jackknifed in the light snowfall on the outskirts of town, spilling his entire load of live turkeys.

Only in Haven Point.

This kind of snowfall could be misleading. The clouds had dropped only an inch or so of snow on the ground that was supposed to melt the next day. Some people didn't bother shoveling until more covered the ground, but Marsh knew the light snow could be treacherous, hiding spots of black ice to tangle up unsuspecting drivers.

Christopher hadn't been by to take care of it, but there was no reason Marsh couldn't do it. Why not? The snow was light and fluffy. Even on crutches, he ought to be able to slide the shovel down the walk, just in case anybody happened to drop by.

Maybe that would help ease the restlessness that seemed to have been on a low boil inside him since the day before, ready to explode.

His gaze drifted toward the house down the street, where he had a clear view of her Christmas tree gleaming in the window, the merry twinkling lights around her porch and windows she must have hung herself.

Yeah. He had become a freaking Peeping Tom—except he couldn't see anything except the occasional shadow moving past the windows.

He didn't know what the hell was wrong with

him. A week ago, she had been a virtual stranger to him—his sister's friend, yes, but otherwise an abstract name on a crime report.

So how could he possibly be missing the noise and laughter and chaos of her and her children in his home?

It didn't make sense and it certainly couldn't be right.

The memory of that kiss hadn't stopped bouncing around his head, try as he might to push it away. Those delicious moments spent kissing her had been the first time in a week he had truly forgotten all about his damn broken leg. With her in his arms, how could he think about anything else?

He had completely lost track of time. Now, reliving it, he couldn't believe how consumed he had been by the sweetness of her mouth, the softness of her skin. He had wanted it to go on and on and on.

He didn't know what had distracted him. A sound, perhaps, or a pain signal from his leg that managed to pierce the cloud of desire. Something had yanked him back to awareness of just whom he had been kissing. He had suddenly remem-bered that the delicious-tasting woman in his arms had endured a terrible ordeal with courage and strength.

She deserved gentleness, courtesy, respect.

She certainly deserved more than to be pawed in

the front seat of her SUV by a man who would never be able to offer her anything.

Yes, he definitely needed something to distract himself from the restlessness. Shoveling that walk out there would perfectly fit the bill—with the bonus of helping him feel at least halfway useful.

Ten minutes later, he slipped on his jacket and double-checked the plastic bag he'd shoved his boot into to keep it dry and a little warmer, then headed out onto the porch.

The cold felt invigorating, blowing away the cobwebs that came from spending entirely too much time in a small room in front of a big television set.

He managed to make it down the stairs without falling—even with the plastic bag providing no traction. The hardest part was balancing on the stair railing and using one of his crutches to pull the shovel down to him.

Not the easiest task he had ever undertaken, balancing on the crutches with his armpits and pushing the shovel a few inches at a time, but he was making slow progress when he heard the door slam next door.

"I thought you were supposed to be paying *me* to do that," an annoyed-sounding voice called out through the darkness.

He looked over at the house next door, and for one terrible moment, he couldn't seem to make his brain work to come up with an answer.

His son.

That was all he could manage to think as Christopher shuffled down the steps wearing only skinny jeans, thin skateboarder Vans with skulls on them and a black Nirvana T-shirt.

He had been a big Nirvana fan himself, during his own dark and angry-over-nothing phase. At least they had that much in common.

"Did you decide you don't need my help?" The boy's shaggy ink-black hair hung over his forehead and he had on that same perpetual scowl. "You trying to back out of paying me?"

His son was speaking with him. They were having a conversation.

Marshall cleared his throat. "Not at all. I've been cooped up inside all day—all week, really —and was feeling claustrophobic. The little bit of snow needed clearing, so I figured, two birds."

"Gramp said I have to do it, since you're paying me, so hand over the shovel."

He wanted to tell the kid he could take care of it, that it felt good to actually *do* something instead of sitting on his ass all day, but realized that was stupid. His son was here to help him. How could he turn down the opportunity to let him, especially if it meant they could spend a few minutes actually communicating?

"Great shirt," he said, then felt awkward for not coming up with a better topic of conversation.

The kid looked down. "It was my mom's. She had a thing for Kurt Cobain."

"I remember," he said without thinking.

That caught Christopher's attention. "Did you know my mom?"

In the biblical sense, yeah. Otherwise? Not really.

"A little. She was, uh, older than me by a few years, so our paths didn't really cross in school. Different crowds, you know? But I bumped into her a few years later in California, when I was in the military."

"Weird, you both being from a Podunk Idaho town and bumping into each other a thousand miles away."

"True enough. But I was glad to see a friendly face to remind me of home. We had dinner together a few times." And breakfast, but he wasn't ready to tell the kid that. "I believe Nirvana came up. We were both fans."

He paused. Because it seemed warranted—and was nothing less than the truth—he added, "I was sorry to hear she died."

The only light came from their respective houses, aided by a pale slice of moonlight breaking through the clouds, but Marshall still could clearly see the pain that twisted the boy's features for only a moment before he ducked his head.

"Thanks," he mumbled and seemed to shovel a little harder.

It was clear he didn't want to talk about his mother and Marshall would honor that.

He leaned on the crutches and watched him work. He wanted to tell him it was less strain on the back and arms to lift with the shovel closer to him, but he didn't want to come off sounding like a know-it-all ass. "What other kind of music do you like?" he asked instead after a moment.

Christopher leaned on the shovel handle. "Dude, you don't have to make conversation and pretend to be all interested. All you gotta do is pay me for the time."

His attitude was so patently contrived that Marshall had to smile. "Humor your crazy neighbor who has been trapped inside his house for a week."

The teen didn't seem in a big hurry to return to shoveling. "Nice bag," he said, pointing to the plastic garbage bag Marshall had wrapped around his cast. "So what happened to you? You get popped in the leg or something?"

He didn't really want to talk about it, but he couldn't avoid a direct question. "Nothing so exciting, I'm afraid. I got hit by a car. Hit-and-run driver, actually."

"No shit? Have they caught the guy?"

"Not yet," Marshall said grimly.

The lack of progress in the investigation just might be making him crazier than the cabin fever.

"That blows."

"Definitely."

It had been a really rough week, but he was glad at least he'd had the chance to talk to his son.

"How long you been a cop?"

"Longer than you've been alive," he said truthfully. "I started as a military police officer—an MP—in the Marines, then became a civilian when I left the military. My dad was the chief of police in Haven Point and his dad before him."

"Weird."

That was one word for it. He wanted to tell Christopher he came from a long legacy of men and women who had chosen to protect and serve. He longed to tell the boy he was the spitting image of his uncle who had died one wintry night while helping people in need and about his grandfather who was still much beloved and greatly missed by the people of this community, a year after his death, and about his aunt Wyn, who had been shot in the line of duty while trying to rescue Andrea and her children from a sociopath.

Of course, he couldn't mention any of that.

The list of topics he had to avoid left him very little to talk about, so he settled on the most boring thing an adult could ask a young person. School.

"I guess you don't have many more days left before Christmas vacation."

"Yeah. We get out next week. Can't come a minute too soon for me."

They talked about his classes for a moment, though it was obvious Christopher didn't have much interest in the topic. After a moment the boy made one more swipe with the shovel and Marshall had to regret his driveway wasn't longer.

"There you go. Next time call me, cop. No sense paying me if you're only gonna come out and do it yourself."

"I'll do that. Thank you."

The boy shrugged and set the shovel back up on the porch before he headed back to his house, his fleeting interest in further conversation apparently dying a quick death.

"'Night," he mumbled.

"Good night," Marshall answered. He watched him until he was inside, then turned and hobbled back along the now-cleared sidewalk to his porch and up the few steps.

By the time he made it into the house, everything felt like one big solid ache, but he didn't care. He had just enjoyed a halfway civil conversation with his son. Perhaps there was some reason for optimism that he might actually be able to build a genuine relationship with the boy.

You should tell him.

Amid the heated memories of that stunning kiss he had shared with Andrea, he hadn't forgotten her insistence that he needed to step up and tell the boy's grandparents and Christopher himself that Marshall believed he was his father.

He wasn't ready. Not yet. Better to carefully insert himself in his son's life a tiny step at a time, give them a chance to get to know each other.

His cell phone rang just as he settled back into the recliner with a beer and the remote.

He thought about ignoring it, since he really wasn't in the mood to talk to anyone, but when he saw the caller ID, he sighed and knew he had to answer. He had already ignored three calls from his mother that day, responding instead with a brief text that he was okay but couldn't talk. One more and she would probably be banging on his door to find out for herself why not.

"Hey, Mom."

"Marshall. There you are. How are you, my dear?"

He vowed he would never ask that question again to someone suffering an injury. He had a broken leg. How did she think he was?

"Fine," he lied. "I was just out shoveling snow."

"Oh, stop teasing me. You were not."

He most certainly was, but he decided she would never believe him anyway, so there was little point in arguing.

"Who *is* clearing away your snow? I didn't even think of that! Do you need Mike to come over when it snows? I'm sure he won't mind."

His uncle, who had no children of his own with his first wife, was probably doomed to spend the rest of his married life checking on Charlene's various children.

"I'm good. Thanks. I've actually hired a boy in the neighborhood."

"What boy?"

Your grandson.

The word hovered on the tip of his tongue. He couldn't tell her—not yet and maybe not ever.

Though he knew how desperately Charlene longed for grandchildren, if Louise and Herm didn't want him to intrude into the boy's life, he would have to respect their wishes.

"The Jacobses' grandson. Nikki's son."

You know. The one who looks exactly like Wyatt—you've just never noticed.

His mother made a small sympathetic sound. "Oh, that poor boy. Can you imagine, losing his mother so young. But at least he's got good grandparents who love him. How kind of him to take care of a neighbor."

"Isn't it?" he said without a trace of dryness, though Christopher's kindness extended only as far as Marshall's wallet.

"That's odd, actually," Charlene said. "Louise didn't say a word to me about Christopher taking care of your sidewalk when I talked to her earlier today."

"You talked to Louise?" He tried to ask casually.

He knew his mother was friendly with Louise Jacobs, though not bosom buddies.

"I bumped into her at the dollar store. We were both buying wrapping paper, scissors and tape. It was funny—we had almost the exact same items in our basket!"

Christmas *was* only a week away. No doubt they weren't the only ones in town in need of those particular items.

"We got talking about the Lights on the Lake parade and she mentioned that Christopher hasn't seen it yet as this is his first Christmas in Haven Point, so of course I offered to let them sit with us. With Mike being on the town council, we get VIP seats for up to ten guests and we've got plenty of room, since otherwise it would just be the six of us."

"The six of *us?*" Where did that come from?

"Yes! You were planning to go, weren't you? I hope so, because I've already talked to Andrea about picking you up."

"Andrea."

Apparently he wasn't capable of doing anything but echoing his mother, but he couldn't seem to make sense of her words. Hearing Andrea's name made him ache all over again, to remember their kiss and how perfect she had felt in his arms.

"Well, yes. This is her and her darling children's first Christmas in Haven Point as well, which means they haven't seen the Lights on the Lake parade, either, have they?"

"I suppose that's right."

"I'm so happy she's taken such good care of you these last few days. Having them along to sit with us in our VIP seating area is a tiny thing, really. A very small way of repaying all she has done, but I think that cute little boy and girl of hers will just eat it up. Don't you agree?"

He pictured Chloe and Will, eyes bright as they watched the wildly illuminated boats float past on the last big event on the lake before the shallow edges froze up in January.

His mother was matchmaking, he realized, doing everything she could to throw him together with Andrea Montgomery. And it was his own damn fault.

"So let me get this straight. You called Andie and told her she could sit with you in the VIP seating as long as she stops first to pick up your poor helpless son."

"Not in so many words."

"But that was the gist."

"Did I do something wrong? I thought you would be happy for the chance to spend a little more time with her."

This was his own fault, he thought again. Andie had warned him what would happen if he intentionally fed his mother misinformation. Now she thought the two of them had a budding romance and she would consider it her maternal duty to twist and turn every circumstance so she could facilitate a relationship that didn't exist.

What was he supposed to do now? If he told Charlene the two of them were merely neighbors, she would be upset at his deliberate deception, yes. Worse, she would feel obligated to jump in and smother him with her solicitude.

The alternative meant going along with the pretense he had created. He was stuck.

Rock, meet hard place.

"Sure. It will be fun."

As fun as somebody running you down with a stolen SUV on a cold December night.

"I agree. Mike and I will have hot drinks and snacks for the parade, and then we're invited to a party at Ben and McKenzie's house to watch the boats sail back from the warmth of their family room, the one with the big windows overlooking Redemption Bay. Kenzie said dinner will be provided. Are you sure that won't be too much for you?" she asked, voice suddenly anxious.

He had a broken leg. He wasn't dying.

"I don't know. Maybe I better bring an oxygen tank, just in case."

As usual, Charlene missed the joke. "I didn't see you using oxygen the other day when I stopped by," she said, her voice perfectly serious.

He immediately felt guilty. It really wasn't fair

to yank her chain when she was already so concerned about his health.

"I'm just kidding, Mom. I don't need oxygen. I'm fine, actually. Better every day."

"Why do my children all find such delight in teasing me?" she asked, presumably to the universe in general.

"Because we love you. And because you're an easy mark."

She huffed out a breath, but when she spoke, she sounded like her usual cheerful self. "I'll see you tomorrow evening, then. Dress warmly, but the forecast calls for only a little more snow tonight, and then it's supposed to melt right off tomorrow by noon. I understand we've got a warm front coming in tomorrow. That will be perfect for the festival, won't it?"

"I guess."

"I don't know what time Andrea planned to pick you up. If you don't hear from her tomorrow, you might want to give her a call."

He didn't. He needed to put as much distance between them as possible—and spending the evening in the company of her and her very cute children was going to make that increasingly difficult.

Chapter FIFTEEN

Did she have everything? Blanket, hand warmers, snacks, water bottles, extra mittens and hats.

She looked in the cargo area of her SUV to make sure she had everything on her mental list. When she couldn't think of anything she'd forgotten—though, doubtless, she had—she pushed the power button and the hatch door slid with a whoosh.

Though she sometimes missed the minivan she used to drive, she had come to love her new small SUV.

Her first Idaho mountain snowstorm a few months earlier had reinforced that winters around Lake Haven definitely warranted a four-wheel drive. As a result, she had traded the minivan she and Jason purchased together after Will was born for a late-model used vehicle from a dealership in Shelter Springs.

It was the first time she had purchased a car on her own, as she had never been able to afford her own vehicle when she was living on her own and going to school. Somehow it had seemed like one more rite of passage into widowhood.

New town, new house, new vehicle. New life. Sometimes it seemed Chloe and Will were all that remained of the marriage she thought would endure forever.

She paused on her way back into the house to breathe past the familiar grief, aware it had become a mere shadow of what it once was.

As if sensing her distress, Sadie nudged her leg. The little dog planted her haunches on the sidewalk to give her a quizzical look.

"I'm okay. Relax."

From the moment they'd brought her home from the shelter, Sadie seemed to have a particular gift for sensing when one of her new family members was experiencing an excess of emotion and was in need of extra attention.

The dog waited for her to gain control, then with a wag of her tail, Sadie scampered to the rear of the SUV and waited there expectantly.

"You can't go, sweetie. I'm sorry."

The dog's expressive eyes turned reproachful. Andie would swear the dog understood every word she said.

"I would take you if I could, I promise, but we're supposed to go to a party afterward. Lots of boring conversation. You wouldn't enjoy it."

The dog took a few steps to where Andie stood on the sidewalk, then returned to the liftgate of the SUV.

"Why can't we just take her?" Chloe begged from the backseat. "We can keep her on the leash the whole time!"

"Yeah," Will said. "I bet she would *love* seeing the boats."

"Not tonight," she said. "We can't take Sadie to McKenzie's house after the parade."

"Why not?" Chloe begged. "She could play with Hondo and Rika! It will be like a doggie playdate!"

She couldn't deny, she was tempted by their entreaties. All of them loved having the little dog along. In this case, though, she was already going to be taking Marshall with them. She was nervous enough about spending the evening with him. She didn't need to add the chaos and further responsibility of taking along a little dog.

She shouldn't be so nervous. She knew it and had been trying all afternoon to tell herself all the reasons her anxiety was ridiculous. Still, she couldn't seem to shake it off.

After that stunning kiss, she wasn't in a hurry to spend the evening with him, especially when his mother thought they had a budding relationship.

Oh, she wanted to *smack* him for giving Charlene that impression.

"Not tonight," she repeated firmly. "When you're a guest of someone, it is poor manners to take an uninvited dog to their home, especially when there will be others there who might not love dogs. We'll make arrangements for a playdate with Hondo and Paprika another day. Now, we need to hurry or we'll miss the beginning of the parade. Sorry, Sadie. Not you," she said to the dog.

When she scooped up the little brown-and-white Havachon, Sadie wagged her tail harder, apparently convinced Andie had changed her mind.

Her tail wagging turned into a whine when Andie carried her back inside and set her down in the family room.

"We'll be home before you know it. Take care of the house for us. Both of you, behave," she said to the room in general.

Sadie gave a disgruntled sigh and sadly made her way to her favorite rug. A moment later, a silky black feline head with green eyes poked out from under the sofa. The cat they had also picked up at the shelter—the one Chloe had named Mrs. Finnegan, for reasons that escaped Andie— stalked over to stretch out beside the dog.

After more than a month, the cat was still shy with all of them except Chloe. Mrs. Finnegan adored the little dog, however, and the two of them seemed to be best friends, which set her mind at ease when she had to leave them alone.

Satisfied they could entertain each other, she returned to the vehicle, double-checked the children's seat belts, then backed out of the driveway, butterflies chasing each other around in her stomach.

Though she had spoken briefly on the phone with Marshall earlier that day to make arrangements for picking him up, she hadn't seen the man in two days, not since the memorable afternoon of that stunning kiss.

The kiss had replayed through her head dozens of times since then. She hadn't slept well and her dreams had been wild, tangled affairs, all featuring the hard-eyed sheriff. She awoke each morning feeling restless, achy and out of sorts.

She had to stop this, especially as she understood completely that she could never fall for a man like him.

The fact that he was in law enforcement was a huge part of it but not the only obstacle, she had come to realize over the last few days.

If she ever allowed another man into her life, he would have to be spectacular father material. Her children deserved nothing less, especially since their own father had been somewhat lacking in that department.

The thought made her feel disloyal, though she had accepted it as hard truth. Jason had loved their children but hadn't seemed particularly motivated to interact with them.

When Chloe was a baby and then a toddler, Andie had chalked up his disinterest in their child to age and perhaps also that Chloe was very much a girlie girl who wanted to play with dolls and have tea parties and dress up like a princess.

After Will came along, though, Jason's detachment continued and she had been forced to accept that he might never be a super engaged, hands-on father, at least not to their young children.

He loved the *idea* of children and proudly showed off their pictures on his desk and around the department. He wasn't as crazy about the hard, endless, usually thankless work required to nurture them well.

In his spare time, he preferred to watch sports or escape to the golf course or ride motorcycles with his buddies. He would begrudgingly consent to "watch" them for her when she needed a break or to get her hair done or finish a work project, but he didn't actively seek out opportunities to engage with them.

She had come to the sobering and enlightening realization after he died that the actual logistics of parenting as a widowed mother hadn't differed significantly from when Jason was ostensibly still there to help.

She was older and wiser this time. If she ever grew serious enough to let someone into their lives on a regular basis, she would choose a man who didn't simply tolerate her children because he loved *her* but who loved them as well for the remarkable humans they were becoming.

A gruff, taciturn sheriff would not even make the first cut.

"Can we come inside with you?" Will asked when she pulled into Marshall's driveway.

"No. Stay in your chairs. I'll just be a moment."

Before she could even open her door, though, Marshall was making his way down the few steps of his porch.

The late afternoon glowed in his dark hair. Even on crutches, he looked big and rough and masculine. The silly butterflies started dancing around inside her again, until she wanted to smack them.

"Who knew you would be so excited to watch the Lights on the Lake parade that you would literally be waiting for us on the doorstep?"

He made a face. "Funny. I just didn't see the point in making you come all the way to the door when I was ready to go."

He was the sort of man who would charge through life. She admired that, especially as she still had much room for improvement in that area.

"Watch for ice. It stays pretty shady on this side of the house."

"Christopher cleared most of the snow last night and the warm temperatures this afternoon did the rest."

The night was unusually warm for December. She wouldn't call it balmy, but it was not at all unpleasant.

"Isn't this weather strange?"

"Don't get used to it. You know the saying about

the calm before the storm? We often get a warm spell just before a big snow. I've heard we're in for a serious storm tomorrow night and Monday."

"I hope we get a white Christmas."

"From the sound of it, you'll get that and more."

He reached her vehicle before she could answer and she hurried to open the door for him and offer help if he needed.

He seemed to be moving around even better on the crutches than he had two days earlier and slid in easily. He tucked the crutches at his feet, with the ends extending between their two seats.

"Hi, Marshall!" Will chirped from his booster seat.

"Hi!" Chloe added her voice.

"Hey, Will. Miss Chloe. Been decorating any Christmas trees lately?"

They both giggled.

"Nope. Just yours." Chloe gave her sweet smile.

Andie couldn't hear Marshall's response as she moved around the vehicle and slid in behind the wheel. When she climbed in, Will was talking.

"Guess what? Santa Claus comes in only one more week!" her son exclaimed, as if nobody else on earth knew Christmas Eve was on the way.

"Is that right?"

"Yep. We only have seven more days left on our 'vent calendar."

"What are you asking Santa to bring?"

It was the sort of question guaranteed to keep

two kids chattering the entire drive from Riverbend Road down to the lakeshore and the downtown park where most of the festivities would be.

"Oooh, look!" Chloe breathed when the park and all its holiday lights came into view. "It's so beautiful!"

The long, narrow lakeside park served as the nadir of Haven Point's holiday decorations. While the town itself and the property owners and downtown merchants all did an excellent job of holiday decorating, with wreaths on all the vintage-looking streetlamps and lights in all the windows, here the holiday spirit was in over-drive. Each massive pine tree was lit up with hundreds of thousands of lights, and bulbs were strung from tree to tree. In an open space of the park, a life-size winter village provided interest the entire month.

She and the children and Sadie had walked through the park one evening in November, just after the lights had been turned on. Now the entire north section of the park was covered with more lights and several rows of booths that would be selling crafts, food and gifts.

"This is gonna be so awesome!" Will exclaimed, just about jumping out of his booster seat with excitement.

Marshall turned in his seat and did something wholly unexpected. He smiled. Not just a perfunctory, casual sort of thing, but a full-on, ladies-grab-your-britches smile, overflowing with warmth and delight.

Those butterflies could hardly contain themselves. Andie wanted to simply stare at him all evening, but she swallowed and forced herself to move. She parked, then climbed out and walked around the vehicle, wishing the air were a little more brisk to cool her down.

He didn't need her help, apparently, and was already pulling himself to stand, balancing on his good leg, so she turned her attention to the children.

"I'll need both of you to help me carry things," she said, fumbling for a moment with the key until she found the right button that would release the cargo door.

She handed Chloe one of the blankets and gave Will the small bag of snacks, then reached for the other blankets and the soft-sided cooler with the water bottles.

"I can take the cooler," Marshall said.

"You're going to have enough trouble navigating through that crowd as it is. It's not heavy at all."

"Then I should be able to carry it just fine."

With an implacable expression, he held out a hand. Arguing only made her look foolish, she knew, so she finally handed over the bag, which he pulled on cross-body style, as he had his laptop bag the other day.

"Perfect," he claimed, though she knew it couldn't possibly be comfortable.

Will looked as if he was ready to race through the crowd at top speed, but Chloe was watching, eyes worried, as Marshall moved slowly on the crutches toward the area of the park where Charlene Bailey told Andie the VIP seating could be found.

"Will and me will go in front of you to make sure everyone gets out of your way," Chloe announced. "Otherwise you might trip on people."

"We don't want that, do we?" Marshall said with another one of those potent smiles. "That's a great idea."

Chloe seemed to relish his approval. "Come on, Will," she ordered her brother, then the two of them walked side by side with a slow formality normally reserved for royal standard bearers.

They made quite a procession, she couldn't help thinking with amusement.

"Hey there, Sheriff!" A man with a bald head, thick mustache and leather jacket that made him look like a middle-aged motorcycle bandit waved and offered a friendly smile.

"Dennis. How's it going?"

"Can't complain. But then, I'm not the one on crutches." The guy guffawed and Marshall smiled in return, before Helen Mickelson, the director of the community center where Andie attended yoga and self-defense classes, stopped to exchange greetings and offer her sympathy for his injury.

The first minute out of the car set the pattern for the rest of their short walk to the VIP seating. Everyone seemed to want to talk to him. She supposed she shouldn't have been surprised at it—nor at his reaction. Instead of rebuffing their well-wishes, Marshall showed courtesy to all and even warmth to many.

For some reason—probably because of his enforced isolation the past week and his resistance to accepting her help—she had thought he was some kind of loner who preferred his own company. As he stopped his slow progress to shake hands with a couple of elderly men along the way, she was reminded that Marshall was not only a native son of Haven Point but also a county elected official. He couldn't have attained his position at such a relatively young age if he had been cold and unapproachable.

Apparently the man contained dimensions she was only now encountering.

As they made their slow way to the VIP spot, a few other mothers she'd met through Chloe's elementary school and Will's preschool greeted her and then seemed to do a double take when it became apparent that Marshall and her family had come together.

Only then did it occur to her that people might think they were *together* together. She really hoped everyone in town didn't get the idea she was dating the county sheriff.

Their journey of about a hundred feet took three times as long as it should have because so many people wanted to greet him, until Andie had to bite her lip to keep from telling people to just let the poor man sit down already. At this rate, he would be exhausted before they even reached their seats.

Finally they made it to the roped-off VIP area and Will and Chloe were immediately surrounded by the friends they had made in town, particularly Ty and Jazmyn Barrett and Maddie Hayward, all chattering a mile a minute.

"Mom," Will said in excitement, "Ty says there are sparkly cookies over there at the refreshments and we can have as many as we want!"

"How about you start with one, kiddo," she said.

Will looked disappointed. "Can I go get one now?"

She needed to get Marshall settled, but she figured with all the adults around, Will and Chloe would be well supervised. Devin Shaw and Cole Barrett stood by the refreshments and Eliza was not far away.

"Sure. Grab a cookie and then come find me."

"Okay."

"Can I go, too?" Chloe asked.

She nodded and her daughter handed over her blanket into Andrea's full arms.

"I can take some of that," Marshall said.

Where? On top of his head?

"Let's go find you an empty chair," she said, ignoring him. "Oh, look, there's your mom. She must have a spot for us."

She nodded toward Charlene and Mike Bailey, who both were waving with enthusiasm.

"They're a little hard to miss," he murmured.

"Can you make it there on the uneven grass? I'm sure it's not as easy as the sidewalk."

"I'm fine."

He would never say otherwise, she was quite certain. Still carrying the cooler, he made his way over the frozen ground. Before they could reach his family, the mayor of Haven Point waylaid them. "Marsh! And Andie. Hi, you two."

McKenzie Kilpatrick gave her a quick hug, blankets and all, then gestured to the crutches.

"I heard what happened to you. This doesn't look like a fun way to spend Christmas."

"Just about as fun as sticking pine needles in your eyes."

"I'm so sorry. I couldn't believe it when Chief Emmett briefed me on what happened. No leads yet on who might have hit you?"

"Not yet."

"That's crazy! I've told Cade to put all his officers on high alert. I'm just hoping someone isn't deliberately targeting law enforcement officers in the community."

"So far it seems an isolated incident, but I've asked my deputies to be on alert, as well."

McKenzie asked more questions about the incident, and while he answered her cordially, Marshall shifted several times and Andie could tell his leg was bothering him.

She loved McKenzie and didn't want to be rude, but she knew Marshall would never admit he needed to sit down.

"Sorry, do you mind if I carry these things over to our chairs?" she broke in during a gap in the conversation. "My arms are a little overloaded here."

"Oh yes. Of course. Of course. I've got a hundred things to do anyway before the parade starts."

She rushed off, but Marshall didn't seem in a hurry to continue toward the chairs. Instead, he gave her an odd look with an expression she couldn't quite identify.

"Don't think for a minute I missed what you did there."

"What?" she asked innocently. "I don't know what you're talking about."

He simply shook his head, still with that odd expression. He maneuvered toward the chairs and a moment later sank into a seat with a barely perceptible sigh of relief.

"Oh, I'm so glad you made it on time!" Charlene enthused. "Isn't it a beautiful evening? This is the best weather we've had for the festival in *forever*. Did you have a hard time finding a place to park?"

"No, actually. We were lucky."

"Where are your cute kids?"

"The Barrett children are showing them the cookie selection."

Andie scanned the area with studied casualness. "Are Louise and Herm still joining us?"

"Supposed to be. I just texted her and she said they got a late start. Apparently that rascal grandson of theirs didn't come home when he was supposed to, but they eventually found him at a friend's house. They're all on their way."

The moment Andie had spoken the Jacobses' name, Marshall tensed beside her and the rest of his mother's words didn't do anything to ease it. Andie wanted to give his arm a reassuring squeeze but, for multiple reasons, was hesitant to draw his mother's attention.

"We'll be sure to save them seats, then," Andie answered, then casually changed the subject. "So tell me about your honeymoon cruise."

"Oh, we had the *best* time—isn't that right, honey?"

Mike nodded, giving his new wife a besotted sort of look. "I'll be working off all the food we ate until our first anniversary," he said. "Two entrées and three desserts every night for a week. Good thing I'm not riding one of those boats in the parade or the thing would sink."

She laughed, charmed by Marshall's uncle. Her impression of him was of a sweet, quiet man who simply adored Charlene.

"What ports did you stop at? Did you do much shopping? What were your favorite excursions?"

Charlene launched into a long travelogue, which carried the conversation until the children returned and the parade began to start.

Chapter SIXTEEN

Marshall couldn't remember when he had last sat on the sidelines to enjoy the Lights on the Lake parade.

It had probably been back in high school, when he had been dating a girl in Shelter Springs and they had watched it with some of her friends around a bonfire in somebody's backyard. In the years since, he'd either been away in the military or been helping out with crowd and traffic control—a sometimes cold job on a Lake Haven December evening.

He had forgotten how charming the parade could be, when boat owners in Haven Point and Shelter Springs would decorate their watercraft with fanciful holiday lights and motor from the marina here to the one five nautical miles away in Shelter Springs.

He could get used to enjoying it this way, with propane heaters all around and mugs of hot cocoa and the extra blankets Andie had brought. Not that he would likely have the chance. Next year, everything would be back to normal. He certainly wouldn't be here with Andrea Montgomery and her cute kids, though that thought caused a sharp little pang in his chest.

"The boats are so beautiful," Chloe breathed, her eyes huge.

A big part of his own enjoyment had been watching her and her brother. They both seemed enchanted, just like every other child he could see.

"I wish we had a boat parade every night," Will said from his mother's lap, where he was snuggled under a blanket.

"It's wonderful, isn't it?" Andie agreed. With her eyes sparkling with the reflection of the lights and her cheeks pink from the cold and a cute little blue knit cap with a tasseled pompom on top, she was every bit as enchanting as the parade.

"We never saw anything like this in Portland," Chloe said softly. "I'm so glad we moved here, Mama."

"I am, too, honey." Andie's chin wobbled a little and her eyes looked suspiciously bright for a moment. He couldn't resist nudging her shoulder with his and she gave him a tremulous smile.

Marshall gazed down at her, aware of a weird shifting and settling in his chest. It took about five more boats passing by before he identified the feeling.

Tenderness. That's what it was.

He frowned. He was starting to have feelings for Andie and for her kids. When he wasn't looking, they had started to sneak their way into his life, into his heart.

How the hell had *that* happened?

And what was he supposed to do about it now?

He was still reeling from that and trying to figure out a way out of the mess when another huge complication in his life showed up in the form of Louise and Herm Jacobs and their grandson.

His heart pounded at the sight of his son, who looked sullen and angry with a stocking cap pulled almost over his eyes.

"Sorry we're so late," Herm Jacobs said. He shook Mike's hand and Louise kissed Charlene's cheek. "Somebody didn't come home when he was supposed to and didn't answer his cell phone, either."

"I was at a friend's house," Christopher snapped. "What's the big deal? It's not like we were shooting heroin or something. We were watching a movie."

If Marshall had the right to step in, he would have said it was rude and disrespectful for Christopher not to let his grandparents know where he was and to ignore his phone when they tried to reach him. That was the thing he should say as the boy's father—if he were in a position to step up, anyway.

His whole life suddenly felt like a tangled knot of Christmas lights wrapped around tinsel and tied up with fraying ribbon.

"You're here now—that's the important thing,"

Marshall's mother said with a cheery smile. "The parade has only been under way for about ten minutes, so there's plenty more to see. Grab a chair. We've put warmers on all of them, so they should be a little more bearable."

To make room, Andrea gestured for Chloe to come sit on her lap as well, tucking her in beside Will. As a result, Christopher ended up sitting next to Marshall.

"This is lame," Christopher muttered. He slouched in his seat and crossed his arms over his chest. "I don't get why everyone makes such a deal about sitting out in the cold and watching a bunch of stupid boats."

"It's more about the sense of community and being with friends and family."

"I was *with* my friends, until the geezers showed up and dragged me away."

It would be tough on any kid to lose his mother and be forced to move in with grandparents he apparently didn't know well. That didn't give him the right to be disrespectful.

"If you previously had plans with your grand-parents," he said mildly, "it was kind of *lame* to leave them hanging like that, worried about you and not knowing where you were."

Christopher glowered at him. "I was going to call them," he muttered.

Marshall hesitated. He didn't want to risk the fledgling relationship he was starting to establish with Christopher, but he couldn't stand by and let the kid mistreat the only two people who had his back right now.

"None of this is your grandparents' fault. I know they make a convenient target for your grief and anger, but that's not really fair, is it?"

Christopher glared at him. "Mind your own business, cop," he snarled. "You don't know anything about it."

The kid slumped even farther in the chair and pointedly looked out at the water, every inch of him radiating pissed-off teenager.

Marshall sighed, thinking he should have kept his mouth shut. "You're right. I don't know how you feel. I lost my dad earlier this year and miss him like crazy, but I was an adult. It's not the same thing at all."

He thought of John Bailey and how his father would reach out to this hurting young man. He had no doubt whatsoever his father would try—of course he would. Just as he had stepped up to help Cade Emmett when Cade was about the same age as Christopher.

Marshall and Cade had been in the same grade, but he had hardly known the other boy. They certainly hadn't been friends. Marsh had been a little afraid of him, actually.

The Emmetts were a wild, lawless bunch. Cade didn't seem to have any respect for rules, for teachers, for other people's property.

John had seen something in him—probably his devoted care to his younger brothers—and had enlisted Marshall to help him show Cade a different way. His father had somehow persuaded Marsh to invite Cade to their house to hang out after school one day and then the next and the next. Before he knew it, he and Cade had been inseparable and had formed a bond that endured to this day.

John would have tried to help this boy, too, whether Christopher was his acknowledged grandson or not. Marshall had to do the same. A paternity test might make things more clear-cut, but even without it, he still had to do what he could.

"You know, your grandparents are good people who love you."

Christopher's jaw jutted out. "Then maybe they should stop trying to tell me what to do every freaking minute of my life."

Marshall met his gaze. "You just might want to consider that maybe their plan for their retirement never included raising a grandson who goes out of his way to make them suffer, just because *he's* hurting and doesn't want to be here."

Christopher didn't appear to have a response to that. He only stared straight ahead.

Aware he may have just screwed up any chance of building something with his son, Marshall turned back to the parade. A moment later, he felt

271

a hand squeeze his arm through his coat. He glanced down and found Andie looking at him, her features soft with sympathy and, he was quite certain, glowing approval.

He felt that weird tug of tenderness again and fought the urge to reach for her hand. Knowing the foolishness of that, he turned back to Christopher and decided to work at unraveling one tangled complication in his life at a time.

"That wooden boat right there with the big Christmas tree on it is an early model Kilpatrick. That's a beautiful boat, with a ride so smooth a guy in the passenger seat could shave with a straight razor and not end up with a single nick."

Christopher didn't answer for a long moment, until Marshall thought maybe he was going to ignore him. Finally he spoke. "Why would any idiot be stupid enough to shave while he's on a boat?"

Marshall let out his breath and managed a smile. "That's what you call hyperbole. I just meant it's easy sailing, no matter the conditions out on the water. The Killies are legendary in these parts. They were built right here on the lake by Ben Kilpatrick's family, up until about five or six years ago when Ben closed up shop. That particular boat probably goes for six figures, easy."

"No way."

"True story. They're highly prized by collectors.

One went up for auction back East a few months ago and sold for nearly half a million dollars."

"For a boat?" Christopher did a double take. "I could see paying that for a yacht or something, but that's just a glorified dinghy. For that kind of money, you could buy a freaking Lamborghini and have change left over!"

When the weather warmed up, he ought to see if Ben would take them out on his beautiful restored Delphine. It was a nice thought—until he remembered he didn't have the right to take Christopher anywhere.

"I've been lucky enough to drive both, and I can tell you with complete honesty, a Killy is more fun—but just by a hair."

"Right. You want me to believe a cop in the middle of frigging nowhere Idaho drives a Lamborghini?"

He shrugged. "I never said I drive one on a regular basis. But when I was a rookie deputy just out of the Marines and back from Iraq, I worked undercover on a drug case. As part of my cover, I drove a Lamborghini Gallardo that had been confiscated from another case."

"No shit?" As soon as he swore, Christopher sent a guilty look in the direction of his grandmother, who didn't seem to be paying them any attention.

"True story. It was only a weeklong operation, but it was absolutely unforgettable. When you drive a Lambo, you can feel the engine rumbling in your bones. When you accelerate, you're sucked into the back of your seat and you feel like you own the world."

If he wasn't mistaken, Christopher seemed to look at him with awe and respect, all annoyance forgotten. Apparently fast cars were the way to his son's heart.

"What color was it?" he asked.

"Ice blue."

"Sweet."

He had pictures somewhere of him behind the wheel. He'd have to dig them out for the kid so he could prove it.

"Look, Mama," Will suddenly exclaimed, breaking into the conversation. "There he is! Look! Santa's riding on a boat!"

"I see it. Isn't it wonderful?"

In that moment, the whole evening felt wonderful, even with the throbbing of his leg. Marshall wouldn't have traded it for anything.

"I never went to a parade at night before. That was *fun*," Chloe declared when all they could see was the long line of lights heading toward Shelter Springs with the Santa Claus boat in the rear.

"The best parade I ever went to," Will agreed.

"I agree." Andrea smiled at her children.

As everyone stood up and started gathering up their belongings, a couple of boys around

Christopher's age approached their group. Marshall recognized one as being the son of a friend of his who owned one of several art galleries in Haven Point. He didn't know the other one.

Christopher headed over to talk to them, with much gesturing and pointing. Marshall couldn't hear the conversation, but he did hear when Christopher approached his grandparents.

"Can I go with Cody and Jonas? They want to walk around and look at stuff."

Herm and Louise looked at each other, then back at their grandson. "I'm inclined to say no," Herm said sternly. "You haven't demonstrated much reason why we should trust you today."

Christopher's jaw jutted out and it took Marshall a moment to realize why the expression looked familiar—because he did the same thing.

"I was a jerk, okay? I'm sorry." The boy glanced at Marshall and he had to hope something he said might have made an impact. "It's just . . . Cody is pretty good at art. His mom and dad have a booth selling pottery and paintings and stuff and he wanted us to see a couple bowls he made."

The Jacobs conferred for a moment, then turned back to their grandson. "Meet us back here in forty-five minutes," Herm said. He reached into the pocket of his coat and handed over a black cell phone. "Take your phone so we can reach you and answer us when we call this time. If you don't —or if we have to come find you—the phone and the Wi-Fi password at home will both be gone until after Christmas."

The boy's smile made him look even younger than his thirteen years.

"Thanks, Grandpa," he said, then jerked his head in a nod that encompassed the rest of them. "See you."

He and the two other boys hurried away as if afraid his grandparents would change their minds.

After he left, Marshall released his breath, aware of a soft, fragile optimism that hadn't been there earlier in the day.

"You and Christopher seemed to have a lot to talk about," Andie said in a low voice.

He looked around, noting the boy's grandparents were busy talking to Eliza and Aidan Caine. "I guess you could say we bonded a little, talking about fast cars."

"He was more animated, speaking with you, than I've ever seen him. Maybe he feels a connection."

He wasn't sure about that, but it was nice to think about. "Maybe," he said in a noncommittal voice.

She was quiet for a long moment, then gave him a searching look. "Have you thought more about telling his grandparents the truth?"

Instantly, the warm feelings from before seemed to take a running leap into the lake. "No. The timing isn't right. They have enough to deal with at the moment."

She looked as if she wanted to press him, but Chloe and Will both came back from comparing notes with Cole Barrett's kids.

"Mom, can we go look at the fair?" Chloe asked. She clasped her hands together in the same sort of pleading gesture she might use when asking a wicked queen to spare her family from the guillotine. "Jazmyn said they have kettle corn. You know I *love* kettle corn."

Andrea's gaze darted from her daughter to Marshall and back. "I do know that. Probably not this year. We'll have a chance for kettle corn again."

She was refraining from taking them to the fair because of *him* and his stupid broken leg. She didn't think him capable of moving through the crowded booths and displays.

He stood up, intent on showing her she was wrong.

"Come on. It will be fun," he said. "I wanted to see some of the booths myself. And kettle corn would really hit the spot right now."

"Yay!" Chloe exclaimed with delight, beaming at him as if she were a teenage boy and he had just handed her the keys to a Lamborghini Gallardo.

Andie, on the other hand, frowned at him with a worried look. "Are you sure you're up to it?"

She apparently thought he had all the strength and endurance of a ninety-year-old man with emphysema.

"If I need to stop for a break, I'm sure I can find a spot to sit down."

"We're happy to take your blankets home for you, if you'd like," Charlene offered. "That way you don't have to come back here for them. I can drop them off at your house tomorrow."

"Why don't we take them?" Louise offered. "Christopher can run them to you in the morning."

Andie apparently decided she was overruled. "Fine. All right. Charlene and Mike, thank you for inviting us to share your prime spot here. It was truly lovely."

"You are so welcome. And I mean that, Andie. I couldn't be happier to have you and your children here. I'm so thrilled we'll be seeing more of each other now."

His mother squeezed her hands, then kissed her cheek. Andie flashed Marshall a telling look and he sighed.

He was going to have to tell his mother not to expect anything between him and Andie. It would break her heart, but it was probably better to do it now, before anyone's messy feelings were involved.

They slowly made their way through the series of booths set up in the park with the children again walking in front of Marshall to help him manage through the crowd.

At least the tents and booths were set up along paved paths in the park so he didn't have to tackle more of the uneven ground. The crowds of people had to be difficult enough.

"Don't worry," she told him. "The kids will lose interest as soon as they realize the booths mostly have arts and crafts and not toys. We'll grab the kettle corn first so that's out of the way, then just stop at a few booths and call it good."

"I'm doing fine," he answered. "Feel free to look as long as you'd like. If I need to, I can go into the main food tent to sit down and warm up."

He did seem to be doing okay, much to her relief. His color was good and she could see no sign of those pain lines etched too often at the edges of his mouth. He was only a week out of surgery and she knew his leg had to be hurting, but she had a feeling he would never admit it, even if it felt like rats were gnawing on his ankle bone.

In only a few moments, she was reminded again that he appeared to be well liked and well respected. He greeted many of the people they passed by name and stopped to chat with a few.

She was interested to see he nodded to—but didn't stop to chat with—a couple of his deputies who were wearing uniforms but didn't seem to be doing anything official other than talking to each other and a man in a fancy Stetson. All three of the men greeted him cordially, but she sensed the enmity simmering in them.

"Do you know everyone from Shelter Springs and Haven Point?" she asked in wonder, when they finally made their way to the concessions tents.

He gave a gruff laugh. "Not even close. It's good to see so many new people moving in—especially now that the Caine Tech facility is up and running. New blood is good for a town. You keep things fresh and interesting."

He wasn't talking about her specifically, she reminded herself. Just her status as a newcomer to town.

She had to wonder how long it might take for the transition from newcomer to old-timer. Probably a few decades, at least.

"Something smells *so good,*" Will exclaimed.

"You got that right, kid," Marshall said.

Andie had to agree with them. Kettle corn just might be one of the more addictive smells in the universe.

The kettle corn was a hit, of course. Sugar and popcorn. What was there not to like in that particular pairing? Chloe and Will both begged for their own small bag and she relented, even though she knew neither would be able to finish. They could always take it home. Remembering

Marshall's sweet tooth, she bought another medium-sized bag for him. After the cashier handed it to her, she held it out to the sheriff. "This one's yours. I'll carry it until we're back in the car, but do you want some now?"

He gave her a "hell yeah" kind of look that made her smile.

"Unlike the rest of us, you're not going to be able to walk and eat. This looks like a good place to stop for a minute."

They paused beside one of the convenient kerosene heaters and she opened the bag and held it out to him. He leaned on one of the crutches and ate a few kernels from the bag.

It was a strangely intimate moment. He had to be close enough to reach the popcorn and she could feel the heat emanating from him, smell the woodsy, outdoorsy scent of his aftershave.

These were the sort of memories that stuck with a person for a long time—the delectable scents drifting around, the magical Christmas lights twinkling along with the stars overhead and the lake gleaming in the background. The sounds of holiday music and conversation and children's laughter.

In that moment, she couldn't imagine anywhere she would rather be.

"Sheriff Bailey! What are you doing here?"

At the shocked exclamation, Andie turned to find a woman in her forties staring at Marshall as if he had just dropped in out of nowhere by parachute.

He flashed the woman a warmer smile than anything he'd yet to give *Andie*. "Hi, Jackie. Right now, I'm eating some excellent kettle corn. Really excellent. You should try some."

The other woman looked aghast. "I mean, what are you doing here at the festival? These crowds can't be good for you. You should be home with your leg up where it's warm and safe."

He didn't look very excited about that suggestion.

"Jackie, this is my neighbor Andie Montgomery. These are her kids, Chloe and Will. Andie, this is my administrative assistant, Jackie Scott."

Andie smiled, but Jackie barely paid her any attention as she looked at Marshall like a mother cat wanting to pick up one of her kittens by the scruff of the neck. "I can't imagine your doctors would agree a crowded festival is a safe place for you. It's wall-to-wall people and nobody is watching where he's going. You're still trying to heal. You should be home in bed with your leg up."

That was exactly the wrong thing to say to Marshall, as Andie had quickly discovered.

"Thanks for your concern, Jackie, but I'm really fine. Yes, it's a challenge to get through the crowd, but nothing I can't handle, especially with Andrea and her kids watching out for me."

Mouth tight, Jackie slanted a dismissive look at

her before shifting her gaze back to Marshall. "I don't like this," the woman said, all but wringing her hands. "Until they catch the person who did this, I think you're better off staying home, where you're safe."

"That's not going to happen. In fact, I'm hoping to return to work next week, at least part-time. If I don't try to stay on top of things, we'll both be drowning in work next month."

The assistant looked horrified. "I would rather work thirty hours a week in overtime all through January than have you push yourself too hard and end up doing permanent damage to yourself," she said in an impassioned voice.

Jackie's concern was beginning to annoy him. Andie had enough experience annoying him herself to recognize the signs.

"You're sweet to worry about me," he said, "but you really don't need to. Especially not tonight, when we're all here to enjoy ourselves. Have a good evening."

It was a clear dismissal and Marshall punctuated it by hobbling away, leaving Andie and her kids to scramble after him.

"She's very protective of you," Andie observed as they moved to the next booth.

"She and my mother ought to form a club. I'm sure you could join, too."

She refused to feel guilty for her concern over him, though she did wonder why all the women in his life felt compelled to look out for him. He was tough and hard and perfectly capable of taking care of himself, yet he still managed to bring out her protective instincts—maybe because that hard shell concealed that gooey core of sweetness he would probably deny to his dying breath.

"I inherited Jackie from the previous sheriff when I took over a year ago. She's extremely efficient and keeps the department running, really, but she can be a bit of a worrier."

She didn't have a chance to respond before they reached the white tent with the Haven Point Helping Hands sign hanging on the front. The smell of cinnamon and cloves poured through the doorway, along with an enticing warmth that drew passersby inside.

Megan Hamilton and Samantha Fremont were working inside the tent, Andie saw at a glance. Samantha was helping a customer, but Megan greeted her and the children with enthusiasm.

"Why, look who's here! My favorite boy named Will and my favorite girl named Chloe!" she exclaimed, in such a cheerful, over-the-top voice that the children giggled. "How did you like your first Lights on the Lake parade?"

"I didn't like it, I *loved* it!" Chloe said. "The boats were awesome."

"Especially the one with Santa Claus on it," Will said.

"That's my favorite, too," the innkeeper said with an affectionate smile for him.

"Have you ever been on one of the boats in the parade?" Chloe asked. "I think it would be so fun!"

Will's eyes widened at the novel idea. "Yeah! Hey, Mom, we should get a boat, then we can ride in the parade next year!"

"Maybe we could ask Santa Claus for one," Chloe suggested.

She had heard Marshall talking to Christopher about the astronomical price tag of one of the wooden Killies, which was a little far out of her budget.

The idea of owning any boat was way out of her comfort zone—though it was a shame, really, since one of the most beautiful lakes in the country was right in her backyard.

"Are there any ornaments here that might work on my tree?" Marshall asked. "Since you two are my master decorators, maybe you could help me pick out a couple."

The kids jumped at the chance to help him with anything. Grateful for the diversion, she headed over to talk to Sam and Megan about how sales were going. The proceeds from selling the crafts they made throughout the year helped fund some of the group's charitable work.

The two women apparently didn't want to talk about the Helping Hands.

"Marshall Bailey!" Megan said in an undertone, giving the tall sheriff a sideways look at the other end of the booth. "Seriously? Are you two a thing?"

The memory of that delicious kiss suddenly surged to the front of her brain and Andie shivered but quickly pushed it back. "If by *thing* you mean neighbors, then yes. But that's all. Wyn asked me to keep an eye on him after he broke his leg, since I'm the closest one to him."

"Lucky. I'd be happy to keep *anything* on him," Samantha said with a little sigh. "I've had a crush on the man *forever*. With those blue, blue eyes, he's always reminded me of Paul Newman in *Butch Cassidy and the Sundance Kid*. If Paul Newman had dark hair, anyway. But don't you dare tell Katrina, okay? She would *freak* if she had any idea I'm seriously in lust with her big brother."

"I won't tell. I promise."

"You two would make a great couple," Megan said. "He's always been so serious. He needs to laugh more and those adorable kids of yours would melt even the hardest heart."

"Yes, they would. But we're not a couple," she stressed.

"But look how cute they are together," Megan said. She pointed to Marshall, who was bent over on his crutches listening to her kids as they appeared to be arguing the merits of certain ornaments over others.

Her heart gave a little twist. They *were* cute together. Despite their rocky beginnings, both Will and Chloe obviously adored him.

She was coming to, as well. Entirely too much.

"It looks like the note cards Louise painted are almost sold out," she said, trying to change the subject.

"They've been really popular this year."

"Because she's wonderful. I'll buy the last box."

By the time they paid for their purchases, Andie could see Marshall had overdone things— just as she knew he would never admit to it, even if tortured. He kept shifting on his crutches, mouth tight and his expression remote.

She resolved to usher them all to her vehicle quickly and get him home, where he could elevate his leg.

The crowd seemed to be even heavier as they made their way out of the warm tent and the unnaturally mild temperatures had begun to drop with the cold front forecasters said would be moving down from Canada later that night.

The going was tough for him on the crutches and he had to stop several times when people moved in front of him without paying any attention.

"Sorry about this. I thought the crowd would thin by now."

"I'm doing fine. We're almost to the end of the row."

Just before they reached the last few tents, she spotted Charlene and Mike coming the other direction. They saw them at the same time and made their way through the mass of people.

"Oh, you're still here!" Charlene exclaimed. "I thought for sure you would have left for Snow Angel Cove by now."

"We're heading to the car now," she started to say.

Before she could squeeze out the last word, she heard a grunt at the same moment she became aware of movement out of the corner of her eye.

She turned instinctively and reached out a hand, an instant too late to help Marshall, who seemed to have lost his balance and was toppling forward —directly onto his broken leg in the protective boot.

Chapter SEVENTEEN

He managed to keep most of his weight off the leg as he toppled, but it still banged into the frozen ground and pain growled through him, hot and vicious.

He rolled to his back and started to curse, then caught himself when he saw Chloe and Will looking down at him with big, frightened eyes.

His mother looked just as frightened. "Somebody call an ambulance!" Charlene shrieked.

"On it," Uncle Mike said, reaching for his cell phone.

Marshall managed to breathe through the pain and held up a hand. "Stop. Don't call an ambulance. I'm okay. Honest."

"You are *not* okay," Andie said, kneeling on the concrete beside him. Though her eyes were a deep, concerned green and he didn't miss the flickers of panic in them, her voice sounded remarkably calm.

"I will be, as soon as we both get up from the cold ground."

"I don't think we should move you until the paramedics come!" Charlene said. "Mike, call 911."

His uncle looked like he was in an impossible position, forced to choose between two conflicting orders.

"Don't call the ambulance, Mike," he said firmly, hoping common sense would overrule the man's desire to please his new bride. "I'm fine, I promise. Just stabilize the crutch so I can pull myself up. Andie, he might need help."

Though in his sixties, Mike was strong as a plow horse from his years of manual labor at the body shop. As he hoped, though, Andie quickly rose from the cold concrete to grip the crutches.

This was so humiliating, finding himself on the ground like that, but he had a bigger concern and couldn't stay here like a turtle that had landed on its shell.

He grabbed the crutches as high as he could reach and pulled himself up, cursing the awkwardness of the heavy brace that he was already so damn sick of. He supposed it beat a plaster cast, but not by much.

When he was once more balanced on his good leg, he reached into the pocket of his coat, aware his fingers were shaking a little in reaction to the pain that made him feel weak and helpless.

"You're making a phone call? *Now?*" Andie exclaimed when he pulled it out. "You can barely stand up! Can't it wait until we get to the car?"

"No. I thought I saw Ruben earlier and I need to find him. I don't know if he can hear me with all the crowd noise, but I have to try."

He dialed his friend's number, but it went straight to voice mail. He frowned, wondering if he ought to try Cade. Haven Point was his jurisdiction, after all, even if the incident was part of an ongoing investigation.

As he was dialing Cade's number, though, he spotted Ruben back at the opening of the Helping Hands tent, talking to Samantha Fremont and Meg Hamilton.

"There's Ruben. I need to see if I can catch him."

Andie glared at him. "Stay here. If it's so important that you have to talk to him right this minute, I'll grab him."

She hurried back the way they had come and returned a minute later with his deputy.

"What's going on? Andrea said you just fell. Do you need help getting to your car? Do I need to call an ambulance?"

His mother and the kids were still watching with wide eyes. Charlene would completely *freak* if she heard what he needed to tell his deputy, so Marsh jerked his head away from the group and started walking a few steps away for privacy.

"I did fall," he said, when they were out of earshot of the rest, "but it wasn't an accident. Somebody very deliberately came up behind me and kicked my crutch out from under me."

Ruben looked alarmed. "Are you sure? It's a big crowd. Somebody could have just bumped you."

"Positive. The first time didn't do it so they kicked again."

"Did you see anybody?"

"No. I thought the first kick was an accident, too, so I didn't turn around until the second one. I thought I saw somebody heading through the gap in the tents where we were, but all I could make out was a dark shape rushing away."

"You're thinking this was connected to the hit-and-run."

"What else?"

He could tell Ruben didn't quite believe him. He would have thought he was crazy, too, if not for that second sharp kick. "I saw Wall and Kramer earlier, talking to Bill Newbold. None of them looked happy to see me."

"You think it might have been one of them?"

"Who else?"

"What do you need from me?"

"Ask around. See if you can find a witness, maybe somebody who's running the booths in this area. Somebody had to have seen *something*."

"You got it."

Ruben took off and Marsh watched him go for a moment before returning to Andie and the others.

"Darling, are you sure we can't call an ambulance?" his mother pressed.

"No. I'll be fine."

Andie gave him a close look and he was quite sure she didn't miss that he didn't say he *was* fine but spoke instead in the future tense.

"Let's get you to the car and I'll take you home," Andie said.

"What about the party?" Chloe complained.

"We'll get there eventually," Andie said.

"Maddie said she was waiting for me, though," Chloe complained. "She wants to show me their new puppies!"

"She can wait a few moments longer."

"We can take the children with us," Charlene suggested. "You can meet us there after you take Marshall home."

If his leg hadn't still been howling with pain, he might have found it amusing that his mother didn't offer to take him home instead of Andie doing it.

Because he hadn't yet confessed that he had misled her, she still thought something was going on between them. He should probably come clean, but the truth was Charlene completely exhausted him, while Andie's presence filled him with an odd sort of peace.

"Good idea," he said instead. "Thanks, Mom."

"You don't have booster seats for the kids," Andie protested.

"We can grab yours. No problem," Mike said. "I would feel better anyway if we walk with you back to the parking lot to make sure Mr. Wobbly Knees here doesn't decide to take another header."

Andie looked as if she wanted to argue, but she must have decided the combined force of three Baileys was more than she could take on.

"Are you sure you're ready?" she asked him.

As ever. He nodded and swung the crutches forward, keeping a careful eye on the crowd for potential threats.

Just before they left the collection of booths, he spotted Ken Kramer in a knot of people standing around one of the propane heaters and enjoying a slice of pizza.

He could swear the deputy smirked as he watched Marshall make his slow way on the crutches. Hot anger burned through him and he hoped to hell Ruben could find something.

Ten minutes later, they were all settled in their respective vehicles and Andie pulled out of the parking lot and headed in the direction of Riverbend Road.

"How are you *really* feeling?" she asked when they were finally on their way.

He wanted to lie but didn't see much point. "Hurts like hell," he admitted.

"Maybe you need another X-ray so we can be sure you didn't do more damage in there when you fell."

He didn't even want to think about that possibility. "Cade is supposed to be off tomorrow and was planning on coming over. If it still hurts, I'll have him take me."

Her mouth tightened. "I was afraid the festival would be too much for you, but I never expected you to reinjure your leg."

"It's fine, really," he assured her. "Don't worry about me."

"That's not as easy as it sounds," she answered, just as his phone buzzed with a text.

He pulled it out and frowned at the message from Ruben.

"I'm still not clear on what exactly happened. I saw you go down, but I didn't see what happened just before that. Did your crutches hit an uneven spot on the sidewalk or something? And why did you need to talk to Deputy Morales?"

He debated about telling her. She didn't need more worry. That hardly seemed fair, though, when she had done so much to help him.

"It wasn't an accident," he said with conviction. "Somebody kicked my crutch out from under me."

She jerked her gaze from the road just for an instant, but it was enough for him to see the shock and dismay on her features. "That's impossible! I'm sure you must be mistaken. Somebody behind you probably stumbled into you. That's all."

"Exactly what Ruben said. And as I told him, once might have been a mistake. The first time I was able to stay upright, so they kicked it again."

"*That's* why you tried to call him," she said, turning onto Riverbend Road.

He nodded. "I asked Ruben to talk to vendors in that area to see if anybody saw anything. He just texted me that he came up empty."

Her hands tightened on the steering wheel. "You could have been seriously injured," she said. "Who would want to hurt you deliberately like that?"

"I don't know. Maybe someone who hit me with an SUV a week ago and broke my leg in the first place?"

"You think it was the same person, right there at the Lights on the Lake festival?"

"Seems to me that's the logical answer. Either that or I've got an entire army of enemies out there. I don't know . . . I think I like the first option better."

She didn't appear to like either of the possibilities.

As soon as she parked, he quickly opened his door and was halfway out of the vehicle before she could make her way around to help him with the door.

He hated being so damned needy, a guy who couldn't even get out of a car by himself.

He wanted her to see him as more than that. The thought sidled through his head. Though he tried to dismiss it—reminding himself of all the reasons he shouldn't want more with her— he couldn't seem to shake it.

"You don't have to come in," he told her, but he

didn't add that it would probably be best if she didn't, given his current mood.

"I'll make sure you're settled inside."

He didn't want to argue with her, so he unlocked the door and let himself into the house through the side kitchen door, with her following close behind.

"You should head straight for the sofa or the recliner, where you can elevate your leg. Where are your pain pills? I'll grab them and some water for you before I leave."

She sounded like his mother, like Jackie, and it suddenly pissed him off. He didn't need her taking care of him. Not like that, anyway.

"That's not necessary. I said I was fine."

"Funny. You don't sound fine and you certainly don't look it. It's taking every ounce of energy you have not to grimace, isn't it? Don't try to be a hero, Marshall. You're in pain. Take a pill, for crying out loud."

He scowled. He hadn't had a pill in three days and didn't want to backtrack, but he knew she was right.

"You're not my nurse."

"No." She stepped close enough for him to catch the wildflower scent of her. "I'm your fake girl-friend, whom you're using to keep your mother at bay."

He thought of that weird tenderness, the ache inside him to touch her, and realized in that

297

instant with fierce certainty that he didn't want her to be his fake anything.

He wanted the real thing.

"As your fake girlfriend—and your genuine friend—I'm ordering you to take a pill."

She was worried about him. The sweetness of it seemed to fill him, leaving little room for most of the pain.

"Some fake girlfriend you are," he complained. "Seems like all I did was trade one bossy, managing female for another."

Her laugh was quick, genuine. "You seem to be surrounded by them, aren't you?"

"It's a curse."

She smiled and it took all his remaining strength not to take one more step, press her against the kitchen table and kiss every inch of that delectable mouth.

His fingers tightened on the handgrips of the crutches to keep from reaching for her. He couldn't. Whatever he wanted, he had to think about what was best for Andie and her children.

He wasn't it.

His life was a freaking mess right now. He couldn't put her in harm's way, not after everything she had endured at the hands of a fellow law enforcement officer. She was just beginning to find peace again and he couldn't do that to her.

Beyond that, the whole situation with Christopher

was a land mine, complication after complication just waiting to explode.

"I'll take a pill, okay? First, I need to change into more comfortable clothes. After that, I promise, I'll take one of the damn pain pills and plop into the recliner—and then I probably won't move until morning."

She studied him suspiciously for a moment, as if she didn't quite believe him. "I don't feel right about leaving you alone when somebody out there has twice tried to cause you harm," she said slowly. "You don't even have a watchdog to warn you if someone tries to enter the premises."

"You could send Sadie down, but I'm not sure she would do much good."

"What you need is a big, tough German shepherd. I ought to call Ben and McKenzie and have them lend you Hondo, except you would have to take Rika, too, because I don't think McKenzie's dog lets him out of her sight for long."

Unlike the smothering from his mother or Jackie's somewhat neurotic worry, Andie's concern seeped in, warming all the cold spots inside him.

"I don't need a watchdog. They won't come at me in my own house. This is about putting me out of commission, not causing permanent damage. Somebody doesn't want me doing my job."

He was sure of the *what*. He just didn't yet know the *who* or exactly the *why*, though a few of his suspicions were beginning to solidify.

"So, naturally, that's exactly what you're determined to do."

"I need to flush out whoever is behind this." He shrugged. "That will be much better medicine than any pain pills."

She sighed. "You're a hard man to argue with, Sheriff Bailey."

"Funny, I've heard that before."

"From your other fake girlfriends, no doubt."

"Trust me, you're the only fake girlfriend I can handle."

He meant the words lightly, but somehow as he smiled down at her, the mood shifted between them, became charged, electric, crackling with energy and heat and a fine-edged, seductive tension.

Her gaze shifted to his mouth, and with a hard, shocking thump of his heart, he realized she wanted him to kiss her.

He wanted to, more than he remembered wanting anything in his life.

Just as he knew he couldn't.

"Andie—" he began.

She swallowed quickly and gazed up at him out of those huge green eyes, color soaking her cheeks in the delectable blush that seemed to come so easily with her coloring.

"Well, good night," she said in a deceptively casual voice. "I hope you get some rest."

Before he realized what she was up to, she took a step forward. He was about a good six or seven inches taller than her under normal circumstances, but he was leaning down a little on the crutches while he balanced on one leg and she only had to stand on tiptoe to reach him.

He felt the tantalizing touch of her breath against his skin and waited for a kiss that didn't come. Instead, she stepped back again, a mischievous smile in her eyes that reminded him very much of her son.

"That's what you call a fake kiss. You know. To add to the illusion."

He wasn't sure what had brought it out of her, but he loved seeing this lighthearted side of her that he sensed had been dormant too long since her husband's death. He decided to play along, only for a moment. This had been one of the toughest weeks of his life. Didn't he deserve a little sweetness as a counterpoint?

"Is that what you were doing? I missed it. Better try again. I'll be ready this time."

Her eyes gleamed at the challenge and she leaned forward to torment him again with an almost-kiss. This time he was ready and moved his own mouth so he could kiss her firmly, decisively.

Any thought he had of only teasing her for a

moment disappeared the moment his mouth tasted her again. She was sweet, salty, addicting, just like that kettle corn, and he couldn't get enough.

She gave a little sigh, as if she'd been waiting for just this moment. He leaned back against the kitchen counter and she stepped closer, her curves pressed against him, and he forgot all about the ache in his leg.

They kissed far longer than they should have —and not nearly long enough. He wanted desperately to pull her into the other room, to sink down onto the sofa with her and hold her on his lap and explore every delicious inch of her.

She was aroused. He tasted it in her kiss and felt it in the trembling hands resting at his hips.

That strange tenderness he had experienced at the parade seemed to curl and dance around them, stronger than ever, and he wanted to tuck her against him and keep her safe forever.

She seemed to come to her senses much earlier than he did. He knew the instant she returned to reality. She hitched in a ragged little breath and then eased her mouth away from his, leaving him cold.

"This is a dangerous game, Marshall," she said, her expression serious, intent. "One I'm not sure I'm strong enough to play with you."

He wanted to argue with her. He'd like to tell

her no harm could come from sharing more of those delicious sugar-salt kisses, but both of them would know it was a lie.

"For the record, you're one of the strongest women I've ever met," he murmured.

Without answering, she took another step back and shoved her hands in the pockets of her parka. "I'd better go find my children. Are you sure you're all right?"

No. Something had changed during that intense, emotional kiss, something he didn't want to examine closely right now.

"Fine," he lied.

"I'll see you later," she said.

She gazed at him for a long moment, then turned around and headed into the night.

Outside, the first fragile snowflakes of the coming storm had begun to spiral down, catching the moonlight as they spun to earth. She lifted her face and they fell on her cheeks like that first whisper of a kiss between them, the one that never should have happened.

She shivered—but knew it wasn't from the temperature, which had plummeted precipitously. Despite all the precautions she had taken, the entirely prudent and necessary defenses she had tried to build around her heart, she was coming to care for Marshall Bailey entirely too much.

She was halfway to being in love with him.

Maybe even a little further than that, if she were perfectly honest with herself.

She wouldn't allow it. End of story. She had fought too hard, climbed too far to reach this desperately needed state of peace and calm. For the first time in two years, she was in a good place, a healthy place. Her children were happy and content here in Haven Point, she had friends, her work was interesting and fulfilling.

At long last, her dreams were no longer haunted by grief, shame, fear.

Marshall called her strong. She wasn't, not at all. But she was tenacious and she wanted to think she was resilient. She would draw on every ounce of strength she could muster—from anywhere she could find it—to protect her heart.

He didn't need her help now. Not really. He was getting around better on the crutches and could probably fend for himself, for the most part. She had done as Wyn asked and helped him through the first difficult days after he was released from the hospital.

While he couldn't yet drive, his mother and new stepfather were back in town. Charlene or Mike could step up if he needed a ride somewhere and Wynona and Katrina would both be coming home the following week for the holidays. He didn't need Andrea anymore and she couldn't risk further breaches in the defenses around her heart.

From now on, she would do her best to stay away from the man. It shouldn't be that difficult —until Wynona asked Andie to help him, their worlds had hardly intersected. She had no reason to think that would change, moving forward.

She would leave it to Marshall to explain to his family that he and Andie were nothing to each other but neighbors.

With hands that trembled only a little, she opened the door, climbed into her vehicle and started the engine. Once she wasn't in his company so often, she thought, these fledgling feelings would die a natural death.

She was almost sure of it.

Chapter EIGHTEEN

For three days, Andrea managed to keep her resolution to stay away from that lovely stone house by the river.

As she predicted, it hadn't been easy. A dozen times a day, she fought the urge to call him or walk up the street to check on him, just to make sure he was all right.

At every mealtime, she worried that he wasn't eating, though she knew that was an unwarranted concern as she had seen Charlene stop by twice in those three days, loaded with bags of groceries each time.

Whether he liked it or not, his family would take care of him, she assured herself. He didn't need her anymore. That didn't stop her dreams from tormenting her or her thoughts from constantly wanting to travel down Riverbend Road to his house.

Her children had made it more difficult by asking constantly if they could go visit "Sheriff Marshall"—if they could see his Christmas tree from their house, if his broken leg was all better now, if he might want to play with Sadie.

The weather didn't help her restless mood, with three days of uncertain, on-and-off-again storms. Though no significant precipitation fell, it was cold and bleak, with a steady, moaning wind and a low pressure system that made her bones ache.

Finally the long-anticipated major storm started in earnest late Tuesday afternoon, five days before Christmas. The snows started just before dark—lightly at first, with huge flakes that seemed to hover in the air and spin in place before plummeting to the ground.

When she looked out the window twenty moments later, all she could see was a curtain of white.

"Look at all that snow!" Will breathed, his eyes wide.

"Maybe we'll have a snow day tomorrow," Chloe exclaimed, looking more excited about that than the prospect of Christmas in a few days.

By their bedtime, that was looking more and more likely. Everything was covered in white and the wind blew hard, rattling the windows of her house, moaning under the eaves, whipping branches against the glass.

She stayed up later than usual, sitting by the fire and wrapping the last of the children's presents while she listened to the wind and watched a sweetly romantic Christmas movie on TV. The happy ending made her sigh through her sniffles, though it did nothing to help her restlessness.

When she looked out the window after hiding the gifts and then brushing her teeth, she saw five inches of new snow crowning the fence posts.

The forecasters had said another eight to twelve inches could be on its way before morning.

It took her a long time to fall asleep. When she did, her dreams were once more haunted by a certain county sheriff with a slow smile and serious blue eyes.

She dreamed someone she couldn't see was chasing them through the booths at the Haven Point Lights on the Lake festival, waving a crutch at them.

Marshall carried Will and Chloe on his back, though he had the thick black boot on one leg, but she still had to run hard to keep up with him as they ducked in and out of tents and people and the Christmas village.

And then they were cornered just on the other side of the biggest Christmas tree at Lakeside Park, with nowhere left to run, and the crutch wielded by a menacing form in a parka and balaclava turned into the same cold and deadly Sig Sauer that Rob Warren had used to pistol-whip her and had pressed to her chin that horrible summer evening mere months ago.

Just as terrified as she had been that night, she screamed and tried to push Marsh and her children out of harm's way, but she was too late. She heard a fierce crack and the huge town Christmas tree exploded and she awoke abruptly with her heart pounding fiercely and every muscle tense and alert.

She lay in her bed, her breathing sawing in and out. That crack had sounded so real!

Had the dream awakened her or had something else? She heard a small, whining sound and realized after a beat that it was Sadie outside her door.

She reached for the lamp beside her bed and flipped the switch, but nothing happened. The wind must have blown out the power. Grateful for cell phones and the ever-present flashlight app, she reached for hers, turned on the light and slid out of bed.

Her room was freezing. The furnace was powered by natural gas, but the blower couldn't turn on without electricity, which she had always thought was poor engineering.

Sadie rushed inside the moment Andie opened the door. She plopped at her feet and whined again.

"What's going on, girl? We don't have a well, so I know nobody could have fallen in."

The dog gave her a quizzical look, which led Andie to conclude her lame humor wasn't particularly well received at 2:00 a.m.

"Don't worry. The power has gone out, no big deal. We'll figure out what's going on."

She shoved her feet into her fuzzy slippers with multicolored owls on them and pulled her robe off the chair by the bed. When she peered out her second-floor bedroom to the ground below, she saw the snow had eased somewhat. It wasn't blowing as hard, anyway, and the intensity of the flakes had diminished.

Across the street, she saw the porch lights on Cade Emmett's log home were on and a few more inside. As she watched, more lights came on. Apparently the chief of police wasn't sleeping, either.

"The power outage must be only this side of the street," she told Sadie. She couldn't see any other houses but Cade's from her bedroom window at the front of the house, but when she walked out of her bedroom to the landing, she could see toward Marshall's house and the Jacobses' at the end of the street, where Christmas lights gleamed in muted colors beneath a layer of thick snow.

She tried the hall switch, but again, no welcoming lights burst on.

Maybe it was only her house. She stood for just a moment, aware of a vague feeling of misgiving. She was trying to remember where the fuse box was when she suddenly heard a soft knock at the front door.

The lingering tendrils of her nightmare and that entirely too-real memory of Rob Warren's hand-gun pressed to her chin raced through her head and panic spurted through her.

It was 2:00 a.m. in the middle of a snowstorm. Who would be knocking at her door?

She hesitated, wildly tempted to gather her children and lock them all in the bathroom.

No. Rob Warren was in prison. She no longer had reason to be afraid.

That didn't mean she was stupid, either. She didn't feel right about having firearms in the house with young children, but she did have a Taser and pepper spray. She hurried to the hallway and dug through her purse until she found the small child-resistant bag she kept both in.

Another trio of knocks sounded through the quiet house while she was trying to open the bag with fingers that trembled. She pulled both out and hurried to the door, wishing she had installed a security peephole.

"Who is it?" she called through the door.

"Andie?" She heard a male voice. "It's Cade Emmett, from across the street. Is everybody okay in there?"

She frowned at the odd question and opened the door. In the glow from her phone flashlight, she saw the Haven Point police chief standing on her porch wearing boots and a parka.

"Yes. Everyone's fine. Why wouldn't we be? It's just a power outage."

"It's not just a power outage, I'm afraid. That big elm on the south side of your property just blew over, onto your garage. It must have taken the power line with it. It made a horrible crash. You didn't hear it?"

She remembered that crack in her dream that had sounded so real and terrifying. "Are you sure?"

"Positive. Marsh just called me and ordered me to get my ass over here. Apparently he was looking out the window and saw the whole thing blow over. He tried to call you first, but you didn't answer, so he called me next."

She had put her phone on "do not disturb" before she went to bed, which in retrospect seemed like a stupid idea. She switched it on now and the phone immediately rang.

"Andie! What's going on?" Marshall's urgent voice came over the line. "Are you okay? Are the kids okay?"

"I don't know. I . . . I haven't checked, but their rooms are on the opposite side of the house from the garage. I'll call you back."

She raced to their rooms just as Chloe cried out. "Mama? Where are you? Mama! My light won't turn on!"

Andie opened the door. "I'm here, darling. Right here. The power's gone out, but we're okay."

Chloe jumped into her arms and flung her arms around her neck so abruptly that Andie staggered backward a little. Her daughter burst into tears and buried her head against her.

"What's wrong? Are you hurt? Why are you crying?

"No." Chloe sobbed. "I thought I heard a man."

"Oh, honey." Her arms tightened as she felt her

heart break a little more. Chloe had witnessed too much for a six-year-old girl. She had stumbled out of her room that terrible June night when Rob Warren had found them, had seen her| mother bleeding, bruised, had seen Rob shove the gun to her chin and Wyn and Cade pull their own weapons.

Chloe had watched a man she had trusted and liked—her father's friend and former partner—fire on Wynona when the officer had tried to protect them all from him.

"It's only Chief Emmett from across the street," she said now. "You know Cade. He came to check on us because Marshall saw a tree fall on our garage."

"A tree?" In the dim light from her phone, Andie saw her daughter's eyes go wide. "Was that the big noise that woke me up?"

"I imagine so."

Chloe hitched in a breath, but her sobs slowed a little. Though she was growing bigger, Andie still held her in her arms as if she were a toddler, sensing both of them needed it. "Come on. Let's go check on Will."

She had often found her daughter handled her fears and insecurities much better when she felt useful. Much like Andie did herself.

"I've got a flashlight. The *Frozen* one. Should I use that?"

"That would be great, if you know where it is."

"Under my pillow." Her mouth twisted with guilt. "I might have been reading my book a little past my bedtime."

It was difficult to get too mad at her for that when Andie frequently did the same. Judging that her daughter had her emotions under better control now, she set her down, then used her phone for light while Chloe found her own flashlight.

When they opened the door to Will's room, Sadie immediately trotted to his bed and jumped up, where the dog proceeded to lick his salty little-boy cheek.

Will opened his eyes blearily. "Sadie," he mumbled, still mostly asleep. "Get down. You're not supposed to be on the bed."

The light caught his attention and he squinted at it and his eyes opened more. "Chloe! Why did you put Sadie on my bed?"

He always had such a croaky little voice when he first woke up. Normally it made her smile, but not in the middle of a crisis.

"I didn't. She put herself there."

"Why is it so dark? Where's my night-light?"

"The power is out. A tree fell on the garage," Chloe announced. Now that the initial crisis had passed and her worst fears allayed, she seemed to be relishing the dramatic events.

"Did it smash my bike?" Will asked.

Oh. She had been so worried about the children

she hadn't given a thought to possible consequences. Her new SUV was in that garage. Had it been damaged? Wouldn't that be just her luck?

Cars could be replaced, she reminded herself. That was the entire reason for insurance. Her children were safe and that was the only thing that mattered.

"I'm sorry I had to wake you. We only needed to make sure you're all right. You can stay here under your blankets where it's warm for now, since the furnace can't come on without electricity."

"Are we going to freeze to death?" Chloe asked, some of her anxiety returning.

"No, honey. You know I wouldn't let that happen. For now, we'll bundle up to keep warm. If we have to, we'll go stay at a hotel."

"Maybe the tree smashed our car," Will said. "If it did, how will we even get to a hotel?"

"I promise we'll figure something out. Chloe, you can climb back into your bed if you want and read your book. Or both of you can climb into my big one, and just this once, you can take Sadie with you."

They chose that option and she settled them into her bed with Chloe's flashlight, an extra blanket and a wriggly, warm little Havachon and then headed back to the living room.

The temperature of the house had dropped another few degrees while she was in with the children. She couldn't see Cade at first and thought perhaps he had gone outside to check the situation. She was changing her slippers for boots to join him when she thought she heard two distinct male voices, raised and angry.

A moment later, the door opened and to her complete shock, Marshall hobbled in on his crutches with a plastic bag tied around his orthopedic boot and Cade right behind him, his handsome features furious.

"I told you the situation was under control. You didn't need to come down here."

"I wanted to make sure everybody was okay," Marshall said stubbornly.

"So you walked through nine inches of fresh snow on crutches."

"All of three hundred feet. It's not like I trekked to the top of Mount Solace."

Despite his nonchalance, she could see he was in pain and she quickly pulled a chair around so the stubborn man could sit down.

Looking a little embarrassed, he sank down. He had walked through deep powder on crutches to make sure she and her children were all right.

How on earth was she supposed to resist that?

"You are certifiable," Cade declared.

"Yeah. Probably. So what's the story?"

"I was in the middle of assessing the situation when I got a little distracted by the sight of some idiot hobbling down the snowy street. From what

I could see, the roof of the garage is damaged but not completely destroyed. Looks like it barely missed your car, which is good, but I hope you're done with your Christmas shopping because it likely will be a day or two before you'll be able to go anywhere."

She released a breath. "What about the power?"

"The tree took out the line from the street. I've already called the power company, but they're backed up and probably won't be out until late tomorrow or the next day. You're going to have to find somewhere else to sleep for tonight and possibly tomorrow, but all in all, you're lucky. If that tree had fallen the other way, it would have come down right where you were sleeping."

As the reality of what might have happened began to soak in, Andie suddenly felt like the tree *had* just fallen on her. They might have been killed. All of them.

Her knees suddenly felt weak and she didn't quite trust them to hold her up, so she sank onto the sofa as raw relief, gratitude and, okay, a little smidgen of self-pity battled inside her.

For heaven's sake, hadn't her children been through enough? Other people were sleeping soundly in their beds, getting ready for Christmas, carrying on with their safe, normal world without having to worry about where they were going to live for the next few days. Now here she was having yet one more crisis to contend with.

"You'll stay at my place," Marshall said instantly. "There are two extra bedrooms, which should be plenty, if the kids don't mind doubling up."

"I can stay in a hotel."

"You think you'll find one that will take Sadie and the cat I just saw peeking out from under the couch?"

She had forgotten about the dog and Mrs. Finnegan. "I can try."

"Or you can just say, *thank you, Marshall,* pack a change of clothes for the kids and walk those three hundred feet to my place."

She didn't want to be alone with him.

That seemed a ludicrous thing to worry about in the middle of a crisis, but she couldn't help it. She had been doing her best to prevent their lives from becoming more intertwined. Where Marshall was concerned, she didn't appear to have an ounce of common sense and was a kiss or two from losing her head over the man.

What was the alternative? Eliza and Aidan would probably be happy to put them up at Snow Angel Cove and there would be plenty of room in the sprawling house, but Andie didn't feel right calling them.

She had other friends she could call, but the idea wasn't appealing. She was certain any of the Helping Hands would be willing, but, really, who wanted unexpected houseguests—pets included—a few days before Christmas?

318

She was still trying to figure out what to do when the children wandered in, Chloe leading with the flashlight and Sadie bringing up the rear.

"I'm cold, Mommy," Will complained.

"It was too dark in your room and the wind is scary. What if another tree blows onto the house?" Chloe said.

"It won't, honey," she assured her daughter, pulling them both close.

Her first—and only—priority was doing what was best for her children. They counted on her to keep them safe and she was all they had.

Marshall's house was familiar to them and close enough to their own place if they needed to run back and forth for things. Staying with him made the most sense—even if it was the option that left her the most uncomfortable.

"Fine. Thank you, Marshall. I appreciate your kindness. We'll stay at your house for now while we figure out how long it will take to get things straightened out here."

He gave a brief nod and she thought she saw relief in his features. "Good decision," he said.

"Very wise," Cade agreed. "Why don't you pack up what you might need for a few days and I'll pull my SUV over and drive you all to Marshall's place? That way you don't have to trudge up the street with your things."

She was once more indebted to Cade. Here he

was, coming to her rescue again, just as he had the night Rob Warren had come to Haven Point.

How grateful she was for good neighbors and friends who were willing to step up in the middle of a crisis, she thought as she started making mental lists of all the things the three of them—and Sadie and Mrs. Finnegan—might need for a few days.

When she had random moments of self-pity, of feeling her burdens and troubles were heavier than she could carry, she only had to remember she didn't carry them alone anymore. She had a support network here in Haven Point, one she cherished more every day.

Hosting three unexpected houseguests—not to mention a shy cat and one friendly little mop of a dog—turned out to be less of a burden than Marshall might have expected.

By the time Cade helped Andie and her children load a couple of suitcases into his SUV, then drove the lot of them back to Marsh's house, the children were wrung out from the early-morning adventure and more than ready to climb into bed.

Andie settled them into the larger of the guest rooms, then made her excuses and quickly took her pets and the rest of their belongings into the other guest room. Marsh did his best to help, ignoring her protests that she could do it herself and carrying in a few of the lighter bags.

She needed to rest—he could see it in the shadows under her eyes, the pallor of her skin. She looked thin-boned and fragile, as if that December wind out there would blow her all the way to Shelter Springs.

He didn't expect to sleep—it had been his inability to get there that had led to him gazing out the window at 2:00 a.m. in time to see her tree fall—but the moment he made his painstaking way to his own bed and crashed, he fell asleep in an instant.

He awoke with weak winter sun trying feebly to push itself through the window and the unmistakable morning smells of fresh coffee and sizzling bacon.

And pain, of course. Since his bout with the SUV, it had become his constant, unfailing companion. First thing in the morning and just before bed seemed to be the worst, and he'd figured out if he could ride those moments out, he could usually manage the rest of the day.

By the time he finished the delightful process of trying to shower without being able to stand on both legs—and then the ordeal of trying to shave, comb his hair and dress himself—he was almost ready to go back to bed.

He needed to at least go say hi to his guests, he decided, and hobbled out of his bedroom and down the hall.

As he approached the kitchen, he heard Andie laughing at something one of the kids said. He spotted her standing by the sink, her lovely features alive with happiness and humor. His chest ached a little and he wanted to stand there all morning and just drink in the sight that seemed so warm and perfect for a snowy winter's morning.

"Hi, Sheriff Marshall," Will said, spotting him first. "We ate your bacon and some eggs. I hope that's okay. I didn't think we should, but we were hungry and my mom said she would pay you back."

"I will," Andie assured him. Though she was smiling as she said it, he thought she looked a little embarrassed. He was embarrassed, too—and more than a little shocked—by his urge to hobble across the kitchen and kiss away that blush, right in front of her kids.

"You're welcome to anything you find. Please. Help yourself."

"Don't worry. We didn't eat it all. We saved some for you," Chloe assured him.

"Good. I'm starving."

"Sit down," Andie urged. "I've got another batch of bacon just about ready, along with some scrambled eggs and toast."

His stomach rumbled. He hadn't been hungry the night before at dinnertime and had contented himself with a yogurt and a banana. Right now, bacon and eggs sounded fantastic.

"You really don't have to wait on me, you know. I can get it."

"Sit," she ordered with a stern look.

He decided not to point out it was *his* kitchen. Well, his sister's, anyway. Only a fool would argue with a woman who wanted to feed him. Instead, he made his way to the table and sat across from Chloe. Instantly, Andie poured him coffee and set it down in front of him and Sadie scampered over to sit beside him.

How odd, that they all seemed to fit right in here.

"Aren't you supposed to be in school?" he asked Chloe after his first restorative sip.

"Snow day," she said, beaming in clear delight. "It's my first one *ever!*"

"Count yourself lucky. Schools don't close on account of weather all that often around here."

It felt wrong to just be sitting here. In serious weather, he was usually right out in the middle of the mess, directing traffic, investigating accidents, helping the utility companies restore power and gas if necessary, doing welfare checks on older people who couldn't get around.

He would check in with dispatch as soon as he ate so he could see if there was anything he could do to help.

A moment later, Andie slid a plate piled high with food in front of him.

"Wow. This looks delicious. Thanks."

She sat across from him. "You're going to need your strength to put up with us today, especially since we won't be able to go anywhere."

A few days earlier, the thought of being stuck in his house with a woman and a couple of kids would have had him wanting to chew off his own cast to escape.

Now it seemed infinitely appealing. The quiet domesticity, the giggling children, the dog under the table, eager for scraps.

The lovely woman sitting across from him, smelling like summer flowers and heaven.

He wanted all of it—which scared the hell out of him.

"Is something wrong with the eggs?"

"No. Why?"

"You're frowning at them like they're contraband. Do you want ketchup or salsa or something on them?"

"No. They're fine. Delicious, actually. Thanks."

He attacked the rest of the breakfast with vigor, mostly to keep from thinking about how empty the kitchen would feel when they were gone again. He was finishing his last bit of perfectly cooked bacon when the doorbell rang.

"I'll get it!" Will sang out, jumping down from his chair and racing from the room before his mother could stop him.

Andie shook her head. "Sorry! I guess we need to have a talk about not running to answer the door in someone else's house."

"Don't worry about it."

"It's Wynona and the police," Will announced, just a moment before Cade walked in, accompanied by, shock of shocks, Wynona.

"Wyn!" Andie exclaimed. She jumped up and hugged her friend as if they hadn't seen each other in years.

"I leave town for a few months and what happens? My brother breaks his leg and my dear friend and her kids end up on the streets. Maybe I better reconsider spring semester! Who knows what might happen next?"

His sister turned her attention to him next, giving his leg a fierce once-over, then reaching in and hugging him. "Hey, Marsh. I hear you saved the day when their tree fell down."

"I didn't do much. Just called Cade and he did all the legwork. What are you doing here? How'd you get here? Don't you know we just had a blizzard?"

"I finished my last final yesterday and decided I couldn't wait until the roads were clear to come home, so I caught a ride with a friend of mine who drives a plow through the canyon."

Impulsive and focused. That was Wynona. She wanted something, so she went after it, however she could figure it out.

He turned to his friend. "Anything new on the situation at Andie's place?"

"The power won't be back on until tomorrow afternoon, I'm afraid, and that's with crews working around the clock. With that wind and sleet, we've got over five hundred people in Haven Point alone without power, including two entire downtown blocks."

"Oh no!" Andie exclaimed. "What terrible timing, the last few shopping days before Christmas."

"Apparently the representative from the power company told McKenzie that fixing the outages that impact multiple families is the first priority, then downtown businesses. You're a ways down on the list, I'm afraid."

"I understand. Thank you for letting me know."

"I also talked to your landlord. Gerald said he would have a crew out later today to work on cutting the tree that fell, so you can at least get your car out."

"But even so, we can't go back home without power and heat."

"Does that mean we get to stay with Sheriff Marshall another day?" Will asked.

"You can stay as long as you need to," he promised. "Even if it's after Christmas before your house gets fixed, you're welcome here."

"Thanks! It would be *cold* if we really had to sleep in the streets."

Will grinned and gave one of those quick, impulsive hugs Marshall had figured out were the kid's specialty, the ones that never failed to make him smile.

When Will climbed down, Marshall happened to catch his sister's gaze and found Wyn watching them with a baffled look.

What? Hadn't she ever seen him interact with kids before?

"I still hate to put you to so much trouble," Andie fretted. "I'm sure I could find a hotel room in Shelter Springs. You need to focus your attention on healing, not on entertaining a houseful of guests and pets."

"Yes, it's a real hardship, being forced to endure having someone around to put on a fresh pot of coffee and make me breakfast."

He smiled at Chloe's infectious giggle.

"Let's not argue about this again, okay? You're more than welcome to stay here. I insist on it. It's the most convenient option and this way I don't have to worry about you being on the snowy roads between here and Shelter Springs."

He almost wished they indeed could stay through the holidays.

Okay, where did *that* come from? He was supposed to be keeping her at a distance, not finding more excuses to spend more time with the Montgomerys. He shouldn't be imagining Christmas Eve around the fire with the kids in their pajamas, reading holiday stories and eating cookies and bouncing off the walls with excitement.

"Hey, since I had to ditch my car at the road department lot to catch a ride with the plow, I'm in need of wheels for a couple days," Wyn said. "Can I borrow your truck, since you're not using it?"

Wyn could outdrive most of his deputies, as she'd proved at the last high-speed chase training, when she was still Cade's number one officer. She was an excellent driver and he could see no reason to refuse.

"The keys are hanging by the front door." He paused for just a beat and had to add, "Just don't scratch it."

She finished the rest of the refrain along with him. "Or bring it home with an empty gas tank," they both said in unison, and Wyn laughed.

It was one of John Bailey's familiar refrains, one he repeated to all of his children each time they took out one of his vehicles.

He felt a deep pang for his father, missing the guidance he had always provided. Maybe if John were here, Marshall wouldn't be making such a mess of things with his *own* son.

"Andie, why don't you come help me, to make sure I get the right keys?"

She looked surprised but rose to follow Wyn out of the kitchen.

Were they talking about him? Or did that particular assumption only make him narcissistic?

He wasn't sure. He only knew he suddenly didn't know if he liked the idea that his sister was close friends with his . . . Andie.

Not his anything, he reminded himself. She wasn't his fake girlfriend or his real one. Just a neighbor who needed help. He might not be able to find himself out on the front lines of the storm, but he could offer safe shelter for a woman and her children who needed it.

Chapter NINETEEN

"What have you been feeding my brother?"

The question didn't exactly sound like an accusation from her friend, but Andie wasn't quite sure. "Um. This morning, bacon, eggs and toast," she said warily. "I made him beef stew last week. And Louise Jacobs sent over some homemade shortbread he seemed to enjoy."

"I'm sure he did. Marsh has always had a soft spot for cookies or sweets of any variety."

"That is an understatement."

Andie wasn't sure she liked the way Wyn studied her. Marsh's sister had been a very good police officer. She had a great deal of experience interrogating people, persuading them to reveal things they had no intention of doing when they first sat down with her.

"I'm stunned. I hurried back to town at the earliest opportunity because I figured he was well on his way to going stir-crazy—and taking everybody else along with him. Marsh hardly ever sits still. When he's not on the job—which is most of the time—he's working out or helping my mom with something at the house or enjoying the backcountry by hiking or mountaineering."

She could easily picture him scaling some of the local high mountain ranges, looking tanned and fit and much more relaxed than he had since his injury.

"He's also the most serious of my brothers and the least tolerant of his own human weaknesses," Wyn went on. "I'm sure this whole thing is his worst nightmare—not just because they haven't yet found the idiot who hit him but because Marsh finds purpose and meaning in his life through his work. He's like my dad that way. It's got to be killing him—not being able to meet what he considers his sacred responsibilities because of something as inconvenient as a compound fracture."

How was it possible that she could admire him so much for that dedication to duty while still finding it an insurmountable obstacle to any relationship between them? "He hasn't just been sitting around. I took him into the office last week for a briefing and he's been going through cold cases. I heard him tell a woman who works with him that he wants to go back to work this week, but maybe the storm and the holidays will complicate that."

"I doubt it. I'm astonished he didn't go back the day he was released from the hospital."

She smiled. "I'm quite sure he wanted to. He just couldn't get a ride."

Wyn squeezed her arm. "I can't thank you enough for helping him."

It seemed a lifetime ago that she had stood on his doorstep, wishing she didn't have to go inside and face the man who made her so nervous.

The same man who had hobbled through deep snow with a broken leg to make sure she and her children were safe the night before.

"I'm really glad you asked me," she said truthfully. As long as she could keep her heart from being broken, she would never be sorry she had been able to help him through a difficult time and in the process had come to know him better.

"Cade told me I should never have asked you."

"Why?" she asked, hurt and confused. As her friendship with Wyn had deepened over the summer, Andie and Cade had subsequently become good friends, as well. She'd had the two of them over for dinner several times, they exchanged vegetables from their respective gardens, and she and the kids had carved a pumpkin for Cade at Halloween.

"He said it was unfair of me. He said you would feel obligated to do whatever I asked, even if you didn't want to, because of what happened last summer. I believe he called it subtle emotional coercion."

Marshall called it emotional blackmail. Cade's version sounded only slightly better.

"Maybe he's the one who should be taking all the psychology classes."

"No. He's just an expert at people. Unfortunately, I think he's right on this one. I should have found someone else. Megan or Samantha or Julia

Winston. Someone else who would have felt free to tell me no."

Andie must really have it bad. Why else would she feel so territorial and find it completely abhorrent to think of any of her other friends stepping up to help Marshall after his accident?

"I'm glad you asked me," she said again. "And anyway, I really haven't done much. A few meals, a little grocery shopping, running him to Shelter Springs that day. That's about it."

"That's not what I heard. Mom said you've been taking great care of him."

Andie froze, her face suddenly hot. Rats. What had Charlene told her daughter? Did *Wyn* think she and Marshall were romantically involved, too?

What was she supposed to say? She didn't want to lie to her friend, but she couldn't leave her with any misconceptions.

"You should know, Marsh might have, um, misled your mother about the two of us."

"How so?" Wyn asked, her features deceptively innocent.

"We're not, um, you know. Seeing each other. He just gave her that impression so she would focus on that instead of stepping in to smother him."

Again, Wyn studied her like a sharp-eyed investigator. "Are you sure?"

She fiercely wished she could control her coloring. "I think I would know if I were dating your brother," she said tartly. "We're friends. That's all."

"Too bad," Wyn said. "Don't get me wrong— that was freaking brilliant of him to throw Charlene a distraction like that. I just think the two of you would be great together."

She had to wonder if Wynona had been talking to Eliza and Megan. Did all her friends think she needed matchmaking help like Marshall needed someone to drive him around?

"We're friends. That's all," she repeated.

Wynona didn't look convinced. "If you say so. I do think it's interesting that I hurried back to Haven Point expecting to find Marshall miserable, in pain and driving everyone crazy. Instead, he looks relaxed, well fed and happier than I've seen him in a long time."

"Maybe he just needed a break from being sheriff for a few days."

"Or maybe he looks happy because he *is* happy. My brother has spent entirely too much of his life and his energy focused on being in law enforcement. He needs to remember his life doesn't begin and end with the badge. Whether there's anything romantic between you two or not, I think you and your adorable kids have helped remind him of that. So thank you. Now I owe *you* a favor."

Before she could protest, Cade came in search of Wyn.

"I've got to run. We've got more slide-offs and accidents than I've got guys to take care of."

"Be safe," Wyn said. "I'll see you when you're done."

"Counting on it." He wrapped his arms around her and she kissed him fiercely.

The two of them were so sweet together. It made Andie's heart happy to see the love they shared even as she tried to ignore the little niggle of envy.

Much to Andie's relief, her children were on their best behavior throughout the day. No bickering, no tantrums, no claims of "I'm bored."

She didn't give them a chance to misbehave, really. They cleaned his house from top to bottom, went out several times to help Christopher shovel snow that started again and fell steadily throughout the rest of the day, and even helped Christopher build a huge, fat-bottomed snowman while Sadie scampered around up to her belly in snow and Marshall watched from the porch.

When they were cold and wet, they went back inside and she put them to work helping her bake the cupcakes Will needed for his party the next day, then Christmas cookies to take around to the neighbors.

Her strategy seemed to be paying off. Over the late dinner—a perennial favorite pasta bake casserole the children had helped her throw together—Chloe was in the middle of telling a patient Marshall a story about playing reindeer tag at recess the week before when she suddenly gave a huge, jaw-popping yawn.

"Wow," Marshall said with an admiring look. "That was impressive."

Will giggled, but the sweet ripple of sound ended abruptly in a yawn that just might have been bigger than his sister's.

"Must be bedtime," Marshall said.

"I'm not tired *at all,*" Chloe insisted.

"Neither am I," Will said.

"That's weird," Marshall said. "Because I'm totally *exhausted.*"

Hearing his hero admit to it was apparently enough for Will to concede the same. "Okay, I might be a *little* tired."

"I'm not," Chloe said. "It's not even eight yet."

Her daughter was firmly convinced that going to sleep before her bedtime would violate some grand cosmic law.

Chloe was still learning how to tell time on a clock with hands, so she always went by the digital clock on the stove. On particularly long days, when parenting two children by herself seemed singularly exhausting, Andrea may or may not have been guilty of adjusting that digital readout ahead by fifteen minutes.

"Let's clean up the kitchen and then take your baths. By the time we're out, it will be eight." Or close enough, anyway.

"I'll take care of the kitchen," Marshall said. "You worry about the baths."

She wanted to tell him she could clean it when she was done putting the children to bed, but his firm expression convinced her it would be useless to argue.

"Thank you. Come on, kids."

They didn't argue, either too exhausted from their chaotic night and a day packed with activity or simply intrigued at the novelty of bathing in the old claw-foot tub in the guest bathroom.

The children wanted to linger in their respective baths. Finally they were both clean, dried and dressed in clean pajamas.

This was her favorite part of being a mother, when she knew they'd had a good day filled with discoveries and they were now sleepy, sweet-smelling and cuddly.

"Where's our book?" Will asked. "Did you bring it?"

"Yes. It's by the bed in the room I'm using. I packed it last night."

She loved children's books and collected holiday stories all year long. For the past few days, they'd been reading *The Best Christmas Pageant Ever*, about the wild Herdman kids and the lessons they learned about giving.

"Do you think Marshall will read to us?"

At some point that day, Will had dropped calling him Sheriff Bailey or Sheriff Marshall. Now he was just plain Marshall.

"I don't know," she said, not sure how she felt about giving up the sweet, quiet bonding time she considered her payoff for all the hard work of the day. "I'm sure we've bothered him enough for today. We should probably give the guy a break."

"I'm gonna ask him anyway," Will said.

Before she could call him back, he padded into the family room in his superhero pajamas. She could hear Will's high-pitched voice and then a lower one in reply, and a moment later, her son hurried back.

"He said he would," he announced gleefully.

"Yay!" Chloe exclaimed. She was out the door almost before Andie finished brushing out the tangles in her hair.

Feeling a little let down, Andie cleaned up after them in the bathroom, wondering as she frequently did how it was possible for two small children to make such a mess and spill half the bathwater. When she was satisfied Marshall could safely maneuver in here on his crutches if he needed to, she followed the sound of his voice to the den.

She paused out of his view to listen. He had a beautiful, deep reading voice and inserted the perfect amount of inflection and dramatic pauses. He even changed his voice a little higher to read dialogue bits spoken by the younger children in the story.

As Andie listened, a soft, tender warmth soaked through her.

He was so good with them. She had thought him so brusque at first. Harsh and austere, even. How could she ever have guessed he would be sweet and patient and loving? He was inordinately kind to them, even though she assumed it couldn't be comfortable for him to hold Will on his lap like that or have Chloe squeezed in next to him on the recliner, leaning on his arm so he could barely turn the page.

They needed a male figure in their life. It hurt her heart that her children didn't have a grand-father or an uncle to help Will become a good, decent man and Chloe to know what things to look for in one.

Marshall could show them that. He was exactly the sort of man she would like her son to emulate and her daughter to someday seek for herself—full of strength and determination, yet also kind-ness and compassion.

She was falling in love with him.

The realization didn't tumble over her like a clump of snow falling from a tree branch so much as it whispered in an insistent voice she couldn't ignore.

She drew in a sharp breath. Oh. This would never do.

She *couldn't* fall for him. The implications were as disastrous as they were inevitable.

She had made a terrible mistake, letting him so far into their lives. When their paths diverged, Chloe and Will would see it as another blow, the loss of yet another important male in their world.

Anything more than friendship between them was completely impossible—and she suddenly wasn't sure she was strong enough even for that.

How could she hover on the outskirts of his life, content to see him only once in a while at some barbecue at Wyn and Cade's house, when she wanted so much more?

Regardless of how much her children might be coming to care about him and regardless of her own growing feelings, it was completely impossible.

He was a dedicated lawman. It was as much a part of him as his skin, his bones, his heart. She had lost one man she loved because of his dedication to the job—because he had tried to save someone else, instead of thinking of the family waiting for him at home. She couldn't put herself in that precarious position again and she refused to do it to Chloe and Will.

For her own sake and for her children's, she needed to do her best to return their relationship to the semi-cordial but distant one of the first few days after his injury.

How was she supposed to do that when they were living in his house for now?

She sighed quietly, but it was loud enough that Sadie, stretched out beside his chair, lifted her head to look at her. This in turn caught Marshall's attention just as he read the last page.

"What am I doing wrong?" he asked.

Besides breaking my heart? "Nothing," she answered. "Why would you ask?"

"You were frowning," he said. "It's been a while since I've read aloud to kids and I thought maybe I was going too fast or too slow."

She scrambled to think up a convincing excuse. "No. Sorry. I was thinking what a pain this must be for you, having your space suddenly invaded by us while you're still trying to heal."

"Yeah. I'm doing my best to endure it."

She didn't miss his dry tone or the affectionate look he gave her children, which wasn't helping at all.

"Story's done now. Time for bed, you two."

"Do we have to?" Will said, a telltale sleepy whine in his voice.

"Yes. You and Chloe both have school tomorrow."

"Unless we have another snow day," Chloe said hopefully.

"I wouldn't count on it," Marshall told her. "The snow stopped a few hours ago and I think we're done with it for a while, which means the plows will have plenty of time through the night to clear the roads for the buses."

They groaned in unison as they slid down,

341

both careful not to bump his outstretched cast.

"What are you complaining about? You've both got Christmas parties tomorrow that you don't want to miss, remember? But if you want to have fun tomorrow, you need to sleep tonight."

That cheered them both up enough that they brushed their teeth without further complaint. After going through the regular routine of prayers and kisses and tucking them in, she headed for the kitchen to return the nearly full glass of water Will had insisted he couldn't sleep without—then had handed back to her after taking only two swallows.

She stopped short when she realized Marshall stood by the sink. He turned when he heard her and her heart pounded. He looked big and tough and gorgeous and she felt like a stupid, silly girl who had forgotten how to talk to a boy.

They were alone, she suddenly realized. The children were in bed and would probably sleep soundly through the night. The smartest thing to do right now would be to take care of the task that had brought her in here, then escape to her bedroom, close the door and hide out where she was safe until morning.

"I, um, just need to add this to the dishwasher," she said.

He moved out of the way and she opened the door and found a spot for the glass on the top rack, then closed it again.

She was intensely aware of him—the hint of evening shadow on his face, the way his hair was a little messed in the back, the woodsy scent of his soap.

She forced a smile, doing her best to ignore the impact all that had on her resolve.

"Thanks for reading to Will and Chloe. They really seemed to enjoy it."

"So did I," he answered. "It was a great story."

"It's one of my favorites," she said. "Will is probably still a little young for it, but I read it last year to Chloe and she loved it."

He gave that rare smile that never failed to make butterflies jump in her stomach.

She firmly ignored them. "I should let Sadie out one more time, and then she and I will try to get out of your way for the evening."

"You don't have to do that," he said. "You're not in my way, I mean."

He was in *her* way—so much that she didn't know how she was ever going to dislodge him.

"We've invaded your space enough for the day," she said after she opened the door for the dog to trot outside. "I'm sure you're ready for a break from the noisy Montgomerys."

He gazed down at her, his eyes gleaming with an emotion she couldn't immediately identify. "What if I'm not?" he murmured.

She caught her breath as the refrigerator compressor hummed on and everything inside her hummed to life, too.

His question seemed to hover between them, arcing and crackling like her downed power line, and she couldn't help thinking how easy it would be to step forward, to press her mouth to his, to spend the rest of the cold December night in his arms.

And wouldn't that be a disaster of epic proportion?

She released her breath and decided her only hope of protecting herself was brutal honesty. "I don't believe it's a good idea for me to spend time alone with you."

"Why not?" he demanded. His surprised expression intensified. She couldn't tell if he was shocked, outraged or hurt—or some combination of all three. "You're not afraid of me, are you? I hope you know I would never hurt you."

For a moment, she didn't know how he could possibly say that. Of course he would hurt her. Maybe he wouldn't do it intentionally, but she would be left emotionally bruised anyway when she walked away.

An instant later, she realized he was referring to more than her inevitable heartache.

He was thinking of what Rob Warren had done to her.

She couldn't even think of the two men at the same time, they were so very different.

"No," she whispered. "I could never be afraid of you, Marshall. Not like that."

"Are you sure? Right now, your eyes tell a different story."

Brutal honesty. She didn't know how else to move forward. She couldn't let him think she could ever put him in the same category as vermin like Rob.

"I'm afraid of myself," she admitted.

Though his expression was baffled, he studied her with the same sort of probing look she had received from his sister earlier in the day. "What does that mean?"

She swallowed, wishing she had just left the glass of water in the children's room and avoided this whole encounter.

"I don't know if you've noticed this, but when we're alone together, we have a little habit of, um, kissing."

Instantly, that current sizzled again between them, wild and dangerous.

"I believe I have noticed that," he drawled, his voice low. His gaze dipped to her mouth and her insides ached with the overwhelming need to throw up her hands already and just kiss him.

"We both know that's not the smartest thing we could do. I just . . . thought it would be better to avoid temptation altogether."

"Temptation. You find me . . . tempting."

Beyond words. Like he had been dipped in the very best Belgian chocolate and she couldn't wait to lick it away.

"Yes," she said softly. "I shouldn't, but I do."

His expression arrested, he nodded. "That's fair, I guess. Because I've spent all day trying not to think about kissing you again and tasting that soft mouth of yours and hearing your sexy little sighs. Ever try to not think about something? Yeah. It ends up being the only thing rattling around in your head."

She hitched in a breath at the hunger in his eyes and she felt like she was going to burn away to cinders right here in his kitchen. She opened her mouth to respond, but now it was the only thought in her head, too.

She swallowed and licked at lips that suddenly felt swollen and achy. He made a strangled sound and moved forward.

"I want to kiss you right now, Andie. I think you want it, too, but I won't do it if you tell me no, I swear. I'll turn around and hobble out of here."

No. It was one of the first words her kids ever learned, but sometimes it was the hardest possible word to say. "I . . ." she began, *don't want you to kiss me.*

She couldn't say the rest because both of them would know it was a lie.

"Was that a no?" he asked, watching her intently.

She couldn't do it. One kiss. Surely she was strong enough for one kiss. Like him, she had thought about it all day, since that morning when he had first come out of his room with his hair damp from the shower.

He wouldn't kiss her until she made a move. Somehow she knew it with firm assurance. She shook her head and stepped forward and kissed him before she could give herself a chance to come to her senses.

Instantly, she knew it was a dire mistake. The other times they kissed had been tiny, gentle little snowflakes compared to the wild, frenzied storm that churned and sparked between them.

It was raw and intense, heat and hunger and need, and she wanted the kiss to go on and on and on. She forgot about the real storm outside, her damaged house, all the reasons she shouldn't be doing this.

The only thing that mattered right now was this man she was coming to care for entirely too much.

"You know, I would really love to kiss you somewhere besides my kitchen," he murmured long moments later. Andie closed her eyes, her imagination going crazy.

"And," he added, pressing another kiss to the edge of her mouth, "I would really love to do it sometime when I'm not on these damn crutches."

They could go into his bedroom. He could lie back and she would do all the work. Tease him and touch him and explore all those muscles.

She came within a heartbeat of throwing every last shred of caution into that whirlwind.

Fortunately, her dog saved her. Sadie whined outside the door, shredding the hazy, impossible dreams she had begun to weave.

No. She couldn't do this. She stepped away from him feeling shaky and weak.

"See what I'm talking about? I don't have much self-control when it comes to you and it's obvious neither of us has very good judgment when we're alone."

"We kissed. It's not the end of the world."

He was right, but she didn't know how to tell him why she couldn't afford to keep tormenting herself like this, discovering the possibilities between them when she knew it could never be anything more.

Again, she wished she had just slipped into her room the moment the kids were in bed so she could have avoided him completely. She really didn't want to bare her soul to him, but right now she didn't see any other option.

"I'm very attracted to you, Marshall. That's probably obvious the moment you touch me. I'm attracted to you and I . . . think I could care about you very easily. If I'm not careful, I could see myself doing something entirely self-destructive like falling in love with you."

He looked as stunned as if she'd just kicked his cast out from under him. "Self-destructive."

"What else would you call it? Stupid. Thoughtless. Masochistic. All of the above. You're the worst possible man in Haven Point for me!"

If she didn't know better, she might think he looked hurt.

"The worst. That's quite a generalization."

"That doesn't make it any less true." Her fingers were trembling and she tucked them into fists, hoping he didn't notice. "I've already loved one man in a uniform. I can't let myself do it again. I know my own strengths and weaknesses and the simple truth is that I'm not strong enough to let myself care for someone who insists on putting himself in harm's way."

He seemed carved in stone—except for his eyes, which blazed with heat and desire. "You're going to discount me and an entire segment of the male population because of an occupation?"

"It's more than an occupation. We both know that. I was married to a cop. I know it's a mind-set, part of who you are. You want to jump right in and save people, no matter the consequences. You feel like it's your job to watch over the whole world. That's the reason you hobbled down the street through the snow last night to make sure the children and I were all right."

"What's wrong with worrying about the people you . . . care about?"

"There's nothing wrong with it. It's admirable, Marshall. The world needs more people like you. I was incredibly touched that you would go to such lengths because you were worried about us and had to make certain yourself that we were okay."

This entire argument was moot. It was already far too late. She had already fallen for him and talking about it was only making her more aware that a vast chasm of pain waited for her.

"Don't make such a big deal out of that," he said gruffly. "Anybody would have done the same."

He looked embarrassed, uncomfortable and unsure of himself.

She sighed. "No. Not everyone. But you will, a hundred times over, whatever it takes. I respect that and admire it so much, but I can't let myself care for you."

"I guess that's clear enough," he said, his features remote and his tone stiff.

Again, she had the impression she had hurt him, though she couldn't imagine how that was possible. Oh, she hoped her house would be habitable early the next day so she didn't have to deal with this awkwardness much longer.

"I'm sorry."

"No need to apologize."

He said one thing, but she couldn't shake the feeling the truth was quite the opposite.

"Good night," she murmured. Her throat felt tight, achy, but she told herself that was a small price to pay for holding on to the last safe remnant of her heart.

Chapter TWENTY

After a restless, uneven sleep, he woke early the next morning, when the sun was just starting to think about rising above the mountains through the curtains he hadn't closed the night before.

As soon as he awoke, her words seemed to echo in his head all over again, as if she had programmed it into an alarm for him.

You're the worst possible man in Haven Point for me.

That was clear enough. A guy couldn't argue with a woman who could make that kind of definitive statement. *The worst.* Not just questionable or even bad. He was the worst. She had her mind made up and he was pretty damn sure he could say nothing that would change her mind.

Did he *want* to change her mind, even if he could?

He didn't know how to answer that and his restless sleep certainly hadn't provided any insight.

He was still trying to figure it out when he heard a vague sound from the kitchen, a little whimper.

Sadie, he realized. That must have been what awakened him. Somehow the dog must have slipped out of Andie's room and was now waiting by the door for someone to come and let her out.

No reason he couldn't help her so Andie could sleep a little longer.

He forced himself to push past the usual morning pain and pulled sweats on over his stupid brace before he rose from his bed and headed into the kitchen.

The little dog was practically dancing by the back door, desperate to go out.

He opened the door for her and she bulleted out to take care of business. He stood there watching the snow fall in big fat flakes. Up and down Riverbend Road, as people started making ready for the day, early birds with snowblowers and all-terrain vehicles with plows were busy clearing away driveways and sidewalks.

A moment later, his son walked around the side of the Jacobs home with a snow shovel in his hand.

You have to tell him.

He could almost hear the echo of Andie's voice in his head, though he hoped she was still tucked into her bed.

Unable to resist, he hobbled out onto the small covered porch off the kitchen.

The boy spotted the dog first, up to her belly in snow, and pulled out his earbuds.

"Sadie, what are you doing out here?" he asked.

The kid probably couldn't see him, since he was standing on a dark porch.

"Morning," Marshall called softly. "You're out early."

Christopher shrugged inside his big snowboarder coat. "No choice. Gram says I have to finish both driveways before the bus comes."

"You don't have to. I just won't pay you if you don't do the job."

"I'm here, aren't I?" Christopher said. He stuck the shovel in the soft powder and went to work.

Marshall couldn't bring himself to go inside, even after the little dog finished her thing and waddled up the steps to stand beside him.

"Dude, you need a snowblower," Christopher said when his path led him closer to the porch.

Yeah, probably. Before moving to Wyn's house on the river, he had lived in an apartment where snow removal was taken care of by the management company, so he'd never had reason to buy one.

Wyn might have one back in the shed, he just hadn't bothered to look.

"When do you get out of school for the holiday break again?"

"Today's the last day," Christopher's voice sounded muffled as he pushed the snow in the other direction. "Too bad yesterday wasn't."

"Yesterday was a snow day, probably the last one you'll see all winter."

"So I hear. You should know, tomorrow I'm sleeping in. If you want your snow shoveled before noon, you'll have to pay someone else to do it."

353

"I heard we're done with the snow for a few days. Until Christmas Eve, anyway."

Christopher didn't say anything, just continued clearing the driveway in back-and-forth horizontal stripes that sent him away from Marshall every other pass.

With no real incentive to go inside except the cold, which he found more bracing than uncomfortable, Marshall stayed where he was and watched.

After about five minutes, Christopher stopped in front of him. "Okay, what am I doing wrong?"

Marshall blinked at the unexpected attack. "Nothing. Did I *say* you were doing something wrong?"

"No, but you're just standing there like you think I don't know how to shovel a driveway."

He wanted to respond that there was nothing wrong with looking at the son whose life he hadn't been part of for all these years.

"You're not doing anything wrong. I really appreciate the job you're doing, especially since Andie and her kids are here for a couple of days. I know it hasn't been easy, but you've done good work and I'm grateful for it."

The boy studied him for a long moment, then shook his head. "You are one weird cop."

Yeah, didn't he know it?

"I just wanted to say thanks. That's all."

Christopher grunted in response, which Marshall

was going to assume meant *you're welcome.*

The dog was nudging at the door like she wanted to go inside now so she could find some breakfast, and Marsh figured if he stayed out here much longer watching his kid, he was going to be heading into that creepy stalker territory.

With a sigh, he turned around and reached for the door, but it jerked open before he could even turn the knob.

"There you are!" Andie exclaimed. "I've been looking *everywhere.*"

His heart gave a good, hard kick—until he realized she was looking down at the dog.

"Sadie, you rascal. Get in here."

She opened the door wider and stepped out of the way. When the two of them made their way inside, she finally looked at Marshall, her color rising. "Did she wake you? I thought I closed the bedroom door so she couldn't get out on her own, but it must not have been latched tightly. I hope she didn't make a nuisance of herself."

"She didn't. It was no big deal."

"I'm sorry I didn't hear her before you did. It's not safe for you to be out here. I'd hate for you to fall while taking care of my dog."

He had seen combat in Iraq and had averted multiple incidents since he'd been back that easily could have ended with the use of deadly force. Apparently now his biggest worry was slipping on ice.

"The driveway's almost clear. Christopher's taking care of it now before he leaves for school."

"Oh. That's good. He's done an excellent job so far, hasn't he?"

"Yeah. I just hope he can keep it up all winter."

Her gaze shifted to the window overlooking the driveway. She opened her mouth as if to speak but apparently changed her mind and closed it again.

"You might as well say it," he said, bracing himself.

"Say what?"

"You're obviously dying to tell me again how I need to tell him I'm his father."

"Am I?" She gave him a cool stare, worlds away from the soft, yielding woman who had trembled in his arms right here in the kitchen just a few hours earlier. "Why would I waste my breath when you've made it abundantly clear you disagree? It's fine. I get that my opinion doesn't really matter."

In that moment, all the thoughts that had been chasing themselves through his head all night combined into one overriding realization.

Her opinion *did* matter—more than anyone else's in his life.

She mattered.

His hands tightened around the handgrips of the crutches and he felt as if he had, indeed, slipped on the ice and landed hard enough to knock the wind out of him.

He was in love with Andie Montgomery. Her courage, her strength, her kindness. The unexpectedly sly sense of humor that jumped out at the oddest moments.

He had never felt like this about another woman, this urge to cherish her and protect her and spend the rest of his days keeping her happy.

Not just her, but her children. For the first time in his life, he wanted something else besides the job. He wanted a family, a future. Hikes into the mountains with them, taking the kids on fishing trips, summer evenings in the backyard playing catch with the river murmuring past. Christmas mornings and birthday presents and preschool graduations. He wanted all of it—with a woman who had told him in no uncertain terms that he was the worst possible man in Haven Point for her.

"What's wrong?" Andie asked.

Everything. His whole life had gone to hell from the moment he got hit by that damn SUV and his sister sent Andie to his house with hearty stew, delicious pie and that warm compassion that drew him like a fire in a blizzard.

Once, he thought he didn't need anyone else, that he could be perfectly content the rest of his life doing his job and helping the people of his community.

How big an idiot could one man possibly be?

"Marshall?"

"Nothing's wrong. I'm fine. Just not in the mood

for conversation this morning, I guess." He spoke brusquely to hide the chaos inside him and saw her eyes widen briefly with hurt.

"Good news for you, then." She produced a smile that didn't come close to looking genuine. "I had an email from my landlord first thing this morning. He said the repairs on the house should be finished by the end of the day, then we can all get out of your way and leave you alone with your own company."

The only problem was that he didn't want them out of his way and he could think of few things as miserable as his own company right now.

He wanted to spend Christmas with Chloe and Will, watching Christmas movies and playing games and eating cookies.

Instead, he faced a bleak, solitary holiday spent without their laughter and joy, staring at the walls of his sister's den while unable to even walk next door to wish his own son a merry Christmas.

The hell of it was, the rest of his life stretched out ahead of him, just as desolate.

"I'm sure that's a relief for you," he said.

"For all of us."

He was spared from having to come up with a response by the appearance of her children clamoring for breakfast.

The afternoon couldn't come soon enough for her, Andie thought as she and Will walked through the light but steady snow on their way back from walking Chloe to the bus stop later that morning.

She needed to get back to her comfort zone, away from the tension and awkwardness.

"I like it here. I want to stay with Marshall," Will announced when they were almost to the stone house with the green shutters that looked so charming and warm with its windows lit up against the wintry landscape.

"He's been very nice to let us stay with him, hasn't he?" she said. "But everything will be all fixed at our house this afternoon, so tonight we'll be sleeping in our own beds."

Will looked back at their house down the street with an uncharacteristic frown. "What if another tree falls on the house?" he asked, clear nervousness in his voice. "Chloe said we were almost squished."

She didn't want to think about it, nor did she want him being so nervous he couldn't sleep.

"That was a very strange accident. It's not going to happen again."

"How do you know? Our house has more trees around it. Maybe they will fall, too, and then we *will* be squished."

She stopped there in the snow and hugged her son. "How many nights have we already been sleeping in the house?"

"I don't know. A lot."

"Right. And no other trees have fallen while we

were there, have they? Marshall's house has many trees all around it and no trees have fallen the two nights we've been here. It happened once and it was scary for me, too, honey. But we can't spend the rest of our lives worrying and waiting for the worst to happen again."

Her words struck a strange chord in her mind, but she didn't have time to puzzle out why.

"Why can't we just cut down all the trees at our house?" Will demanded. "Then it would never happen again."

"Yes. But if we cut down all the trees, think of everything we would miss. Trees are wonderful. We need them. They give us shade overhead in the summer and leaves to pile up and jump into in the fall. You wouldn't have a place to climb or that tire swing in the back you and Chloe both love. They clean the air and give a home for birds and insects. The world would be a pretty sad place without them, wouldn't it?"

He appeared to consider that, studying the big pine trees outside Marshall's house. "I guess. I just wish they didn't have to fall down some-times."

"The great thing about trees is that when one falls down, you can plant another one. It won't be exactly the same and it will take time to grow, but if you pick carefully and take care of it, it can even be stronger and healthier than the one that fell."

The echo of her own words seemed to resonate deep into her heart, so deeply she hardly felt the chill of the snowflakes falling on her cheeks.

She was talking to Will about a tree, but it could easily be a metaphor for her life right now.

Like her son, she was terrified about the possibility of another tree crashing through the safe, secure life she had finally started rebuilding.

Jason's death had nearly destroyed her. For the last two years, she had spent all her time and effort to make a safe, comfortable life for herself and her children—with a few delays and complications along the way.

To keep herself safe, she was making the same apocalyptic choice Will suggested—cutting down any tree that might threaten that security before it had a chance to grow, all on the random chance that someday the winds might come again. Her deepest fear, she realized, was that this time she would be left with nothing but splinters and no way to hammer them back together.

She was so terrified of letting herself love Marshall that she wanted to ruthlessly take a chain saw to any sapling of emotion that might be growing between them.

If she continued to do that, yes, she might be safe. Blessedly secure.

But she would also miss out on new leaves in the springtime, a shady spot to rest in the summer. Birds' nests and tire swings and tree houses.

Joy.

The great thing about trees is that when one falls down, you can plant another one. It won't be exactly the same and it will take time to grow, but if you pick carefully and take care of it, it can even be stronger and healthier than the one that fell.

Did she have the strength to take the risk? To wield a watering can instead of a chain saw and let the feelings she already had for Marshall take root and grow?

She wasn't sure.

"Can we go in? My feet are cold," Will announced, just as impatient as he was that first day she had stood at this doorstep, afraid to walk inside and face Wyn's grouchy injured bear of a brother.

Only this time the injured bear was *hers* and she was afraid to face him for entirely different reasons.

She forced herself to set aside her turmoil to focus on her son for now. "Yes. Of course."

They didn't see Marshall when they went inside and Andie assumed he must be in the den again or his nearby bedroom.

As she had a work project to finish before the holidays, she and Will retreated to her bedroom. She was lucky he could entertain himself so well and was content to color or play with Sadie and the few toys he had brought along from their house, but after about an hour, his four-year-old patience wore out.

"I need a drink of water," he announced.

She looked up, her eyes a little unfocused from staring at the computer screen. "Okay. But I don't want you bothering Marshall."

"I won't," he promised and left the room with Sadie at his heels.

A moment later, though, she heard the deep notes of Marshall's voice followed by the higher ones of her son's through the doorway Will had left open.

She wasn't ready to talk to him yet, but she also didn't want Will to pester him if he was busy. Needing a break anyway, she rose from the small desk in the guest room and headed for the kitchen.

She found both males leaning against the cabinet in almost identical poses—though Marshall was on crutches. They both held glasses of water and one of the sugar cookies she and the children had made the previous afternoon and they both wore the same guilty expression at being caught eating them when she walked in.

She tried to quash the little burst of tenderness but didn't completely succeed. "We were trying to stay out of your way, as I assumed you would be working."

"No need," he said. "I was working, but I'm kind of at an impasse right now. I was just asking Will if he wanted to watch a movie. Wyn has a whole collection of Christmas movies, just about every one ever made."

She thought of the work she still needed to finish and her own limited options for entertaining her son.

"Sounds like fun."

"You can watch, too, if you want," Will said.

"That sounds really nice. Heavenly, actually. But I've got a few more phone calls to make and need to finish my project."

"You go," Marshall said. "Meantime, we'll be busy watching *The Grinch*."

"I love Max in that show," her son informed him. "That dog is almost as cute as Sadie."

"Almost," Marshall agreed.

"Can Sadie watch with us? She likes Max, too."

"Don't know why not," he said.

The two of them headed into the den, talking about Whos and roast beast and looking completely adorable together, and she, with regret, returned to her work.

Sometime later, she looked up from her computer and realized more than an hour had passed since they started the movie. Where did the time go when she was working?

She stood and stretched, rotating her neck and shoulders, then decided it would probably be a good idea to see if Marshall needed rescuing from a boy and a dog.

When she walked into the den, she first spotted

the cheerful Christmas tree Chloe and Will had decorated, with its humble mix of hand-cut snowflakes and paper chain garland. Snowflakes fluttered down outside, creating a picture pretty enough to use on a website.

"How's the—" *movie,* she started to say but cut her words off when she spotted the two of them.

Marshall was sound asleep in the easy chair, his head back and his mouth open a little. Will was asleep tucked in next to him, his cheek resting on Marshall's arm. Even Sadie was in on the napping action, curled up on the floor next to both of them.

For a moment, all she could do was stand and stare at them as her emotions bubbled over.

Tree houses and tire swings and birds' nests.

Could she find the courage to embrace all the possibilities? The risks, yes, but also the immeasurable rewards?

His eyes fluttered open, and for a brief second, they were unguarded, vulnerable—and filled with a tenderness that made her catch her breath. Too soon, he blinked and seemed to awaken more fully.

"Some babysitter I am," he said, his voice low. "I can't believe I'm sleeping on the job."

"Are you kidding?" she whispered back, her voice a little ragged as she tried to gather her jumble of emotions. "I can't believe you actually got Willie to take a nap. He always has such a better day when he does, but he's been claiming since he could string full sentences together that big boys don't take naps."

"Apparently some of us do," Marshall said. He cleared his throat. At the sound, Will woke up and looked around in confusion. His gaze landed on the big television, still running.

"I missed the movie!" he exclaimed, his lower lip quivering.

"We'll catch it another time, pal," Marshall promised.

"No, we won't," he whined. When he *did* nap, Will invariably woke up cranky, unfortunately. "My mom says we're going back to our house today."

"But, honey, we have this movie at our house. You can watch the end again there," she soothed.

"I don't want to watch it there. I want to watch it with Marshall."

He was gearing up for a full-fledged tantrum and she needed to head it off before it began.

Marshall beat her to the punch. "Tell you what," he said. "We can still watch it. You come back here after your Christmas party this afternoon and we'll try to figure out where we both fell asleep and watch until the end. Does that work?"

"I guess," he said, drawing that pouty lower lip in a few millimeters.

"Maybe we can even have popcorn," Marshall said.

That did the trick. "I *love* popcorn," he said, getting more animated.

"Who doesn't?" Marshall said.

"Speaking of parties," Andie said, "we need to get moving if we're going to make it on time. Go find your shoes and coat."

He started to slide down, careful of Marshall's leg, but paused for a moment to throw his arms around him. "Bye," he said, then hit the floor and took off, his postnap cranky mood entirely gone now in the excitement of being almost five and heading to a Christmas party with his friends.

She watched him go, now with Sadie at his heels again, before she turned back to Marshall.

"Thanks again for keeping him entertained," she said. "I was able to finish my project and clear my slate for the holidays."

"I'm glad."

"I have a few errands to run this afternoon. I'll do those while Will is at the party and be back here before Chloe gets home."

"Sounds good."

"Do you mind if Sadie and Mrs. Finnegan stay with you?"

"No. Why would I mind? I hardly see the cat and Sadie is pretty good company."

"I'll put her out now so you won't have to do it while I'm gone."

The tension again shivered between them. She wanted to say something else, but Will came back in, chattering about his boots and his friend Ty and the games they would play at the party, and the moment was gone.

The house seemed empty without any of the Montgomerys—except the cheerful little dog and the shy cat, anyway.

Marshall couldn't seem to settle. He moved from the sofa to the recliner to a chair at the kitchen table. He even tried stretching out on his bed but couldn't get comfortable anywhere.

The cute little fur ball seemed to pick up on his restlessness. When he finally headed back to the kitchen to take some ibuprofen, she went to the back door and circled around a few times.

"Need to go out again?" he said, and she yipped in response.

He opened the door for her and stood for a minute enjoying the cold air and the stellar view of the vast mountains.

The day had been full of surprising pleasures. He never would have imagined the quiet, sweet joy he'd felt when Will had insisted on sitting next to him to watch the movie.

He was going to miss both the boy and his sister like crazy when they went home later that day He wasn't sure why, but they both seemed to like him. That morning before school, Chloe had rushed in to tell him goodbye, and she had hugged him, too, as well as kissed his cheek, then giggled at the stubble he hadn't shaved away yet, which had just about stolen his heart.

For most of his life, he had convinced himself he wasn't good with kids. Wyn and Wyatt—and Kat, for that matter—had been such wild little creatures, always in and out of trouble, and whenever he tended them for his mom, it seemed like one or the other ended up crying and making him crazy.

He had always told himself he didn't want anything to do with kids, that he would probably be a lousy father. Maybe that had been at the core of why he didn't fight harder when Nikki asked him to sign away his parental rights.

He had always thought he wasn't patient enough or loving enough to provide what a kid needed. If that were so, why would Will and Chloe seem to like him?

And if he had something to offer them, what about his own son?

The dog came back to the porch quickly. Marshall opened the door for her but didn't go inside himself.

He had a son who needed him and it was past time he stepped up, no matter the consequences. He needed to tell the Jacobses' and he suddenly had the burning assurance that he had to do it now, before he lost his nerve.

Without giving himself time to reconsider, he hobbled back into the kitchen and found the envelope he had prepared months ago, right after he found out Nikki had died.

The snow had been falling steadily, but it wasn't heavy. Still, he had to take care as he maneuvered the crutches through the few inches that covered the sidewalk.

He rang their doorbell and waited, impatient now to get everything out in the open finally. Louise Jacobs answered, her eyes red and upset, her face blotchy. It looked as if she had been crying and he was about to make things worse.

"Sheriff Bailey! Come in! Are you all right? Is Andrea all right?"

"Yes. Fine. I needed to talk to you about something. About Christopher, actually. But it can wait. This looks like a bad time. I'll come back."

"What has he done now?" she asked, her voice defeated and her eyes welling with tears.

"Nothing. I—" He couldn't think how to begin, the words all tangling together in his head.

He shouldn't have come. He should have just waited until after the holidays.

Herm Jacobs came into the room then, round and bald with an expression that had always seemed kind to Marshall.

"What's going on?"

"The sheriff needs to talk to us about Christopher," Louise said, her voice hitching with emotion. "It's bad enough he's been suspended until the week after school starts in January. Now he's in trouble with the law, too!"

Marshall straightened. "He's been suspended? Why?"

"Fighting with another student," Herm said. "A younger boy, too. One of those Laird kids from Sulfur Hollow."

He knew the family, as several members had come through his jail. They were all rough and rowdy, quick to fight and mean. The week before he broke his leg, he'd caught one young Laird stealing beer at the convenience store, bold enough to do it even with the county sheriff in full uniform just one aisle over.

"He claims the other kid stole a girl's cell phone and he was just trying to get it back for her," Herm went on. "Meanwhile, the other kid said *Christopher* is the one who took it. The principal said either way they shouldn't have been fighting, so they were both suspended for a week."

"If it's any consolation, those Lairds are trouble," Marshall said.

"I appreciate you saying that, but this is just about the last straw. We're at our wit's end with that boy. Fighting, failing his classes, always in trouble." Herm sighed. "But that's not your worry, Sheriff."

He gripped the envelope that contained proof,

as far as he was concerned, that it *was* his worry.

"If the law's not after him, what did you want to talk about? If he's not doing the job you want on the shoveling, tell me and I'll set him straight. We'll go out and practice together."

"He's doing a fine job." He gripped the envelope more tightly again, not sure where the hell to start.

The beginning was as good a place as any. "I came to tell you something. Show you, actually. You, uh, might want to sit down."

Apprehension flickered over both their expressions, but they sank onto the sofa together. Herm reached beside him for his wife's hand, a tender, protective gesture that moved Marshall.

He sat down across from them. After opening the envelope, he extracted the contents and passed over the first form.

Louise took it from him and she and her husband read it together. As he waited for them to finish, Marshall thought this just might be the most excruciating moment of his life.

"What is this?" Herm exclaimed a moment later. "I don't understand."

"It's a legally binding document your daughter's attorney prepared, where I relinquished—from the date on the document into perpetuity—all paternal rights to any child the two of us may have conceived together."

Twin blank stares met this awkward explanation. "I don't understand," Louise said. "Why would you have this? I had no idea you even knew Nicole."

He closed his eyes, wishing he could go back and change that single weekend that had impacted so many lives. "It's a long story, but we bumped into each other when I was just about ready to ship out to Iraq and . . . we spent some time together."

How awkward was it to talk about this? Nikki was dead now and it felt terribly wrong to tell her parents about a brief hookup that hadn't meant anything to either of them. He had been absolutely right to dread this.

"It was a mistake and I take full responsibility for everything. Neither of us expected a child to come out of it, of course. I don't think she wanted to believe it had, but then she found out she was pregnant with Christopher."

"But she was already engaged to Johann when she found out she was pregnant," Louise protested. "They were so excited about it because he'd had fertility problems with his first marriage and doctors had told him he couldn't have children of his own . . ."

Her voice trailed off and she looked suddenly horrified.

"I believe now that she suspected the baby might have been mine by then," he said slowly. "I don't know that for sure, though. I can't know it. I think she was trying to protect herself and her upcoming marriage and just wanted to make sure I was out of the picture. I only know she contacted me in Iraq and begged me to sign the document."

"That doesn't explain why a man would sign away rights to his own child." Herm said, expression taut with a condemnation that Marshall fully deserved.

"I've asked myself that a thousand times over the years. I don't have a good excuse. At the time, I figured it was the logical choice. What could I provide a kid? I was young, single and on a dangerous deployment I wasn't sure I would even survive. On the other hand, Nikki was about to marry a rich, successful, mature doctor who seemed to be everything I wasn't."

With the insight he had gained over the last few days, he decided to lay the rest of it on the table. "Besides that, I was pretty sure I would be a terrible father. That's the main reason I haven't said anything all these months. I told myself I didn't want to interfere or complicate his life more than it already was, but . . . I guess I needed to convince myself I had something to offer."

"And do you?" Louise asked, her gaze narrowed.

"I don't know," he said truthfully. "I would like to try, if you'll give me the chance."

They looked at each other for a moment and seemed to carry on one of those wordless conversations he remembered his mother and father doing at the dinner table while five kids bickered and spilled milk and vied for attention.

"How do we even know you're his father?" Herm said after a moment. "What happens if we let you start a relationship and you find out it was all a mistake and you have no reason to stick around? That boy has lost enough."

"We need some kind of proof," Louise agreed. "All this document says is you would relinquish your rights if you *were* his father. It doesn't say you *are*."

"We can get a DNA test. I want that, though it's going to be tough to get a swab without telling him a little about what's going on."

"That would probably be wise."

He paused, reaching into the envelope for what he considered a second piece of evidence. "This isn't conclusive, but I'd like you to take a look at something."

When he handed them the picture of Wyatt and Wynona he'd found from a hiking trip they took when the twins were about the same age Christopher was now, both of them gazed at it for a long moment, and then Louise started to cry again.

"Oh my. Look at that," she said. "Except for the different hair color, he's the spitting image of Charlene's Wyatt!"

"The first time I saw a picture of him you posted on social media, I knew," Marshall said simply. "To be honest, I can't believe my mother has not been camped out on your doorstep since Christopher came to town, anxious to meet her new grandson. I told Andie that I think my mom couldn't see what was right in front of her eyes because she was too busy planning a wedding."

"Andrea knows?" Louise asked in surprise.

She had been such a source of support to him and he had repaid her by making her think he completely discounted her opinion.

"She guessed, from a few things I told her. She's been pushing me to tell you the truth so that you two can figure out the best way to handle introducing the idea to him."

"I think we should have the DNA results first. No ambiguity," Herm said. He didn't look as wholly convinced as his wife, as Marshall.

"That's fair. There are kits we can get in the mail or I can talk to Devin Shaw about going to her office for them. Either way, we're going to have to figure out together what to tell Christopher."

"To tell me about what?"

Marshall jerked his gaze to the doorway, where Christopher had suddenly appeared. His son had a bruise on his cheek and the beginnings of a black eye. His knuckles were bruised, too, and it looked like his thumb was swollen, the nail damaged.

Apparently one of the first things he needed to

376

teach him was how to tuck his thumb in his fist before punching someone.

"What's going on?" the boy said into the continued silence.

Marshall looked at Herm and Louise, who didn't seem to know what to say.

"You're sending me away, aren't you?" He couldn't miss the fear in the boy's voice.

"I . . . No, honey," his grandmother assured him. "We promised we wouldn't."

He faced Marshall, belligerence clear in every line of his body. "I didn't steal that cell phone! You can't arrest me. I have witnesses who saw the whole thing go down. They didn't want to tell the principal, but they'll tell the cops. I know they will."

"You're not going to jail. I'm not here to arrest you."

"Then what are you doing here?"

Christopher moved into the room and his gaze landed on the picture in his grandmother's hands.

"Who is that?"

Herm and Louise seemed frozen in uncertainty, both looking at Marshall to give them guidance. They had to tell him. He couldn't see any other way around it.

His heart pounding, Marshall pulled the photograph from Louise and handed it to Christopher.

"That's my younger brother, Wyatt. He was a highway patrol officer and was struck and killed by a car five years ago while helping a motorist during a bad storm."

"He looks like me. Why?" Christopher gazed down at the picture and then his eyes—an exact match to Marshall's own—lifted. "Are we related or something?"

Marshall looked one last time at Herm and Louise. After a pause, Herm gave a slight nod, tacit permission, and Marshall turned back to the troubled boy he already cared so deeply about and wanted desperately to help.

"There is a pretty good chance he's your uncle. Which would make me your father."

An hour later, feeling utterly exhausted yet also buoyed by more optimism than he'd known in a long time, Marshall made his slow way across the snow to his house.

He had a son.

Yes, they still needed to do the DNA test, but he had no doubt what the results would be.

Christopher had taken the news with surprising nonchalance, though Marshall knew that could be a temporary state of shock. Really, though, the boy hadn't even seemed all that shocked.

"I knew Johann wasn't my dad. I've known it for a long time," he said, which had made his grandmother burst into more tears.

"How?" she had asked. "Did your mother tell you that?"

He shook his head. "I heard them fighting about it four or five years ago, I think, after my mom's second divorce. She was trying to get more child support, and he refused, and I heard him say he was already paying out the nose for someone else's bastard. They didn't know I heard. I didn't know what bastard meant and had to look it up."

What must that have been like, to be a young boy hearing your father disavow you. No wonder Christopher adopted a smart-ass attitude to the world.

Marshall's chest felt jagged and raw as he contemplated the pain his son had endured because of Marshall's own foolish choices.

"I am so sorry," he had said, knowing the words were wholly inadequate.

His son had shrugged with that indifference Marshall now realized was so carefully cultivated. "In some ways, it made it all easier, you know? Before that, I just thought he didn't love me because of something I did."

Though he had grieved deeply each time, he had tried hard not to weep when Wyatt died or he lost a buddy in Iraq or when his beloved father had been shot.

In that moment, as he listened to Christopher's casual acceptance of another man's cruelty to an innocent child, he felt his eyes burn and his throat close.

He had wanted to hug him even as he sensed

they weren't quite there yet. It would come, but Marshall knew it would take time before Christopher would accept that kind of easy affection from him.

He was grateful when Louise did it for him, wrapping Christopher in her arms and holding tightly while Herm managed to put an arm around both of them.

"I have a lot of regrets in my life," Marshall had admitted. "The biggest, though, is not fighting for you when I found out thirteen years ago there was a chance I might have a son. I should have. I can make a hundred excuses for why I didn't—why at the time I thought I was doing the best thing for you—but they don't really matter. In the end, I'm only left with remorse."

After a few more moments of talking, Christopher finally asked the question on Marshall's mind and, he guessed, the boy's grandparents.

"So what now?"

"We'll do a DNA test if you want, to be sure. It might make your grandparents a little more comfortable with the whole thing, but I know everything I need to. You're my son and, more than anything, I'd like the chance to be your father, if you'll let me."

Christopher had given him a measuring look that contained wariness, doubt and, maybe, just maybe, a little happiness at all the possibilities ahead of them.

Marshall would have to work for those possibilities, he knew. As if to confirm the thought, Christopher tilted his jaw up. "Yeah, but what if I don't want some weird cop for a dad?"

"I can try not to be so weird, I guess. But as for the rest, I'm afraid you're stuck with it. I'm a cop to the bone. Don't know if I can be anything else."

"I guess that's okay," Christopher said, and Marshall had to fight a smile of pure happiness.

After a few more moments of talking, Marshall sensed Herm, Louise and Christopher needed a little time alone to absorb the shocking grenade he had just tossed into their world.

As he said his goodbyes, Christopher walked him to the door. At the last moment, Marshall reached out and hugged the boy. To hell with what he should or shouldn't do or what Christopher might want. To his great joy, his son had hugged him back, just for a moment, before he stepped away.

"I never thought I wanted children," Marshall had admitted to his son, that raw emotion back in his throat and chest. "I had no idea until I found you how very wrong I was."

Now, as he made his way to his house, he couldn't wait for Andie to get home. He wanted to tell her everything, the entire word-for-word conversation.

He wanted to hold her close and tell her she was right and to thank her for showing him by example how to find the strength and courage he needed to move forward with the hard choices he had needed to make.

To his disappointment, the house was empty of all but Sadie and her slinky black feline friend, who peeked around the corner when he walked in the back door, stared at him for a long moment out of hypnotic green eyes, then bounded back to parts unknown.

He stood for a moment, knowing the last half hour had changed his life irrevocably—and Christopher's, as well.

How would he tell his mother? His sisters? Elliot?

He didn't want to rush into anything. After the DNA test results, when all the formalities had been followed, he would sit his family down and explain the situation.

He didn't question how they would respond. The Baileys would embrace his son completely. He knew his family and he had no doubt whatsoever. Charlene would be in ecstasy to have someone else to fuss over and Uncle Mike would probably want to give the kid a job down at the body shop, just like he'd done for Elliot, Marshall and Wyatt. As for Wyn and Katrina, he imagined his sisters would instantly be crazy about Christopher, not least of which because he looked so very much like Wyatt.

Wyn would sob when she saw him, and Kat would probably want to teach him to drive in her little sports car, and both of them would spoil him horribly.

That wasn't even counting all the other great-aunts and uncles and cousins who lived in Lake Haven County.

Poor kid. He would have so much family he wouldn't know what to do with it.

How would the kid feel about adding a younger stepbrother and stepsister to their little tribe?

The thought came out of nowhere and Marshall had to grip the edge of the table as a deep yearning just about knocked him over.

Whoa. That wasn't going to happen. He wasn't going to marry anyone, especially not a lovely widow who had told him in blunt, unmistakable terms that he was the worst possible man in Haven Point for her. She didn't want to marry another police officer with the accompanying risks and he had already established that he couldn't imagine being anything else.

That sharp ache seemed to have lodged permanently in his chest at the heartbreaking impossibility of the situation. He wanted Andie in his life and he wanted Will and Chloe as well, while she wanted a different man than he could ever be.

The doorbell rang suddenly. His pulse jumped, but he knew instantly it couldn't be Andie. For one thing, she had a key and wouldn't need to ring the doorbell. For another, Sadie—normally so sweet and easygoing—snarled and hurried to the front door, where she waited, hackles raised, for Marshall to make his way down the narrow hallway on his crutches.

When he opened the door, Marshall stared. "Jackie! What are you doing here? What's wrong?"

It didn't take a crack detective to recognize someone who had reached a precipice and stumbled over the edge. She wasn't wearing a coat, despite the weather, just a shirt with the buttons not quite matched up. Her hair was wild, tangled, in a crooked ponytail that looked as if it hadn't been combed in at least two or three days and the circles he had noted a week earlier under her eyes looked several shades darker.

"Come in. What's wrong?" he asked again.

Instead of answering, she let out a low, keening sort of moan. "I can't fix it. I can't. I tried and I can't."

"Fix what?"

In answer, she burst into tears—noisy, ugly sobs that made Sadie whine and duck into Andie's bedroom.

Marshall stood in the entry on his crutches, wondering what the hell he was supposed to do. He could handle hostage situations, vehicle chases, bank robberies.

So why did a woman's tears send him straight into panic mode?

This was the second time that day he had faced them and he wasn't any better prepared now than he had been with Louise Jacobs.

"Come in, out of the cold," he ordered her again. "Don't cry. Whatever is wrong, we'll figure out how to make it right."

"I can't. I thought I could, but I can't," she cried.

She was heading for full-on hysteria in a minute. If that happened, he wouldn't be able to get anything out of her.

"Let's get you a glass of water, and then you can tell me what has you so upset."

"Don't be nice to me. I don't deserve it."

"Sure you do."

He didn't give her a chance to refuse; he simply swung around and made his way back down the hall, sensing maybe she needed someone to take the lead.

As he had hoped, she followed him after a beat.

"Sit down. I'll get you something to drink." He had been on plenty of calls involving someone in the midst of a mental health crisis. This was no different, except it was someone he knew.

"Is there somebody I can call? Your sister or a doctor or that counselor who helped you after your divorce?" he prompted.

"No. They can't help me. Nobody can help me."

Her emotional state bordered on despair, which worried him. He reached in his pocket for his cell phone, wondering how she might react if he called paramedics. Better to keep her talking for a moment to assess the situation, he decided.

"That's not true," he said gently. "I'm trying to help, but I can't unless you tell me what's going on. Why are you so upset? Did somebody hurt you?"

"No. It's me."

He frowned. "You hurt yourself?"

"I made terrible mistakes. So many terrible mistakes." Jackie buried her head in her hands. "I was trying to do the right thing—to help my boy. That's all I wanted. But I messed everything up and you got hurt and I'm sick about it now. I can't fix it and I'm so sorry."

She lifted her wild-eyed gaze to his, and for the first time, in the better light of the kitchen, he realized her pupils didn't look normal. She was obviously on some kind of narcotic. What the hell? Jackie wasn't a user, at least as far as he'd ever witnessed—though he'd never seen any sign of acute mental illness, either, other than a few bouts of depression as her divorce worked its way through the courts and her son struggled with substance abuse.

He had worked beside Jackie for years when he had been a deputy and she worked for his predecessor, and then very closely for the last year as the sheriff, but this frantic, distressed woman seemed like someone he didn't even recognize.

"I'm sorry," she said again. "I had to tell you I'm sorry. I'm so sorry."

"Okay. Sorry for what? Let's start there?"

She burst into more noisy tears and buried her head in her hands. For a long moment, she didn't seem capable of answering him. This was above his pay grade. She was either high on something or having a mental breakdown. Either way, she needed medical help.

He pulled his phone out, but before he could dial 911, she lifted her head again.

"That," she said, pointing at him. "I did that."

He was completely baffled, until he realized she wasn't pointing at *him,* she was pointing at the crutches holding him up.

He felt cold and hot at the same time. "What are you talking about?"

"I didn't want to hurt you. I just needed you to stay away from work for a few weeks so I could make things right. I only wanted to make things right again, Marshall, I swear. I was going to fix everything. I just needed more time."

He knew. Suddenly he knew.

He dredged up his memories of that secretive phone call from the confidential informant; the vehicle racing toward him through the snow; the dark shape in a ski mask, escaping between tents at the Lights on the Lake festival, right after he had seen Jackie there. It was a struggle to reconcile those bits of evidence, given this jarring paradigm shift, but yeah. Any of those suspects could have been a woman.

"You were driving the car. You tried to kill me."

Eyes haunted, she swiped at her nose with the back of her hand. "Not kill you," she sniffled. "You were always so nice to me. I didn't want to even *hurt* you, but I didn't know what else to do. I just needed you to stay home so I could make things right."

"You took the money from evidence, didn't you? This was all about trying to hide what you did."

She closed her eyes at the accusation and he knew his guess had found its target.

"I knew you suspected me. I knew it, especially when you came into the office last week, even though the doctors told you not to."

"Why? How did you think you'd get away with it? You know the procedures as well as anybody. You knew we would eventually find it missing."

She rose and began to pace around the kitchen in a haphazard way. "It was supposed to be only for a few weeks. That's all. I just needed cash until the divorce settlement came through, so I . . . borrowed it. I thought I could pay it back. I was supposed to get a check this week, and then I could make everything right."

"Why? If you needed a loan, I could have helped you."

"They didn't give me a choice," she sobbed again, and his mind raced, trying to figure out who *they* were. Was somebody blackmailing her? Was she hiding gambling debts?

Suddenly he knew the answer before her next words even confirmed it.

"The rehab center wouldn't take Jeremy unless I paid up front and he needed help," she said. "My boy needed help and I didn't have the money and I couldn't wait for the attorneys to hash out the divorce settlement, so I . . . borrowed it from evidence."

"Oh, Jackie."

"I only took the cash retrieved from that meth bust over the summer. It was only right, wasn't it? They stole my sweet boy from me, so I stole some of their dirty money to help him get clean again. Don't you think that was only fair?"

Her voice had lost some of the hysteria. Now it sounded tired.

"How much have you had to drink today, Jackie?"

She rubbed at her eyes. "Nothing. Not to drink. Pills."

Damn it. He should have called 911 the moment she'd shown up on the doorstep, when he saw she was acting irrational and out of control.

He dialed the number now, hoping to hell he wasn't too late.

"This is Sheriff Bailey. I have an urgent medical

emergency at my house on Riverbend Road. I need an ambulance. Possible overdose." He turned to her. "How many and what kind of medication? We need to get you to the hospital."

"It's too late," she whispered. "Put your phone down, Sheriff. Tell them not to come. It's too late."

She gave a tired-looking smile that chilled him to the bone. "I didn't take that many, anyway. Not enough to do anything. Just enough so maybe it won't hurt as much."

His insides clenched as a dark suspicion bloomed. "So what won't hurt as much?"

In answer, she reached into her purse, pulled out a small black .38 Special and held it to her temple. Though her hands trembled, she still managed to work the safety.

"Women don't kill themselves with guns nearly as often as men. Did you know that?"

Yeah. He knew. The ratio was about two men to one woman—but in this case, once was more than enough, especially when that particular one was someone he knew, standing in his kitchen.

This was surreal, that she could cite statistics to him while holding a loaded handgun to her own head.

"There are a lot of reasons," she said, her voice dreamy now. "Some say it's because women don't like guns and don't have access to them as often. Or maybe it's because women don't want to leave a big mess behind. Men don't care about the messes they leave behind. Just ask my son of a bitch ex-husband. They say women don't use guns as often because it's final. Sometimes they just want the drama. They don't really want to go, right? You can have your stomach pumped after taking pills, but you can't rewind once you've blown the top of your head off."

Now she held the gun under her chin, where they both knew it could do maximum damage. "I don't want to rewind," she said, the words full of a desolate pain. "I can't go to jail. I can't."

"We can work this out, Jackie. You don't have to go to jail. Come on. Give me the gun." He said the word clearly and firmly, hoping the dispatcher could hear it over the line and relay that to the responding officers.

She shook her head. "I stole evidence in a drug case and I can't pay it back. My divorce attorney called this morning and said the money's gone. My settlement. That rat bastard hid it somewhere and we can't find it. He won't pay for our son to go to rehab, but he can take his whore to the Caymans so he can hide everything we built together for twenty years."

"We'll get you a better attorney, then." He tried to keep her talking while he edged ever closer. It was hard to do it by stealth when he was on crutches, but he did his best. "We'll arrest your ex on tax evasion. We'll figure it out. Put down the gun."

"It will be too late. I'll go to jail. I don't want to go to jail." Her hand shook a little more. "I hate the jail. It stinks in there and the ladies are mean."

"Look, you need to give me the gun now. You don't want this, Jackie, I promise. Jeremy will get out of rehab soon and you need to be here for him."

She shook her head. Were her movements slowing down? Could he risk lunging at her? With her finger wedged on the trigger, he wasn't sure.

"He's so mad at me," she said, her words slurred and sorrowful. "So mad. He won't even talk to me, because I made him go to rehab. I made him. If he didn't, I told him I would have you put him in jail."

Where was Cade? Marshall judged approximately two minutes had passed since he called 911 and they should be screaming up within five or six, as long as the dispatcher overheard the call he'd left connected.

"I'm not mad at you. Does that make you feel better? I understand why you ran me down. You were only trying to help your son. Maybe I would have done the same thing."

"You wouldn't. You're so nice. The nicest boss I ever had. I hurt you and I feel *so bad*."

Tears gushed out and she reached to wipe her nose again with the hand holding the weapon before placing it back under her chin.

He could hear noise on the front step and had to hope it was backup. On the other hand, there was always the chance that in her befuddled state, she might instinctively fire at anybody who walked through the door.

"Jackie," he said, his voice stern and loud. "I need you to give me your weapon. Do you hear me? That's an order."

He hoped his firmness would break through the fog of substances clouding her judgment—and would also convey again to dispatch that a weapon was involved.

He thought he had won when she hesitated, but she finally only shook her head. "I can't. I'm sorry I bothered you. I shouldn't have come here. I just wanted you to know I never wanted to hurt you and I'm sorry."

He watched the doorway out of the edge of his vision, trying to avoid looking directly so Jackie didn't notice. When Cade and his guys came in, Marshall hoped they provided enough of a distraction for him to sweep in and disarm her.

And then he spotted someone with her back against the wall, peering into the room.

Andie.

Everything inside him turned to ice. Not Andie.

No. *Go,* he wanted to yell at her. *Get the hell out of here.* But he was afraid if he said anything, Jackie might lose her tenuous hold on reality.

"Who's that? Is someone here?" She waved the gun in the direction of the hallway.

Andie.

"I don't think so," he said. Panic lodged, cold and hard, in his chest and he knew he had to draw her attention back to him and do everything he could to disarm her. "Come on, Jackie. Give me the gun. You don't want to die, right?"

She frowned at him. "Yes. Yes, I do. It's better than jail."

Something was wrong.

She couldn't have said exactly how she knew, but the moment she walked into the house, Andie sensed it. Most likely it was a combination of things—the strange car parked at an odd angle in the driveway or the way Sadie whined from the doorway of the guest bedroom or the tense, hard voices she heard coming from the kitchen.

For an instant, she was tempted to slip back outside the way she had come, to return to her car, where she could call for help. That was the safe choice, the logical one.

But Marshall was in there.

The man she loved.

Someone had tried to kill him a little more than a week ago, then had tried to hurt him just a few days earlier at the Lights festival. What if he was in danger again?

If that were the case, what could she do about it? the rational, cautious side of her brain was quick to ask. She was an artist, a mom. Yes, Wyn had taught her six or seven Krav Maga self-defense moves. Learning a few basic maneuvers to protect herself and her children had felt wonderfully empowering at the time, but she was by no means an expert—and right now the thought of using an eye strike or an outside chop filled her with slick, greasy nausea.

She could do this. To protect him, she would do whatever was necessary. She set down her purse so she would have both hands, then suddenly remembered. She might not need to do Krav Maga. She had a Taser, for heaven's sake.

Heart pounding, she dug through her purse, worked the latch on the child-safe bag and pulled out her Taser and the pepper spray, just in case. She shoved the pepper spray in her pocket, and with both hands on the stun gun, she inched closer to the kitchen.

Her stealth seemed to take forever, but finally she was close enough to see inside the room. Marshall stood near the outside door, and across the width of the kitchen, the woman she had met at the Lights festival—Jackie Scott, she remembered—faced him, holding an ominous-looking black revolver in hands that shook as much as Andie's did right now.

In an instant of blind panic, she could focus on nothing but the gun and she had a flashback to that night in her living room when she had been certain she would die, when Rob had held a gun to her chin with deadly intent in his eyes.

Breathe, Andie. She forced herself to look again. This was different. The woman wasn't pointing the gun at Marshall. She was pointing it at herself.

She hadn't seen Andie yet, she realized—but Marshall knew she was there. His glance flicked toward her and she saw a wild surge of panic in the blue depths, then he looked quickly away. He was trying not to draw attention to her.

Always, always protective.

The woman was obviously having a breakdown of some sort. She was babbling something about not wanting to go to jail, about her son, about being sorry.

"Come on, Jackie. Give me the gun. You don't want to die, right?"

She frowned at him. "Yes. Yes, I do. It's better than jail."

"Dead is dead. You can't fix anything then, only bring more pain to those who love you. Come on, give me the gun."

To Andie's horror, Jackie pointed the gun at Marshall. It wobbled back and forth with her trembling, but she was only ten feet away from him. At that distance, it would be tough to miss.

"I told you to stay back," she said. "You can't stop this."

He was going to try anyway, Andie realized at once. Like Jason, he intended to try saving someone who didn't want to be saved. His muscles were tensed, ready. He shifted all his weight to his left leg and crutch.

His gaze flickered to where Andie waited in the hall and he inclined his head slightly, telling her without words to get out.

He intended to take on a delusional woman holding a handgun, armed with only an aluminum crutch.

Oh, she loved him. In a stunning moment of clarity, she realized a big part of the reason she loved him was *because* he would always be ready to step up, to help where he was needed, no matter the personal cost.

She couldn't let him risk his life. Not this time, at least.

Heart pounding, she armed her Taser and eased into the room. She could do this. She had practiced repeatedly and knew just where to aim. The big downside of a Taser, of course, was that she had only one shot, but she would keep the pepper spray ready just in case.

If she were trained in law enforcement, she would probably have to announce herself and order the woman to put down her weapon or something.

Good thing she was simply a woman trying to protect the man she loved.

From here, she had a perfect shot at the woman's back—the spot she knew from the training she underwent when she purchased the Taser was the absolute most effective place to aim a Taser, as a hit to the large muscle groups there was most likely to result in neuromuscular incapacitation.

She held her breath, took aim and—guided by the laser sight—fired. The two electrodes shot out almost soundlessly and found their target. Instantly, Jackie collapsed like a thousand-pound sandbag had just dropped on her, as every muscle holding her upright contracted.

Andie dropped the Taser—still connected to the convulsing woman by the wires—and rushed forward to pick up the handgun just as the hallway behind her seemed to explode with people.

Cade Emmett was at the front of the line, leading EMTs and a few other police officers from his department. "What happened? Is she having a seizure?" he demanded.

Marshall looked as stunned as if Andie had reloaded and fired at *him*.

"Andie tased her three seconds before you came in."

"Seriously?" Cade gave her an appraising look.

"It worked, didn't it?" she said. "The electrical

charge will continue for a full thirty seconds. I think she has about fifteen more. Here. Take this."

She gave the handgun to Cade, then went straight to Marshall and threw her arms around him. He was safe and warm, and she never wanted to let go.

The sudden impact rocked him back a little on his crutches, but his arms came around her and held her tight. "That was amazing. *You* were amazing," he said.

She had debated even purchasing the weapon, worried she wouldn't be able to actually fire on a human being in a stressful situation. When it came to protecting those she loved, apparently she could.

"What can you tell us about the situation that would help the EMTs?" Cade asked. "This is Jackie Scott, your admin, right?"

Marshall didn't release his hold on her. She knew it couldn't possibly be comfortable for him, balancing on the crutches, but he didn't seem to want to release her. Andie decided she wasn't going anywhere.

"Yes. She took some kind of medication, but she wouldn't tell me what. I don't know what time she took it, only that it seemed to really kick in about ten minutes after she showed up, slurring her speech and slowing her movements. Whatever it is, I don't think she took a fatal dose—on the other hand, she also sustained a full center of mass electric current straight into her back, too, so I can't say how the two things will interact. She was trying to kill herself."

"Any idea why she chose Wynona's kitchen as the location where she wanted to kill herself?"

Andie felt Marshall's chest move as he gave a long exhale. "Apparently she wanted to apologize to me before she killed herself. She was driving the SUV that hit me."

Andie lifted her head to stare at him. Now she *really* had no qualms about tasing the woman. If she had the chance, she might even want to shove in her backup cartridge and do it again.

Who knew she could be so bloodthirsty?

"Your secretary is the one who ran you down? Why?"

"It's a long story," Marshall said. He sounded tired and sore and, if she wasn't mistaken, deeply sad. She hugged him harder, and after a startled moment, his arms tightened around her in return.

"She wanted to keep me from coming into work so I didn't link her to embezzlement in the department," he said to Cade. "I think she knew we were close and decided she would rather die than go to jail."

"Sounds to me that's where she belongs, but we'll get her to the hospital first and stabilize her condition. I'll need full statements from both of you, but why don't you go into the other room and sit down while the EMTs take care of things here?

You're probably ready to fall over, aren't you?"

"No. We're good here, as long as we're out of the way."

The police chief didn't seem to care, returning to talk to his other officers as the EMTs began to load Jackie onto a gurney and wheel her out. Jackie spotted Marshall as the EMT was rolling her out and started sobbing harder. "I'm sorry. I'm so sorry. I'm sorry," she moaned repeatedly.

Marshall gestured for the stretcher to stop and he approached her on his crutches. He reached down and squeezed her hand in a gesture of compassion that brought tears to Andie's eyes.

"I know you were trying to help your boy. I get it," he said. "I just wish you'd come to me first instead of handling things the way you did."

"I'm sorry," she mumbled again. "I don't want to go to jail, Sheriff."

"Just focus on getting better right now. There were extenuating circumstances. We'll get you a good attorney and go from there."

Andie didn't want to feel sorry for the woman. She could have killed Marshall and had caused him severe pain. But it was difficult not to experience some empathy as the EMTs rolled her out, still crying.

When they left, Cade handed the Taser back to Andie with the probes reloaded. "You'd better hang on to this. I don't think we need to keep it in evidence," he said. "Anyway, we know where to find you if we need to take a look at it again."

"Will she be all right?" Andie asked.

Cade shrugged. "The hospital will probably pump her stomach, unless she can tell us what she took and how much."

He took their statements in the den with a crisp efficiency she appreciated. Ten minutes later he was on his way to the hospital to talk to Jackie and the house was empty again except for the two of them.

She felt nervous suddenly, which seemed ridiculous after everything that had just happened.

"How are you doing?" Marshall asked.

"I don't feel like I need to throw up anymore, so that's good. How about you?"

He was quiet. "I wouldn't mind just holding you again."

That was exactly what she needed. Without hesitation she rose from her chair adjacent to the Christmas tree her children had decorated and onto the sofa next to him. He wrapped his arms around her and pulled her halfway across his lap, then buried his face in her neck.

He was trembling. Her big, tough, wonderful sheriff was trembling. When he spoke, his voice was rough. "I've never been so scared in my entire life as when I saw you standing there in the hall when Jackie was waving that .38 Special around."

Wasn't it just like him, to be scared for her but not for himself? "Nothing happened. We're both okay. It sounds like Jackie will be okay, too. At least now you know who hurt you."

"That was some serious kick-ass Taser action."

"Not much to it. Just aim and fire at the red dot."

A low laugh rumbled through him. "You did it, though. Some people wouldn't have the nerve, but you just marched right in and went for center of mass. Remember last night when I told you I thought you were the most courageous woman I've ever met? Yeah. That."

She swallowed hard. She had a long way to go before she could fulfill that expectation of herself, but she wasn't about to argue with him.

"I lost my head when she moved the gun from herself to you. I couldn't let her hurt you." She paused, her pulse abnormally loud in her ears. "Not before I had the chance to tell you how much I love you."

She heard his quick intake of breath against her and lifted her gaze to find him looking down at her with a fierce, wild joy.

"What happened to me being the worst possible man in Haven Point for you? I know you don't want to be with another LEO, and I get it, I do. I don't know how to change that. I can try to do something else, but I'm afraid I would be miserable."

That he would even consider doing something else touched her deeply. A soft, sweet peace seeped through her, pure and lovely and healing. There simply wasn't room for both love and fear in the same heart, she thought.

"Tonight when you were ready to launch yourself at her, broken leg and all, I realized I can't separate that protector out. I wouldn't, even if I could. It's part of you—a huge part. Without it, you wouldn't be the man I love."

His eyes darkened with emotion and he lowered his mouth to hers. The tenderness in the kiss staggered her.

"I love you, Andrea. You should know, I've never said that to a woman before. I've never even wanted to. Only you."

She couldn't say the same—nor would she have wanted to. She had loved another man first. Jason had come into her life at the perfect time, to show her for the first time in her life that she was someone worthy of love.

Their marriage hadn't been perfect, but it had produced two amazing children and had helped her become the woman she was now, someone strong enough to be deeply grateful that she'd been given the chance to love again.

She kissed him and they stayed in the embrace, kissing and touching by the twinkling lights of the Christmas tree her children had decorated, until she was restless and achy and they both were breathing hard. This was not a bad position for a man with a broken leg, she decided. They could certainly figure out how to improvise . . .

The alarm on her phone suddenly went off and she groaned. "That's telling me I have ten minutes before I have to go pick up Chloe at the bus stop," she said.

He made a sound that somehow managed to mingle disappointment and understanding. His mouth found hers again, but right before he kissed her, he drew back, his eyes wide. "With everything that's happened, I can't believe I haven't told you yet!"

"Told me what?" she asked, sitting up beside him and trying to run a hand through the hair he had messed.

"It's been one hell of an afternoon. I had only been back at the house fifteen minutes when Jackie came over. Before that, I was next door, talking to Herm and Louise and to Christopher."

"What?" she exclaimed. "Oh, Marshall! How did it go?"

"Good. Better than I ever imagined. I have a son." His wondering smile made her want to cry, happy tears this time. He leaned forward and kissed her forehead. "I needed to tell him. Yes, you were right. I have a feeling I'd better get used to saying those words."

There was so much promise in his voice, she shivered.

"It's a huge relief to have it out there. He seemed . . . okay with it. Herm and Louise are, too. We're having a DNA test as soon as we can arrange it, but I don't need to see the results to know the truth. I don't think he does, either."

"Oh. I'm so happy."

"He's a troubled teenage boy. Everything won't be roses all the time, I'm afraid, but I can't wait to get to know him."

He paused, his expression both pensive and endearingly tender. "You know, the whole time I was there talking to Herm and Louise and Christopher, all I could think about was telling you. I guess that's what you do when you're in love."

"Oh, Marsh," she whispered.

"I can't believe I'm saying this, but the day Jackie ran me over might have been the luckiest day of my life. Without it, I never would have let you into my life, never would have discovered just how much I needed you. And not just you. Will and Chloe and Sadie and Mrs. Finnegan, too."

How could she *ever* have believed him cold and unfeeling? He had all this tenderness and love inside him, just waiting for him to feel comfortable enough to let them out.

"It's going to be a wonderful Christmas, isn't it?" she said.

"The very best one ever." His gaze held promise and possibilities. "Until next year, anyway. Something tells me that from here on, everything will just get better and better."

EPILOGUE

"All right, give it to me straight, Miss Chloe," Marshall said. "I have it on great authority that my Christmas tree last year was the second-best tree in town. I'm hoping to move up in the ranks this year. What are my chances?"

His seven-year-old stepdaughter pursed her lips and gave serious scrutiny to the tall and bushy blue spruce that took up an entire corner of their den.

"It's so *big*. I don't know. It's like twice as big around as the one Will and me did for you last year. I hope we have enough lights and ornaments."

"Are you kidding?" Christopher exclaimed from the floor, where he and Will were untangling string after string of lights for Marshall to twist around the branches. "How could we possibly not have enough ornaments? You've been cutting out paper snowflakes since the Fourth of July!"

"I have not," she retorted. "Remember? I made all the paper hearts for the wedding, so I didn't even start on snowflakes until after that."

"Okay. Fine. Since September."

Marshall smiled, remembering all those hearts strung around the stone patio in the backyard, where they'd had their reception—just two days

407

after he and Andie signed the papers buying his grandmother's house from Wynona.

He couldn't think of that day without his own heart wanting to burst out of his chest. Random snapshots of that day seemed permanently implanted in his mind, his own little mental slide show he could take out whenever he needed a break from the tough job of county sheriff.

Standing in the front of the little church in Haven Point with Christopher by his side as his best man, palms sweaty and nerves zinging.

His mother in the front row, holding Uncle Mike's hand and already sniffling into a tissue.

His sisters, Cade, Elliot, his aunts and all the people he loved filling the other rows.

And then Andie. His amazing, beautiful Andie, walking down the aisle with an uncharacteristically solemn Will on one side and sweet, pretty Chloe on the other, all three of them prepared to merge their lives with his.

He thought he couldn't possibly ever be as happy as he was in that single moment, watching his future walking toward him—but every single day since had been even better.

Even when his kids were squabbling.

"I *had* to start making snowflakes in September," Chloe insisted to Christopher. "We have fifty trees to decorate."

"Exaggerate much?" Christopher said. Though

his words were a little snide, he smiled when he said it.

Chris adored Chloe and Will. As soon as Marsh accepted that he couldn't imagine any future without Andie and her kids, he had been concerned at first that it wasn't fair to introduce two new young children into the picture when he was still trying to forge a relationship with his son. Christopher didn't seem to mind, though. He seemed to get a kick out of both of them and had relished the chance to have younger siblings for the first time.

"We have to decorate this huge tree that's as big as two other trees," Chloe said now, ticking her count off on her fingers. "I have one in my room. Will has one in his room. You have one in your room in the attic. Mom has one in her new office over the garage. How many is that?"

"Still not fifty," Will pointed out helpfully. "That's only five."

"I also cut out about a billion snowflakes for Grandma Charlene and Grandpa Mike and for Grandma Louise and Grandpa Herm and I made some for Aunt Wynona and Uncle Cade and for Jazmyn and *everybody*."

"If we don't have enough snowflakes for our tree, we'll know it's because you gave them away to everybody else in town," Christopher teased.

"If we don't have enough, Chloe can just make

409

more," Will said. "She's superfast and she has paper in her room and can get more from Mom's office."

"Who can get what from my office?"

After they had been married a year, was his heart still going to pound like this every time he saw her? What about two or ten or twenty? He turned to find Andie coming in, cheeks a little pink from the short walk outside from her new office.

Christopher's room had been carved out under the eaves in the old house. He loved the slanting ceiling and the dormer windows. It was small, but that didn't seem to bother him, since half of his stuff was still at his grandparents' house next door, where he still spent plenty of time with Herm and Louise.

Marshall couldn't believe they'd managed to find room for everyone—including Mrs. Finnegan and Sadie, who right now were both curled together on the rug watching the proceedings.

He was still considering building on to the little house. They were a family of five—plus two pets—and bursting at the seams. The yard was big enough they could easily build on to the house. He was thinking about adding a bigger family room in place of this den and a couple more bedrooms.

For now, it worked. He was never happier than

when he pulled into the driveway, knowing his family waited for him inside.

"I said Chloe can get more paper from your office if she needs more snowflakes," Will said.

"Why on earth would she possibly need more?" Andie asked, eyes wide.

"We're hoping she doesn't," Marshall assured her. "We'll know in a few moments, once I finish with these lights and you all can start decorating the tree."

Andie moved into the room and inhaled deeply of the tree's heady fragrance. "Oh, wow, it smells fantastic in here."

"The smell is about the only good thing about a real tree," Christopher groused. "Unraveling these lights is a *pain*."

"It might be hard, but you guys are doing an amazing job." She placed a hand on the teen's shoulder and Marshall could tell it pleased him. Andie was amazing with his son. Whenever Christopher was in a mood, missing Nikki or simply being a surly teenager full of hormones, Andie could invariably tease a smile out of him.

"I still don't know why we couldn't just get another artificial tree for in here," Chris said now. "I've always had artificial trees and it's tons easier. You just pull them out of the box and plug them in."

"New family, new traditions," Marshall said.

"Exactly." Andie backed him up. "Since this is our first year as a family, isn't it fun to try a few different things so we can figure out which traditions we want to keep in the coming years together?"

"Last night was so fun!" Will said. "I loved when we went swimming and then cut the tree down at Evergreen Springs. My favorite part was the sleigh ride."

"I liked the hot chocolate we had with Jazmyn and Ty," Chloe said. "Especially the little tiny snowman marshmallows."

"Those were cute," Andie agreed.

"You had fun, too. You were lucky," Will said wistfully to Christopher. "You got to cut down the tree. Next year I get to use the chain saw, right?"

Marshall winced at the idea of Will with a dangerous power tool. "We'll have to see on that one, kid. I think I'm ready for the next light string."

"What this party needs is some music," Andie declared. "Christopher, can you stream some on your phone to the speaker?"

"Yeah, if you can come help with the lights. We have, like, three more strands."

They traded places and Christopher found some kind of edgy rock version of "Holly Jolly Christmas," then he followed it up with some classic Sinatra and a bluegrass duet about angels crying on Christmas Eve that had always made Marsh's mother cry.

It was the perfect night, he thought as his family worked together to decorate their tree.

As he reached high to hang the star on the top of the tree, he couldn't help thinking how his life had changed since that snowy December night a year earlier when Jackie Scott thought she could solve her problems with a stolen SUV.

He had been a different man then. Harder. Less giving and less *for*giving.

He had been convinced he didn't need any-thing —certainly not family or laughter, Christmas trees or paper snowflakes or hot cocoa by the fire.

Now, as he watched Chloe direct everyone on proper ornament-hanging in her bossiest tone and Christopher tease Will, who teased him right back, and Andie send him a laughing glance over her shoulder, his chest seemed to expand with joy so big the little house couldn't contain it.

"Okay," Chloe said at last. "I think that should do it. We used all the paper snowflakes and almost all the other ornaments, too."

"Can we turn the lights off now and see it?" Will begged.

"Sure," Marshall said. "Chris, can you do the honors?"

His son turned off the lamp and then the main

lights in the room, leaving only the Christmas tree gleaming against the windows.

"Oh," Will breathed. "It looks *awesome!*"

"I guess it's pretty good, for a real tree," Christopher agreed.

"I love it," Andie said. She smiled at Marshall and slipped her arms around him. They all stood there for a moment, until he realized Chloe hadn't offered her opinion; she was just standing and looking up at the twinkling branches.

"Well, Chloe? What do you think?"

She turned, eyes shining with the reflection of eight hundred colored lights. "Yes," she said in a hushed voice. "This is the best tree in town. Maybe the best one *ever*. We have the best tree and the best house and the best family."

"I can't argue with you there, sweetheart," he said, his own voice low as soft music played and outside the windows a light snow began to fall. "It's absolutely perfect."

Center Point Large Print
600 Brooks Road / PO Box 1
Thorndike, ME 04986-0001 USA

(207) 568-3717

US & Canada:
1 800 929-9108
www.centerpointlargeprint.com